Praise for *A Wolf Apart*

"Vale's second foray into the exquisitely built world of the Pack is as enthralling and exciting as *The Last Wolf*."
—*Booklist*

"An epic story...the total package of romance, passion, betrayal, and a strong plot. I hated for it to end."
—*Night Owl Reviews*, Top Pick

"A wealth of sharply etched detail, snippets of pack history and lore, and a colorful supporting cast add another layer to this remarkable, strangely believable world."
—*Library Journal*

"A feral and fearsome romance that works for its happy ending."
—*Kirkus Reviews*

"What a breathtaking story with exquisite worldbuilding. Just couldn't put it down."
—*Love Bites and Silk*

"A fascinating and unique romance, very different from any other paranormal romance...enthralling from the start!"
—*Harlequin Junkie*

"Maria Vale has created a fantastic world...kept me on the edge of my seat."
—*With Love for Books*

Also by Maria Vale

FOREVER WOLF

MARIA VALE

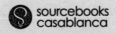

sourcebooks
casablanca

Published by Sourcebooks Casablanca, an imprint of Sourcebooks, Inc.
P.O. Box 4410, Naperville, Illinois 60567-4410
(630) 961-3900
Fax: (630) 961-2168
sourcebooks.com

Printed and bound in the United States of America.
OPM 10 9 8 7 6 5 4 3 2 1

To M, H & G, who have been bemused throughout.

What would the world be, once bereft
Of wet and of wildness? Let them be left,
O let them be left, wildness and wet;
Long live the weeds and the wilderness yet.
　　　　　　　—"Inversnaid," Gerard Manley Hopkins

Chapter 1

THE WOLVES OF THE GREAT NORTH HAVE BEEN SPOILED by peace.

They don't think they are. They imagine they are besieged by enemies. But the raw numbers tell a different story. In the winter when the Shifters came, the Pack lost four. Four out of four hundred.

They mourned them and mounted stones with their names and the dates of their last hunt at the *Gemyndstow*, the memory place, the circles of stones that stretch out from the three-hundred-year-old markers in the center.

One was laid for John, the former Alpha of the Great North, along with another three high-ranked wolves. Then the Pack shuffled papers, buttressing the wall of law that is meant to protect them from outsiders.

And now they have lost another. Celia Sorensdottir, the 9th Echelon's Alpha Shielder. There are fourteen echelons, fourteen age groups among the adults. Each has its own Alpha pair and hierarchies. That should tell them something right there. Packs that are truly under siege are never so fruitful. My birth Pack only had adults and nonadults; there were no echelons.

Celia was shot Offland. Any other time, she would have had a good chance of surviving. She had a half gallon of my blood in her by the end, and I am nothing if not a survivor.

Because it happened right before the Iron Moon,

those three days when the moon is full and we have no choice but to be wild, it came with all the pulling and stretching and torquing and changing and, in Celia's case, tearing and reopening and bleeding and, eventually, dying.

Still, it is only five wolves. Out of fourteen echelons. They don't know what it is like to be truly hunted.

I am here to make sure they never do.

The Great Hall is new and still smells raw. Like stone and wood. In the rebuilding, Evie insisted on using peeled cedar because that is what the burned heart of Homelands smelled like. A cheaper wood might have looked the same, but it would have smelled alien and been a constant reminder of the Pack's loss. Soon it will take on the patina of fur and briar and yarrow and muskrat and sumac and resin and moss and deer.

The world wolves move through and carry with them.

Although it was rebuilt along the same lines as the hall that burned down, it is larger, designed by wolves, for wolves, rather than for the bankrupt industrialist the Pack bought it from way back when. The vaulted ceilings are taller, the staircase wider. The new windows are triple-paned to resist the blustering brutality of winters in the Adirondacks. The outer door is reinforced with iron plates to resist the blustering brutality of thoughtless wolves.

"This table is for the 12th," I growl when one of those thoughtless wolves tries to sit.

He does an odd dance, keeping his raised leg from touching the bench at the communal table that I have claimed for my echelon. "Yes, Shielder," he murmurs, his eyes lowered.

It is as it should be. Only in the absence of higher-ranked wolves would I be called Alpha. But I've always been happiest to be called Shielder. Unlike with *Alpha*, humans have not co-opted the word. A shielder is still distinctive to us: a wolf who assists in the work of herding deer toward the treacherous smooth stones of a dried riverbed or of shelling endless peas for a dinner to feed four hundred hungry wolves in skin.

A wolf who shields us from coyotes through the endless process of shifting when we are blind, deaf, immobile, and horribly vulnerable.

Lorcan, my Alpha, Alpha of the 12th, is big and jovial, with straight blond hair that he keeps tied back in a rubber band, even though his hair isn't particularly long, and if I don't remind him to take the rubber band out before the Iron Moon, it stays in during the change as an undignified sprout of tawny fur at the top of his head.

He slaps shoulders and laughs loud, sitting at the head of the table with a clear view of the Alpha's seat. Where John sat until he was shot and killed and where his mate, Evie Kitwanasdottir, now sits, fully recovered from her lying-in, but never, I think, from the loss of her mate.

Ulrich, the 12th's Epsilon, balances his seax, the sharp dagger that is given to each wolf as they transition to adulthood, on its tip and thoughtlessly twirls it until I reach over and lift hand and knife. With my other hand, I feel the small pit in the newly constructed table.

"You will resand and wax this table after we are finished."

"The whole thing?"

"The whole thing."

Ulrich rubs his finger over the spot. His eyes flit to the wolf sitting next to him, but he says nothing.

I stand away, my hands crossed at the small of my back.

"Shielder," Lorcan says, pointing to a spot next to him. "Will you sit?"

"No, Alpha."

I don't know why he insists on asking, because I never do. Sitting makes for laziness and bad sight lines.

Every time he asks. Every time I refuse. And every time, he turns away visibly relieved. Even Lorcan, my Alpha and my shielder, does not enjoy my company. I am not popular. Wolves do not like me. I don't care that they don't like me. I only care that they fear me. That they obey me. That when the time comes, they will do what needs to be done to keep them alive.

"In our laws are we protected," Evie calls, as the Alpha always does at the beginning of the Iron Moon Table. This meal is the most important event of the month. In skin, at least. Following immediately after the end of the Iron Moon, this is when the Pack is gathered and we all have the words and fingers needed to deal with Pack business.

"And in lawlessness are we destroyed," the Great North calls back. It is a formula for them, but for me, it is the core truth of our existence. In lawlessness is the Pack ripped apart, and without a Pack, wolves die.

Evie calls for all the pups to leave, the juveniles too. She sends them all into the back, toward the kitchen. The juveniles grab big bowls of cereal and pitchers of milk and baskets of bread. Fruit, eggs.

Our Alpha is like me. An outsider. She is older than I am, but not by much, and like me, she is the last survivor of her Pack. The similarities end there. Her Pack was slaughtered with ruthless efficiency by Shifters. Mine was picked off over months, years, by *westends*.

The Great North doesn't much use the Old Tongue word for humans, but I do, because *human* hides what they are. *Westend* doesn't. Just puts it right out there. Destroyer. Waster.

Evie and I also differ in our responses. We both know what it's like to be young and afraid and alone, but while Evie wants to protect the Great North—especially its young—from that knowing, I think they should understand that this existence is balanced on a knife's edge so they will be prepared.

Still, she is Alpha, and I would never speak out against her.

"I am calling the Pack home," she says, and in the silence, someone drops a butter knife.

Chapter 2

"WE LOST ANOTHER WOLF THIS MOON. CELIA Sorensdottir, Alpha Shielder of the 9th Echelon. Her stone will be set as soon as Sten"—she nods to the surly head of carpentry—"has finished carving it."

The Pack looks confused. We would live long lives if the *westends* would let us, but they don't. If they come upon us during the Iron Moon—or anytime, really—when we are wild, they assume we are *æcewulfs*, forever wolves, real wolves, and kill us.

If that was all that had happened, Evie would have said a mournful word or two, and we would have trudged out to the *Gemyndstow* and set this latest stone. No body though. Celia's body has already been consumed as our bodies always are, by the *wulfbyrgenna*. Wolf tombs, we call them. Coyotes.

Only a few of us know that it wasn't a *westend* who mistakenly shot Celia when she was wild. It was a Shifter who, knowing exactly what she was, shot her in skin.

Pack can become wolves whenever we want, but we can't always change back. The Iron Moon, those three days when we must be wolves, makes us both secretive and protective. We must have land that will keep us hidden and provide for our wild. We must have each other.

Shifters aren't bound to the Iron Moon, and because there is simply no advantage to being wolves, they don't bother. They stay as they are, pretending to be human.

Though they aren't: their senses are stronger, their bodies are bigger, their blood and tissue are all wrong.

And, Evie says, their bodies betray them in one other much more important way.

It turns out that the last live Shifter birth was Tiberius Leveraux, born nearly thirty years ago to a Pack mother. Now his mate, Quicksilver, has given birth to four more, and August Leveraux—godfather of Shifters, despoiler of Homelands, father of Tiberius—does not believe in coincidences.

Silver had been with Tiberius for perhaps a minute before she became pregnant. August Leveraux cannot have known Tiberius's mother, Mala, for much longer before she also conceived.

I can tell that the Alpha doesn't believe this is a coincidence either. Pregnancies are infrequent among Pack, because our chromosomes are never static, always sliding between the poles of our nature, rarely alike long enough to make more of us. Evie herself was mated thirty years before she had Nils and Nyala this winter.

"August now believes that we, or rather our females, offer them a way back from the brink of extinction."

Gabi raises her hand. *Raises her hand*, mind you. Still, Evie nods.

"Then why would the Shifters *kill* Celia?"

"As far as we can tell, they intended only to take her, but Celia fought hard. Tristan looked over the bodies before they were left for the coyotes. One Shifter, one human. He says he believes the Shifter shot her before dying."

There's something here that I don't understand, and I put my hand on the hilt of my seax, which unlike raising one's hand, is the proper way wolves signal for the floor.

"Shielder." Evie nods toward me.

"If Celia fought them, they knew she would not be receptive."

"Ah," Evie says, turning to a tall wolf who is wearing pink stockings and a very short, very white skirt with many, many zippers that ping and rustle against each other. "Leonora?"

Leonora Jeansdottir, alone among the Great North, wears clothes that are impossible to run in and hard to clean. It is so that we understand how different humans are, and when we see someone Offland, we will know that to say "How pretty, can I get it online?" is considered conversational, while "How *do* you get bloodstains out of nubuck?" is not.

I have been forced to take ten years of human behavior with her, so I know.

"Humans," Leonora says, fiddling with something catching in her hair—she wears little pieces of shiny metal in her ears that are very distracting—"have a long history of taking other humans who are not receptive. It is a form of conquest visited most particularly on females who by tradition are not taught to fight."

We are sexually profligate. It is our duty, after all, to grow the Pack. But it always starts with finding out through the warmth of the other wolf's scent whether they are receptive. Then the female presents, the male covers, and everyone hopes for the best.

Shifters have been among humans too long. No wonder Celia killed them.

There's a bad feeling in the room. The scent of anger and a low, almost inaudible rumble in large chests. Before the trouble starts, I lean over the middle of our table, the heel of my hand pressed hard into the stout oak, sending a warning glance to the more aggressive members of the 12th.

Then it erupts: the posturing, the growling, the shouting. Within seconds, the 6th Epsilon's mate has a mouth full of someone's flesh. Evie leaps from her seat and slams his face into the table. The gobbet of skin pops out across the table.

Even in skin, it is hard for us to resist the impulse to rip and gouge with our jaws.

"Alphas," she yells, the male's gagging head still squashed beneath her forearm. "Control your echelons before I do."

The other Alphas finally shake themselves out of their torpor and act.

Like I said. The Great North has been spoiled by peace and does not know how little it takes for packs to go feral.

Only when the room settles do I raise my hand from the table, taking my place behind the table with the 12th. Lorcan nods at his echelon, congratulating them on their restraint.

Evie releases the bleeding wolf and returns to her seat.

This has been a difficult transition. The loss of an Alpha always is. It takes time for wolves to get used to a new hand at the helm. Evie is the strongest wolf in the Great North, but she had been weakened by childbirth when her mate died, and there were those who took advantage of that weakness to challenge her primacy.

Or tried. I see him. Elijah Sorensson, the 9th's Alpha, who has just skittered across the hall from the kitchen to the medical station, where the *westend* he calls mate lies using up Pack resources. Victor, our Deemer—our thinker about Pack law, as opposed to human law— quite rightly saw the woman as a threat. She is not just a human but *sum westend þe wat*. A human who knows, the most dangerous enemy we have.

Still, he should not have stabbed her without Evie's permission. The 9th's Alpha took it as badly as a mated wolf would have, and the mark of Elijah's hand is still purpling on the Deemer's neck, while petechiae bloom around his eyes.

The wolves in front of me clear a space for him. He often sits with the 12th. It is a mark of the high regard the Deemer has for our echelon, the largest and best disciplined of the Great North.

The door to the Great Hall opens, and Victor looks only for a moment before turning his back purposefully on the large black wolf and the little silver wolf beside him. Tiberius and Silver ready themselves and their pups for First Marking. The pups were born only three days ago, but the Pack wastes no time before collecting the scents of their newest members and giving them their own.

Silver walks first, her hands cupped in front of her. I'd seen her before, briefly, but then the Deemer stabbed the *westend*, and the 9th's Alpha strangled our lawgiver, and I lost track of what happened to Silver.

Even though she is wearing the long, black shift that our females wear in the weeks around birth so that doctors will have rapid access to their wrecked bodies, it's easy to see how much Silver has lost. Her body is beyond thin, her eyes huge in her fleshless face.

Lying-in is always hard. Early on, the offspring switch species in response to their mother's hormones, but toward the end, they start responding not to their mother's hormones but to one another's. Then the mother must change before her body can reject the alien species inside, killing both mother and young.

The greater the number she carries, the greater the risk, and the runt carried four.

I never did understand this pairing: Tiberius is Silver's opposite—strong, where she is frail; huge, where she is small; worldly, where she is wild—but there is something there. Because Tiberius is half Shifter, I have watched him carefully, but now as he hovers over his worn mate, I see the terror in his usually impassive face.

Packs are for wolves, and Tiberius should never have been given a place in the Great North. But I recognize that there is something between these two that transcends the dutiful mounting that defines my relationship with Lorcan.

Wolves are already marking the two pups cradled in Silver's hands. A little pink mouth opens and snaps closed as Tara, Evie's Beta, rubs her cheeks against one, right first, then left. She repeats it with the second, always with a little pause as the blind, deaf pups draw in her scent. There is a murmured exchange as Silver recites the names of the two pups. Tara then goes through the process again with Tiberius, except that he holds both pups in one enormous hand, keeping the other loose by his side, ready in case Silver might need him.

The pair moves slowly past row after row of wolves until they come to me. I cup my hands under Silver's, a kindness in our ritual to the new mother who is allowed to rest her hands for a moment in those of a stronger wolf.

John, Sigeburg, and Solveig. Powerful names,

reminders of dominant wolves who have died. But then comes the fourth, Theo Tiberiusson, a tiny black runt who even through three-score Pack markings still stinks of *westend* and was named after Thea Villalobos, the *westend* who saved Tiberius, saved Silver, saved Elijah. Or, at least, that's what Elijah claims.

Silver frowns as I lower my head to the air above her hands but says nothing. No one can doubt the strength of my dedication to the Pack. If I choose not to mark its individuals, that is my business.

She continues on her way, with only the occasional waver that most wolves have the grace to pretend they haven't noticed.

"It is a disappointment, isn't it, Shielder?" Victor's voice is still rough from his throttling.

"What is a disappointment?"

"The Shifter and the runt. And now Elijah Sorensson, *who is descended from the wolves of Mercia* and should set an example of respect for discipline and respect the Old Ways."

"What does respect for discipline have to do with Mercia, Deemer? The Alpha is not of Mercia—"

"No, she is not," he says and sniffs disapprovingly, rubbing his nose with his bent knuckle.

"*I* am not of Mercia."

He sucks in his lips for a moment and looks away from me, away from eyes that are too long, under brows that are too black and too straight, set in a face that is too sharp with hair too dark to ever be mistaken for a wolf from the once-upon-a-time forests of England. Victor gathers himself together quickly.

"Ah, but you, Shielder, have proved yourself.

You"—he slices his finger across his torso—"understand the need for law, because you know firsthand the price of lawlessness. You…are *æfast*."

I know the Deemer means it as a compliment when he calls me *firm in the law*, but I am a wolf, and wolves do what they do because they must. We are wary of compliments. Even those from our Deemer.

Perhaps Victor was expecting some more effusive response than cold silence. A moment later, he returns to Lorcan, his head bowed, his voice so low that even my Alpha has to bend in to hear.

At the end of Table, I keep the 12th seated, giving out housing assignments, because nearly half the wolves of my echelon spend the month Offland working or going to school. Evie wants them all home, so we will have to accommodate them, and since Offlanders are fussy about their sleeping arrangements and only rarely willing to sleep wild, Homelands' wolves will have to give up their beds.

Other echelons are still arguing over sleeping arrangements when the last of the 12th's wolves have left to move into their new quarters. Lorcan stands next to me, his hand hovering above my back. I feel the heat of it.

"We make a good team, Shielder."

Every hair stands up on end, every muscle ripples, my eyes burn, and my tongue flicks over my teeth. But I know that this, too, is part of my responsibility, my duty to do what I can to mate power with power and bring strength to the Pack.

"Do you have a towel?"

It proceeds as it always does, at a likely tree a little farther into the woods and a little farther from Home

Pond. Lorcan looks away as I take off my shirt; then I lay my cheek against the smooth bark of the beech tree. The faded orange-brown leaves rustle above me. I wonder how long it will be before they drop, making way for new buds. Lorcan's teeth grasp the join of my neck, holding me firm for him while I stare out into the shady mix of pines and hardwoods and wait for Lorcan's shuddering finish. He stays there, his stomach pressed against my lower back, the small curls of his chest irritating my shoulder blade. He breathes deeply at the back of my ear, a little above the curve of my neck where his teeth have left a mark.

"How is it that you never smell warm?" he says as his detumescent cock slides out.

I pull my shirt back on and shake my hair free from the collar.

"Towel?" I ask.

Sheepishly, he hands it to me.

Chapter 3

An Alpha leads by example. I do not take cabins away from my echelon's Homeland wolves only to return to my own bed at night. A mated pair from the 7th is occupying my sleeping loft. Two other wolves have taken my sofa.

My tiny bathroom is crammed with my new roommates' stuff. Moisturizer: his and hers. Razors: his and hers. Sunscreen: his and hers. As if the sun shines differently on you depending on your genitals.

When I take off my muddy shirt, the sleeve knocks into lip balm (his) that teeters on the edge of my corner sink. It flies into the toilet and twirls around on top of the water like a bicycle wheel in a cyclone, until I pluck it out and set it back in its place.

As soon as I put my clothes in the laundry, I go to the refrigerator to see if my roommates cleaned up the milk spill as I instructed.

They have not, and now it is caked and dried.

The days spent crowded around Home Pond putting out brush fires among fractious wolves are getting on my nerves. I tell Lorcan I will be taking a run. That it might take me a little time to find some place quiet and private. He waves airily, as though I'd asked him for permission. All I wanted to do was to make sure he knew he had the reins.

Everyone has a different way of triggering the

change. For me, I lean into my haunches and stretch until a muscle catches in my left thigh, and when I stretch it a little farther, my wild unravels and fills me. My lungs change, and my ribs narrow and deepen to accommodate them. I take my first real breath since the Iron Moon. My shoulders round, the muscles growing thicker around them. Around my hips too. My hands and feet lengthen and bend, and I collapse, blind and frail, to the ground where I will stay until the end of the elastic thrumming of my body.

My hearing is just returning, but not my voice, when a wolf breaks through the underbrush and steps on my still-paralyzed body.

I don't blame him. He's just trying to do what I am: find a little space, a square with a little retreating snow and a little frilled lichen and drops of ice and no wolf piss-marking it off.

The netted scents of Offlanders are close to the Great Hall; Homelands wolves are more comfortable moving farther up the mountains. Holding my head low, I smell them as I pass the pine and paper birch of the lowlands, farther up to where the sun breaks through the bare branches of the beech and maple. But even up here, the crusted snow reveals the fresh crisscrossed paw prints.

The sky was overcast, as it often is in the last days of winter and early days of spring, but then suddenly the sun breaks through, shining on the bare peak of Westdæl, the most distant part of Homelands, farther from Home Pond than even the High Pines. On the far side is the Utwald, the Outer Woods, which are hard to get to, even on four legs, and too close for comfort to the lands owned by humans.

Almost at the top, the trees thin out and contort until there is nothing left but the bald crown surrounded by the bent and scoured pines of the Krummholz.

It haunts wolves' stories.

> *Winter-bearn, wind-woh,*
> *Se endeweard weorolde.*
> *Eal forsworen, forsacan*
> *Nefne*
> *Æcewulf.*

> *Winter-blasted, wind-twisted,*
> *The world's last sentinel.*
> *Forsworn, forsaken*
> *By all but the forever*
> *Wolf.*

Silver used to come up here, but she has never known anything but the security of the mighty Great North and doesn't have the sense to avoid places without adequate cover.

I should know better. The island of my birth, Vrangelya, was surrounded on all sides by the Arctic Sea. It was infertile, cold, windswept… No, not windswept. Not wind-scrubbed either. The wind came out of the north and sandblasted it, leaving behind either snow or the rubble of stone that bloomed when the snows retreated.

How is it possible that the last survivor of Vrangelya allowed herself to be caught out in the open when the helicopter comes?

The sound bounces around the valleys and mountains to the north, making it impossible to pinpoint. If I were among the trees, I'd curl my body around the base of a pine and stay absolutely still. Up here, there is nothing but snow and rock and lichens and sad, distorted excuses for trees.

Crouching as low as I can, I shuffle toward a rocky fold, then slip down, looking bleakly at the exposed run across hardpan that would take me to the sheltering tree line. Because the rock slopes back from my position, I will be completely exposed if the helicopter comes any nearer. A little farther along is an overhang. It's not much, but if I pull myself close to the rock face and stay utterly still, my gray fur may look like shadow against the granite.

As I move closer, the shade of the overhang resolves into a thicker darkness, and I realize that it is not just an overhang. It's a cave. Shelter. A place to hide. I hesitate, one foot raised above the packed earth. This place doesn't quite belong. The smell is wrong: acrid and sweet and with a single-note intensity that drowns out the softer complexity of the wild.

I remember that smell from before. John, our Alpha, followed Silver's call to Ronan, the exiled wolf who had snuck back into Homelands, stolen food and supplies, and then kidnapped the pup who found him doing it. He'd taped Golan's muzzle closed and shoved him into a backpack.

Ronan knew what was going to happen, and if he didn't resist when we came into the cave, he didn't help either. The four of us—John, Tara, Marco, and I—had to pull the drunken two-legged wolf out by his hands and feet and drag him all the way to the Clearing. Then the Great North did what the law requires we do to an exile who kidnaps a pup: we tore his body apart in a *Slitung*, a tearing. Every member of the Pack took part, as we must, so that we all bear responsibility for our failure to this wolf.

The *thuppa thuppa thuppa* is growing louder, and as much as this is not where I want to hide, there is really no choice between Ronan's cave and a helicopter carrying a *westend* with a gun. Shuffling backward, I creep into the cave, until the sky and the forests and the folded hills of Homelands are nothing but a blink of white and gray in a dark frame of stone.

They can't see me. I know that, but fear makes a mockery of reason, and step by hesitant step, I move deeper into the cave until I can't go any farther and I am pressed shivering against one wall, straining to hear the oddly benign *pop* that means wolves are being killed from the air.

It never comes. I listen the whole time until the *thuppa thuppa thuppa* attenuates, then disappears Offland.

Hesitantly at first, I peel myself away from the wall, shaking out my coat so that no wolf will see that my right flank is matted. I lick my nose and finally remember to breathe. I breathe again because there is something else here. Something that does not smell like Ronan's last days or like any part of the Great North. It's clean and sharp and painfully familiar.

With the helicopter gone, silence returns with a rough wheeze. Maybe a trick of the wind in an enclosed space. At least that's what I think until what seems like minutes go by and I hear it again—a slow and shallow breath, the sound of something living, but not well or for long.

I search through the faded scents of Ronan, Quicksilver, and even of John, until at the very back of the cave, I find a sleeping bag.

Another human, who has ignored our signs and crossed our borders and brought their junk to our territory. I investigate quietly, because if humans know, or even suspect, that there are wolves here, no signage, no law will stop them from bringing their guns to make sure that the former apex predators know who's boss now.

The sleeping bag churns, and my heart stutters and then leaps. Arctic wild has a fragrance so subtle that even wolves can't smell it. For them, it is only the sharp smell of cold. It takes a wolf who has been raised cold to distinguish its subtle varieties. This is somewhere between metal and rock and petrichor, the electric mineral smell before a storm.

This is not only a wolf; it is an Arctic wolf.

Like me.

Chapter 4

SCRATCHING LIGHTLY AT THE NYLON COCOON WITH MY paw, I stick my head in, and my nose is scorched by the heat. With claws, I try desperately to dig the wolf out, but it moves deeper in, and zippers…zippers are made by humans for humans and are the devil's own work with teeth and claws.

I need hands and fingers.

On the floor of the cave, I lean into my haunches once again and feel the snick that will start the whole unbearably slow process in reverse. The bones of my feet turn to rubber and the bony crests of my spine smooth and my eyes turn blindly in my altering skull and skin stretches forward and back and the familiar movement of fur disappears, leaving me only with skin and a shattered whisper of gray fur in the air.

I suck in short, gasping breaths, trying to reacquaint myself with the changes in my lungs.

The mummy pack is pulled tight like a cocoon. But now that I have fingers, I pull open the zipper and unleash a whoosh of heat and the shivering body of a wolf in skin.

Arctic wolves have longer hair in skin, just as we have longer fur when wild, and this wolf's hair falls forward over his pale neck, sweeping his chest. Pale with just a hint of gold underneath, it is the color of bone.

White wolves are rare even among Arctic Packs.

The only one I've ever known was the shielder of my childhood, and he has been dead for nearly thirty years. Now here is another one who isn't long for this world. Even without touching him, I can feel the fevered heat of his skin.

I know Mitya is dead, but I can't help it. My hands still shake with a kind of morbid anticipation, as though I will smooth back the long, white hair and find out that I was wrong and that by some miracle my white wolf survived. That I hadn't actually failed him.

But that's not the way it works, is it? This face is nothing like Mitya's. I knew it couldn't be. In the Great North, pups are almost always wild, so there are many I have never seen in skin and wouldn't recognize if it weren't for their smell. Pack Vrangelya understood that it was always safer to at least look human. Miserable and awkward humans, but still *not* wolves.

In skin, Mitya had a round face, soft with high cheekbones and a short chin. White eyebrows and lashes, too, that rimmed his pale eyes with long fringes, the color of fairy fingers.

This face is gaunt and long, almost bleak, the sharpness picked out by dark brows and lashes. He has to curl up to fit inside even the extra-long sleeping bags the Pack always buys, so I know he's tall.

There is something else unusual about his body. Unwolflike. We are fighters, all of us, and we are crisscrossed with the scars. From the hooves of prey, from a childhood spent tussling with sharp teeth and claws, from juvenile years spent posturing and getting called on it by stronger wolves, from adult years spent challenging for position and mates and respect.

Of course, there are other ways of earning scars. My hand floats across the corrugations that score my torso from left hip to right breast.

His skin, though, is smooth and tight across hard muscle, except for a single hole on his upper chest. A bullet wound that is large but also old and has nothing to do with why he's burning up.

There is one other thing, and it's killing him.

On his right thigh, just above his knee, is a broad, bright-red mountain range. For a moment, I think maybe it was caused by the teeth of another wolf, but the cuts are even and sharp and the flesh is badly mangled both front and back. As soon as I smell the rust, I realize he must have stepped in a trap, a big one with teeth.

It probably happened during the Iron Moon, so he was stuck there, hungry and bleeding and afraid, the teeth sawing into his changing body, until he had the fingers he needed to free himself.

It hasn't been cared for. Not by a *westend*, a Pack doctor, or by the tongue of another wolf, so now his body's rapid healing has sealed over the wound and rust and probably some chunks of fur. If he were stronger, it might not have gotten infected, but he has clearly lost a lot of blood, so he's not and it has.

I lay my hand on the hot, tight mass. My fingers feel like ice by comparison, and the wolf draws a deeper breath through cracked lips, but his eyes do not open. He is unconscious and alive, but only just.

Leaning back on my heels, I suck in another hit of the clean, clear scent of Arctic wolf.

It has taken me years to prove myself to Victor, but I came in the middle of a time of peace. Then the Shifter

came, and all our Deemer's worst fears have been borne
out. Now he clings to Pack traditions like a superstitious
old man spitting over his shoulder: *fu-fu-fu*.

Still, this is not a Shifter or a human. He is a wolf,
and a big one. If I can get him back to strength, I'll talk
to Victor. Then we'll see.

The route to Home Pond is hard enough on two legs
without any other impediment, so I can't possibly get
medical supplies in time, especially since I'd have to
carry them back through the dark, guided only by my
weakened senses in skin.

I look around the cave. It's tidier than I remember
from when I took Ronan's foot in my jaws and helped
drag him out. Bottles are lined up against one wall
next to two backpacks. If the Pack had cleaned it out,
they would've gotten rid of everything that was even
vaguely human.

I dump both backpacks to see what I have to work
with.

The smaller backpack is worn olive canvas and smells
of Arctic wolf. Change of clothes, some protein bars.

A cell phone that turns on when I push the button. No
reception, of course. I turn it off again.

Toothbrush. Floss for getting out those pesky bits of
tendon that stay and stick when a wolf's teeth go flat and
crowd together.

It's like a go-bag for the Iron Moon.

The other larger backpack clearly belonged to Ronan.
I knew that even before I smelled tiny Golan's fear.
What wolf could know so little about his Pack? How
could he not know that they would shred heaven and
earth to find their pup?

It is crammed with things he stole from the Great Hall, mostly food and a bundled collection of threadbare Packish clothes: two pairs of pants, two T-shirts, three Henleys, all bearing the names of schools within a day's drive of Homelands. All XXXL. One particularly worn tee falls to shreds almost as soon as I look at it. I put it aside for bandages.

In the front pocket is a flashlight and Ronan's seax. On the back of the sheath, he carved his name along with a clumsily rendered α. Ronan was certainly big enough to be an Alpha, but size isn't enough. He was too lazy, and when smaller Solveig, who wasn't lazy at all, challenged him, she not only defeated him, but worse, she made him afraid. By the end, he had fallen to the bottom of the 14th Echelon beside Silver, a runt with a dislocated hip.

He might have gotten his spine back and fought his way up the hierarchy again, but he drank. Even though alcohol does terrible things to our bodies, he drank.

He'd been drinking on the day he died.

The bottles are mostly water, as though water in plastic and shipped from exotic places is wetter and better than that of Homelands. I remember because as I was dragging him out, I stepped on a bottle that crackled and snapped loudly under my paw.

There is also a glass bottle half full of—I read the label—Seagram's Seven with several inches of brown liquid.

Even with the bottle closed, the smell burns my nose, but I know what it is and what it's good for.

The Arctic wolf doesn't move at all as I pull his injured leg out of the sleeping bag. I clamp it between my thighs so that when I slice through the length of his abscess with Ronan's seax, he won't jerk involuntarily and kick my teeth out.

As soon as I twist off the cap, the Seagram's hits the back of my nose hard and makes me sneeze. It also stings the inevitable small cuts on my hands when I pour some over the seax and more along the ridge of the infection. Then I clench the flashlight between my teeth.

I measure where the cut should be. He's probably going to die if I do this, but he is certainly going to die if I don't. Thankfully, Ronan was at least wolf enough to occasionally sharpen his seax, but even so, as the knife goes in, this wolf's body jerks.

One exhausted eye swims momentarily up to consciousness. I know eyes that color, the pale, faded blue of old ice. I know the expression too. The one of confused betrayal. I look away and slice deep, then his body relaxes against mine. When I check back, that accusing eye is closed. Thick, yellow pus oozes from the opening. I irrigate it slowly with a mix of clean water and Seagram's until it runs clear.

What most wolves would do now, what I should do now, is debride him, clean him with my mouth and sensitive tongue, but I haven't debrided another wolf since Mitya. Leonora says that *westends* won't do it because they find it disgusting.

I won't do it because of the almost unbearable intimacy of it all, the touch of lips to skin, of tongue to blood. Of giving comfort that is so much more profound than, say, sex, which is nothing but a tree, a towel, and the duty to procreate. Debriding is comfort and healing and belonging.

Instead, I wrap my finger in the shredded T-shirt dipped in whiskey and run it through the cut, cleaning it out, searching for whatever bit of hide or fur or rusted metal keeps it from healing.

A tiny sound, a half a groan, burbles up from his chest, and a burning-hot hand touches the back of my head. At first, I think he's going to grab my hair and yank me away, but he doesn't. He leaves his hand there until the third pass with the third alcohol-dosed rag, when I pull up a large gluey wad of fur.

Then the hand goes limp and falls to the ground. The wolf's breath comes deeper. I pour more alcohol and water into the gash.

He doesn't wake at all when I repeat the whole thing with the back side of his thigh.

Seagram's. Knife. Rags. Seagram's.

Tearing more straps, I wrap his mangled leg before sliding it back into the sleeping bag.

Then I put everything back, starting first with Ronan's bag. I was wrong. This isn't all stuff he'd stolen. There are things like—I turn a tube upside down—mousse à raser and baume après-rasage in a scent called myrrh that makes me gag. A razor, which is odd: Homelands wolves do not shave because if done too close to the Iron Moon, it compromises the guard hairs.

Wolves also don't wear jewelry, except for the neck braid that symbolizes mated wolves' commitment to Pack and land and each other. There is a metal cuff with the words *Alpha male*. Clearly a human thing. He certainly never wore it at Homelands. Too afraid of the half-dozen Alpha females who would line up for a chance to remind him that the words *alpha* and *male* do not necessarily follow and should definitely not be etched in steel.

How, I wonder, could someone like Silver, who is the wildest of us all, have a shielder who was so... I try to think of the *westend* word for it but can't think of anything that comes close to the Old Tongue... *Manweorþung*. Man-esteeming?

Then I put everything back. The Arctic wolf's bag was carefully packed. Aside from the clothes, toiletries, and phone is a wallet with a few dollars, a work schedule at the Walmart Supercenter in Malone, and a fake ID. Not even a good fake. I can tell because the Great North knows how to fake documents.

Frank Carter, it says in a serif font. From *Kearsarge, Mich*.

A broad, flat metal box with colored pencils, eraser and sharpener, and a spiral-bound notebook. The pages are plain and heavy and lightly textured and filled with drawings. Not filled, crowded, clotted with drawings. Mostly black and gray, which explains why those two pencils are so much shorter than their fellows. Some are no more than the roughest outlines—a few lines to hint at a river when the water is low, a somber cathedral of mountains, the dappling of fall hardwoods, mist rising when warm rain hits ice.

Explicit detail is reserved for smaller things: the bark of paper birch, the winter skeleton of Queen Anne's lace, a constellation of striders on dimpled water.

Each drawing is labeled with a place—Ontario. Manitoba, Alberta, Wisconsin, Minnesota, and Michigan—and a date.

I am aware enough of the patterns of our lives to see

the pattern in this life too. A day before or after the Iron Moon spent recording what he sees so that when he moves on, he remembers.

At the front of the journal is the Roman numeral VII.

How long have you been alone, wolf? We are much more social than *westends*. We need more structure, care for our young longer, take losses harder. Usually lone wolves don't last long. That's why exile is really a death sentence.

How long have you been alone, and how did you survive?

I sit back, my legs crossed, my hand to the just-touched hair at the crown, and breathe in the scent of cold. It's so vivid, so present that I almost feel that if I open my eyes, I will be surrounded by my pack. Not by this new pack that hasn't been "new" for decades, but by Vrangelya. Big and hard and, to my young eyes, so invincible. And I would see Mitya. Not like this. Not an injured adult, but little and hopeful in a land that never rewarded that kind of thing.

I don't know how long I sit there watching the slow rise and fall of the body in front of me, sucking in the undeniable and necessary smell of cold. It must have been a while, because wolves howl the midday song, reminding me that I have responsibilities, real responsibilities, to the warm Pack down below.

Putting three bottles of water in front of him where he can't miss them, I get ready to change.

Astille, guðling…

What was the song? And who sang it? And why is it bubbling up from my memory like muck from the bottom of a disturbed pond?

Astille, guðling, þu eart gesund mid me.
Sona, biþ se mona her something,
    something.

Still, little warrior, you are safe with
    me.
Soon the moon will be here, something,
    something.

Astille, guðling,
Still, little warrior.

Chapter 5

TOO MANY OFFLAND WOLVES ARE TREATING THEIR TIME home as something called a "vacation." A vacation is a human concept meaning, as far as I can recall from Leonora's explanation, that an individual suspends their contribution to the survival of the Pack while others pick up the slack.

Well, not in the 12th they don't.

We have been assigned to expand the cold frames in case the Offlanders are still here during harvest season. The echelon is distracted and must be made to focus on their work so the corners are properly squared and the insulation fits without interfering with the lie of the lids.

"You forgot the washers. So you'll have to redo the bolts."

"All of…?" Reinholt asks. "Yes, Shielder."

They take the blessing of this sanctuary for granted.

Tonia throws worms at Lorcan, who giggles, his scent taking on a smell I know too well.

When I suggest they stop throwing worms and just go into the woods and fuck already, Lorcan slams his hammer down, splitting the wood. He is a child who wants to be liked and doesn't understand why I don't want to play. He is very strong of body—he is Alpha, after all—but he is weak of marrow and doesn't understand that being liked is not an Alpha's purpose.

I hand him a new piece of pine. "Now you have to cut it again."

It doesn't matter. I am disliked enough for both of us.

I am the last to leave, screwing in the final lids and making sure everything is tight and well made and that the tools are clean and dry and hung in their proper places. The 12th has already bathed and is probably in the Great Hall, eating.

For now, I sit at the roots of a tight grouping of speckled alder and wait for the line to the Bathhouse to shorten. I am downwind and out of eyeshot, but I can hear the Offlanders grouse about the work or the crowding. I listen, ready in case tempers fray and complaining turns to bloodshed.

Zelda, the 4th's Gamma, complains about her new roommate, saying that she is difficult and severe. *Micclum scripende*.

Very… What would the *westends* here say? Dark, maybe? Hard. Hard is better.

"Ha-ha," titters a familiar voice.

"Ours is *scripendost*!" one of my roommates says with another laugh.

"Whose cabin are you in?" Zelda asks.

"The 12th's Alpha Shiel"—her voice falters—"der?"

"Varya the Indurate?" whispers some subordinate wolf from the 7th.

"*Oh, shut up!*" hisses Zelda. There is a whispered conversation that I can't hear and don't need to. I know my reputation. I know what the Great North whispers about me.

Three minutes later, two of my roommates run,

half-naked, toward the cabin, muttering angrily about who should have cleaned up the dried-milk spill.

So now, without me doing anything, the refrigerator will be cleaned and there are two fewer people in line.

Someone takes the last clean towel, and a fight breaks out. The towel taker is led away quickly because a wolf removed his tooth with her fist. If he doesn't go to medical and have the tooth reset quickly, the missing canine will interfere with his hunting. His bedfellow, who had been sniffing around a receptive male, reluctantly leaves the line.

Now four fewer people in line, and those who remain are furious. One starts arguing with the 6th's Beta who is in charge of crowd control. "Dinner will be over before the rest of us get a chance!"

I nod to Victor, who is not wearing bath shoes or carrying a towel. "Is there some problem here, Alpha?" In the absence of any Alpha-ranked wolf, he calls me Alpha, as is right.

"A squabble, but it is over now, Deemer."

He looks at the band of discontents standing in the churned-up earth. "So, is this what the Great North has come to?" he says loudly and rhetorically. "A group of wet mutts standing in the mud?" His voice has something to it. Scorn? Sarcasm? Anyway, something peculiarly human.

The Offlanders, who are used to privacy and easy access to running water, murmur their assent and listen to the Deemer who speaks to their concerns.

The Pack, he says, is a chain that is only as strong as its weakest link, but we have too many weak links now. The runt, who should by all rights have no say at all, has the ear of the Alpha. He says. The Shifter who has been responsible for peeling back our protections and leaving us vulnerable to his father is a full-fledged member of the Pack. He says. And now the Alpha has allowed a *westend þe wat* to live. A human who knows. With one quick yank, the Pack will fall apart.

He says.

Wolves from the 6th run in with towels. Two others leave the Bathhouse, but the slavering horde that used to be a line seems to have lost interest, so I stretch and stride past.

"Alpha?" says Victor.

I bend my head in deference to his station, but I will not give up a turn at the Bathhouse in order to join a mob.

Tossing my sweaty clothes into the big hamper, I turn to one of the showers. Two wolves look away.

"What do you think?" says one. "You had enough?"

"Yeah, we should get going. We have…tomorrow…" the other says, his voice petering out.

They nod at me, their eyes not lowered so much as averted.

I nod back, but I doubt they see.

None of the wolves of the Great North will look at the scars across my belly. No one else has them, but they all know what they are. They know they don't come from any fight. They know that a *Clifrung*, a clawing, is a punishment just one step short of the ritual flesh tearing by which the Pack ends a wolf's life.

They know that no wolf was allowed to clean the wounds or care for them, so that they would mark me forever as *Wearg*. They also know that I was marked this way when I first came, only a juvenile, to the Great

North. That I had already lost the right to my Pack name and was no longer Varya Timursdottir.

The juvenile who dubbed me Varya the Indurate thought she was being so brave and rebellious. She couldn't possibly know how little I cared.

I was already Varya Wearg: Varya the Bloodthirsty. Varya the Outlaw.

See, now *that* is saying something.

Only Nils, who was Alpha when I came, knew why the Alpha of Pack Vrangelya had ripped his claws through my flesh. Perhaps Nils told John before he died. Perhaps John told Evie before he died. I don't know. They never asked, and I have no interest in telling.

Armed with a rough-bristle brush and a bar of the soap wolves use so that our particular scent isn't obscured, I stand under the icy water, rasping at my skin until I feel nothing.

It's too dark to return to Westdæl on two legs, but I will go back in the morning.

Chapter 6

FIRST THING IN THE MORNING, I HEAD TO THE GREAT HALL and pull together things that the Arctic wolf might need. Water pouch. Ground pad. Antibiotics. Gauze. It will be a while before he is healed enough to go through the change without reopening everything. Unable to hunt, he will need food. In another room in the basement, still-shiny wire shelves carefully bolted into walls and floors and to one another carry row after row of dried and canned foods: beans, rice, fruit, vegetables. The things the Pack eats when they're in skin and can't hunt but will not eat old flesh and carrion the way *westends* do.

Shoving boxes of food willy-nilly into a backpack, I hide what I'm doing from no one, and no one asks.

The coffee is on, and juveniles are in the kitchen making something—date-walnut scones from the look of it—for breakfast.

Gran Tito glances toward me but says nothing as I rummage through the cupboards looking for more food. Instead, he taps on the long scraped-oak table surrounded by juveniles to bring their attention back to him. Usually juveniles knead dough while the adult wolf reads. But it's still called a Knead and Read if they are chopping dates and reciting texts. The previous Alpha, John, taught literature, and Evie, his mate, insists that the Great North be well read.

"Start again," Gran Tito says to a female, who

judging by the awkwardness of her stance, is probably in the Year of First Shoes. "You can do it," he says with an encouraging smile.

Finally, the high-pitched slurry voice pups have until they get used to the shallow mouths and thick tongues of this form rises above the chopping walnuts.

"'As the creeper that gird the tree trunk, the law runneth forward and back…'" She watches me ransack the cupboards with a nervous expression.

"'As the creeper that gird the tree trunk, the law runneth forward and back…'" she starts again, and again her voice dies out.

"Where are the cheese chews?" I ask.

"Top corner pantry," says Gran Tito. "Now keep going, Rainy."

I find the raisins in the top corner pantry as well. The kitchen is still new to me, but this is obviously where they put things they want to keep away from little hands and littler paws.

I take a cheese chew and start gnawing on one end. Even in skin, I like them, though they have the consistency of snow tires. The young female looks at her fellow juveniles, an empty look on her face.

"Rainy, focus," Gran Tito says again. "'The law runneth forward and back…'"

I remember learning this bit under a different elder, in the old kitchen.

Absently, Rainy rolls the sticky bits of date into a ball under her palm and then pops it into her mouth.

It is making me angry, this lack of attention. She is no longer a pup. She has responsibilities now and must learn to take them seriously.

"*Rainy*," I snap. "What comes next?"

Her eyes flicker to her echelon, but the entire table has fallen silent. There is no chopping. The juveniles stare at the table while Gran Tito looks at the dish towel in his hands.

"They are not going to help you. This is your responsibility."

"The law runneth forward and back,'" she finally repeats. "'For the strength of the Pack is the wolf, and the strength of the wolf is the Pack.'"

"Keep going."

"But it's not my turn," she whines. "We're each supposed to take one—"

"I don't care what you are *supposed* to do. It doesn't make any sense unless you learn the whole thing. You can skip the part about elephants."

One of her echelon starts mouthing something to her, but his jaw clamps tight when I look at him.

She becomes misty-eyed and lifts her chin up and to the side, displaying her cheek. It's what pups do when they are feeling insecure and need reassurance.

I do not mark her. Instead, I grab the chair and twirl her around, my eyes boring into hers.

"*We* are wolves. *We* do not have the luxury of being frail and delicate. Now look at me *and do it*!"

Then I growl low and rough, the way dominants do when they are running out of patience and are about to attack.

That gets her attention.

As we stare at each other, her breathing comes steadier and faster, and she pushes my hand away and starts again, this time hissing through gritted teeth.

> "'As the creeper that gird the tree
>   trunk, the law runneth forward and
>   back;
> For the strength of the Pack is the wolf,
>   and the strength of the wolf is the
>   Pack.
> When Pack meets with Pack in the
>   forest, and neither will go from the
>   trail,
> Lie down till the leaders have spoken; it
>   may be fair words shall prevail.
> When ye fight with a wolf of the Pack,
>   ye must fight him alone and afar
> Lest others take part in the quarrel and
>   the Pack is diminished by war.'"

I interrupt her before she gets lost in the dietary restrictions, because this was the important part. "Remember: you are nothing without your Pack. But the Pack is nothing without the law. Without order, we all die."

Gran Tito rocks an imaginary knife back and forth in the air to get his charges going again, then disappears into the pantry.

"Alpha?" he says. "There are still plenty of my soy chips." I shove the two large boxes into my bag.

They wait only until the door has closed before the complaining starts. This little female does not understand the mind-numbing, foot-freezing cold of fear. Or that anger is the only thing hot enough to burn through.

With any luck, I have given her an ember for when the fear comes, as it always does.

My body never feels entirely comfortable in skin. Everything seems far away, as if my eyes, ears, nose, and skin are coated with a thick cotton baffle.

But my mind is never entirely comfortable wild. Wild, I always look over my shoulder, half expecting to find some *westend* looking at me down the barrel of a gun.

When I get back to the cave, the water bottles are untouched. The sleeping bag hasn't moved either. He's either asleep or unconscious. I unzip the bag, slowly. He's not shaking like before, and instead of being curled up tight, he is stretched out, lean and rangy. Tall, muscled chest, lean hips, long legs. Strong, but not in Lorcan's broad and bullish way; more like a mountain lion, lithe and sinewy. It is a body built not for banging on the ground like a hammer but for slicing through the air like a knife. Dark hair starts in the hollow below his navel. Even soft, his cock lies thick against his hip.

I look at his leg.

Our bodies heal rapidly, so the fact that he hasn't is testament to how weak he has become. I think his fever has gone down. Slightly. The skin is knitting together, and the mountain range of infection has lessened. Slightly. More than anything, he needs water.

"Hey."

When he doesn't respond, I shake him.

"Hey, *you*."

His long, solid body is heavy, but I am strong and I lift him up, letting his head droop back against my shoulder. I feel his sinew, so hard and lean against my thighs. The fluid lines of his shoulders against my arms.

The sharp wing of his shoulder blade against my damaged chest.

Holding my thumb across the mouth of the bottle, I drizzle water into his mouth, one half sip at a time.

This is a terrible intimacy, sitting here with a dying wolf between my legs, the heat of his body searing mine, his head lolling against my chest, his pale hair against my cheek, as water runs from the corner of his mouth, along his jaw, behind his ear, and onto my neck, finally dribbling onto my breast.

It takes a long time before he swallows. It is reflex, nothing more, but drip by painstaking drip, he drinks. I hold him there, even when he stops. Let him lean against me, unconscious and unknowing. Let the smell of cold surround me.

I hold him there long after the sun moves overhead and its rays retreat along the rock-strewn floor. I do not hold him when the ground starts to tremble. Then I arrange him back on top of the sleeping bag and tent my fingertips to the packed ground. The dull throb is too regular and too ceaseless to be the earth's natural stirring. It's followed by a distant pounding, a whisper that compresses the air in waves, even here in the tight space of this cave.

I grab a bottle of water and slip outside, though not before I touch the backs of my hands, convulsively checking my long, naked fingers and pale-gold skin to be sure that I at least look human.

One helicopter is a mistake. Two are not. The Great North distributes bribes and threats freely to make sure Homelands isn't on any flight path, so where are these helicopters coming from? If it was from the airport in

Malone, it would be traveling farther east, but this one is coming from the north.

Creeping along the ledge, I grab hold of one of the pines bent close to the ground, then scramble up to the bald peak of Westdæl for a clear view.

The northwest corner of Homelands is cradled by mountains. Not the highest in the Adirondacks, but high enough. Defining much of our northern border is a ridge divided up into parts by shallow ravines. At some point that range was named Norþdæl, the North Part, but mostly they are called the High Pines after their most important feature, the dense, chaotic region of evergreens that flows across them. If something makes the Pack nervous, the High Pines is where they hide.

At the northwest corner, the westernmost slope of the High Pines meets the northernmost slope of the imaginatively named Westdæl, the West Part. Between the two is the Gin—the Old Tongue word for *gap*—though it isn't really, because over the years it has been filled in by downslides, stone fractured by the cycle of freeze and thaw. A few stringy plants cling to the Gin, but trees that try to put down roots on its loose and windblown ridge usually don't last long, so the Gin is mostly bare.

And that's where the helicopter rises.

Thuppathuppathuppathuppathuppa.

Chapter 7

LOOKING OVER HOMELANDS, I SEE WOLVES MOVE through the hardwoods that are still bare and provide nowhere near enough cover. They haven't dealt with men in planes, so they are running by instinct for the High Pines or other evergreen cover, instead of doing what they should: find any tree trunk, wrap themselves around the base, and be still.

Every shadowy movement through the underbrush, every hint of silver or gray against the damp, dark forest floor, every sliver of dark fur against gray stone or retreating snow or beige reeds makes my heart beat against my ears in rhythm with the helicopter blades.

I sit down, because if my legs fail, it's better that I look like a *westend* hiker out of breath. I don't want them landing to help me.

The pilot sees me and comes closer, nearly level with where I sit. The bottle drops from my shaking fingers.

Wolves are not by nature religious. We believe in the sanctity of the land and the Pack and our sacred selves. But that didn't mean Yefim, Vrangelya's last Deemer, was above teaching us a prayer. Just to give us the illusion of control when there wasn't any. The whole thing, if we had time, was *Alys us fram westendum and fram eallum hiera cræftum.*

Save us from humans and all their works.

It got shorter when there were more humans and

their works were deadlier. *Alys us fram westendum*. Or simply. *Alys us*.

Alys us fram westendum and fram eallum hiera cræftum. I pick the bottle up again, holding it so tightly that it cracks and the water drains down my jeans. *Alys us fram westendum*. The life of the forests goes silent and contracts, small and hidden, as the helicopter flies low overhead. *Alys us*.

It is so close that I can see the doors have been removed. A brindle wolf cuts across the Clearing toward the hardwoods to the north.

Thuppathuppathuppathuppathuppa.

A man in a dark-green jacket, jeans, and an oddly fluorescent-pink aviation headset sits harnessed into the back seat looking east, until the pilot, seeing me wave, turns his head toward his passenger and points. The harnessed man looks at me. I touch my smooth skin to remind myself once more that I am human. If they shoot the brindle wolf, it's sport. If they shoot me, it's murder.

The man has something in his hands. *I am human. I am human. I am human*. He won't shoot me. It is a camera. The brindle wolf gets low behind the olive cover of a leather leaf.

I lift the nearly empty bottle to my quivering lips.

Thuppathuppathuppathuppathuppa.

The man waves, his mouth opening and closing. Willing my hand to act, I wave back, then point to my ear with a shrug.

The helicopter keeps moving out over our woods and over the Clearing and over the Great Hall. I watch as it continues over Home Pond and the land that lies between Home Pond and the *westend* lands to the south.

When I am sure that the helicopter is gone, I drop the water bottle and bend over, vomiting up water and air. Then I clap both hands over my mouth and take in a deep breath, reminding myself that I am no longer some quivering pup, so terrified by small planes that the shadow of a passing snow goose makes me weak with terror.

I am Varya the Indurate, the Alpha Shielder of the 12th Echelon of the Great North Pack. What a laugh.

The Great North remains still and quiet. Evie doesn't call the all clear until she is sure that the malignant beat of the blades is not returning north. Once she does, the shadows begin slipping through the leafless hardwoods toward Home Pond. If I had to guess, I'd say that few Pack will be wild tonight, preferring to disguise themselves with skin and words and thumbs and upright posture.

Scrabbling down the side of the ledge, I bend back into the mouth of the cave. The sound of the helicopter did what slicing a knife through the wanderer's abscessed leg could not. It got him up. Somehow, he dragged himself to the front, where he sits folded up and shivering in a corner at the cave's mouth. That's what someone does who knows what it is to be trapped in the back. Who knows it is better to stay in the darkness near the front so that as soon as any intruder passes, you can race for freedom.

Which is what he does. Not race, stumbles. Delirious, starving, bloodless, injured, he keeps going. His leg has reduced him to grabbing onto whatever support comes to hand—mostly the crooked trees that give the Krummholz its name. Here, the trunks are bent low to the earth by the brutal, untamed north winds until they hardly resemble their tall, noble cousins of the more protected lands below; they are the survivors of a harder life.

He collapses, clinging to a bent spruce, the pale hair streaming like an icefall between his broad shoulders.

This is what the Pack needs. No more half Shifters or humans, but a wolf who is not only strong of body, but strong of marrow. A wolf who has the power and will to survive.

He moves faster, but then inevitably topples and steps hard on his injured leg. I leap forward, shoving my foot into the loose earth so I can catch him before he falls. He hops to a standstill against me, his breath hard and ragged. He turns to face me.

Ah.

Now I know.

Now I know why he is alone. Why he has always been alone.

And why he will be alone forever.

I guess I'd only seen one eye before—the pale, ice-blue one. Never the other. Never the one that is the bright, variegated green of the forest canopy.

Dragging him back to the safety of the cave, I settle him onto the open sleeping bag.

Once more, I put a few bottles of water in easy reach. I don't try to talk to him. I've had enough talking to doomed wolves to last a lifetime.

He circles around until he curls up in a ball on the sleeping bag, his head turned slightly, like a wolf without a tail, and falls back into his fevered sleep.

I fold the sleeping bag over again and sit for a little while, my chin on my knees, until it's time for me to leave yet another white wolf I am helpless to save.

Chapter 8

PUTTING THE SCYTHE STONE BACK IN MY POCKET, I SET THE blade parallel to the ground, my feet shoulder width apart, and, with long, smooth strokes, continue cutting.

Ruuucccckkkk, Shhhhh. Ruuucccckkkk, Shhhhh. Ruuucccckkkk, Shhhhh.

Yefim, Vrangelya's Deemer, had given up on teaching the pups anything as sophisticated as law, keeping us entertained with old, invariably grim stories instead.

Ruuucccckkkk, Shhhhh. Ruuucccckkkk, Shhhhh. Ruuucccckkkk, Shhhhh.

"Eormenburh," said Yefim, "was from the Ironwood, the forest that bred and nurtured all wolves."

Ruuucccckkkk, Shhhhh. Ruuucccckkkk, Shhhhh. Ruuucccckkkk, Shhhhh.

"She was the Alpha of the first Pack and, as her name suggests, the great defender of the wood. She was powerful and fierce and a brilliant fighter, and the Ironwood was called the Ironwood because no *westend* could break into it. No ax could fell it; no fire could burn it down for fields. It was iron dark and iron strong."

Ruuucccckkkk, Shhhhh. Ruuucccckkkk, Shhhhh. Ruuucccckkkk, Shhhhh.

"And all was well for the wolves of Ironwood, until the first Alpha burned with need for Loki, the first Shifter."

Ruuucccckkkk, Shhhhh. Ruuucccckkkk, Shhhhh. Ruuucccckkkk, Shhhhh.

Over the years, Yefim went on, Eormenburh bore three children. Fenrir, a wolf, took after his mother and was the wildest of the wild. Jormundgard, a snake, took after his Shifter father and was the strongest of the strong.

Then came little Hela, who took after both parents and was split down the middle: half wolf, wild and divine; half skin, smooth and profane.

Ruuucccckkkk, Shhhhh. Ruuucccckkkk, Shhhhh. Ruuucccckkkk, Shhhhh.

Though the Ironwood was obscured even from Odin, those busybodies Huginn and Muninn had noticed Loki sneaking in and out on more than one occasion and told the big fart.

That's what Yefim called him because wolves owe no debt of respect to the gods of men.

Ruuucccckkkk, Shhhhh. Ruuucccckkkk, Shhhhh. Ruuucccckkkk, Shhhhh.

Odin came with his Aesir and did what hunters of wolves always do. He found Eormenburh's denning young and tortured them until they howled. When the Pack came running, desperate and heartbroken ("slavering," the *westends* say), the Aesir killed them all.

Except one.

Ruuucccckkkk, Shhhhh. Ruuucccckkkk, Shhhhh. Ruuucccckkkk, Shhhhh.

Even after Eormenburh's death, the gods were frightened of Eormenburh and could not bring themselves to say her name. Instead, they called her Angrboda, the Bearer of Sorrows, the "sorrows" being her children, who because they carried a god's blood could not be killed. But they were dangerous enemies who hated the killers of their mother and their Pack, so the gods imprisoned them. Fenrir was tied by magic chains, Jormundgard was bound under the vast oceans, and little Hela was caged so deep in the ground that her jail shared the same bit of real estate as the dead.

Ruuucccckkkk, Shhhhh. Ruuucccckkkk, Shhhhh. Ruuucccckkkk, Shhhhh.

The single survivor of Eormenburh's Pack wandered the earth looking for his Alpha's young until he finally found Hela's scent. He followed her into the abyss that bears her name, and loyal to the end, he guards her there.

Ruuucccckkkk, Shhhhh. Ruuucccckkkk, Shhhhh. Ruuucccckkkk, Shhhhh.

The *westends* call him Garm. Who knows what his name had been in Ironwood—certainly not Garm, which is not a Pack name. But the passing centuries spent underground bleached his fur white as bone. Those centuries spent on guard had changed his eyes too. One became as pale as the sky that he watched for threats from the gods. One became as green as the earth that he watched for threats from humans.

Ruuucccckkkk, Shhhhh. Ruuucccckkkk, Shhhhh. Ruuucccckkkk, Shhhhh.

It is said that he is waiting until Eormenburh's children are big enough and powerful enough. Then the Banwulf, the Bone Wolf, who sees both heaven and earth, will howl and that…that will mark the beginning of the end of both.

Ruuucccckkkk, Shhhhh. Ruuucccckkkk, Shhhhh. Ruuucccckkkk, Shhhhh.

I know packs on the edge, and not one of them is secure enough to look at a white wolf with those haunted eyes and gamble that this is simply an Arctic wolf with pronounced heterochromia, *not* the harbinger of the world's end.

Ruuucccckkkk, Shhhhh. Ruuucccckkkk, Shhhhh. Ruuucccckkkk, Shhhhh.

I will make sure that the white wolf is healed, but then he will have to move on, a wanderer until he dies. A wolf without a pack. I have done what I can; besides, I could do a hundred times that and never be absolved of my failure to save that other white wolf.

They were both strange wolves in a world that has no room for either.

That's what I tell myself when I go back to the tool-shed and switch out the grass blade for the short, thick brush blade.

Then I turn my back on Westdæl and its eye-shaped cave, and with short hacking strokes, I begin attacking the brambles.

Shukk, shukk, shukk, shukk, shukk.

"Shielder?"

I let the stroke run out, lifting the scythe. Sweat runs down my neck, between my shoulder blades, and between my breasts. I cup my hand over my eyes so that I can see a figure so slight, he has to work at casting a shadow.

Arthur, the 12th's *nidling*, is thin with wavy-brown hair that, given the slightest breeze or no breeze at all, whispers like cobwebs around his worried face. He is always hunched, his shoulders curved forward, his arms wrapped around his waist, his chin tucked into his chest. Everything about him is constricted and looks like defeat.

There's an old saying that lone wolves are the only ones who always breed, their children being Frustration and Dissent. To control weak and solitary wolves at the bottom of an echelon's hierarchy, they are consigned to be *nidlings*, servants to the Alpha pair.

Setting the heel of the snath on the ground, I take the file out of my back pocket again and, with long, smooth, curving strokes, bring the blade back to an edge.

There are not many *nidlings*. Not only are they weak, but they are peculiarly prone to outrageous accidents: a fatal hoof to the chest, a careless leap across a gorge, running in a straight line away from a gun when every wolf knows you need to zigzag.

Quicksilver Nilsdottir, the 14th Echelon's runt, was a *nidling* for a few minutes before Tiberius Malasson showed up. Mala, Tiberius's mother, was a *nidling* until she ran away and met August Leveraux and became the root and source of so much trouble.

"The Alpha sent me to inform you that all Alpha pairs are being called to the Meeting House."

Lorcan hasn't spoken a civil word to me since that worm thing.

"Tell the Alpha I'll be there as soon as I clean up."

I dry the bramble blade, then hang it, cleaned and honed, next to the others.

After wiping the damp dirt away, I bend the hoe that Lorcan never repaired back into shape and hang it from the brackets sized for it.

Chapter 9

THE WOLVES OF VRANGELYA HAD LITTLE USE FOR houses and no trust whatsoever for the things that lived inside houses, so it was a tradition of that pack to touch the lintel above any door we passed through. Touching the lintel was our talisman, our fervent wish that no matter what we met upon entering, we would live long enough to exit.

As hopes and aspirations for the future went, it was admittedly small beer.

The Great North is different. The first Alpha bought land here about 350 years ago, and every passing generation added to it whenever possible. Sometime in the last century, the Pack bought a great camp from some bankrupt businessman. It was a windfall of land and nearly sixty buildings: Laundry, Carpentry, Boathouse, the Great Hall that lasted until the Shifters burned it down this winter. The Pack has added other buildings, mostly small cabins used for mated wolves.

Lorcan told me once that the Meeting House had been a chapel to the *westends'* God of Dominion, which I suppose explains the elaborate decorations of curved branches gracing the gabled entryway and the balustrade around the deck.

The Great North uses it for meetings and lyings-in, and when the Great Hall burned this winter, the Meeting House was the crowded heart of Pack life.

I can't help but touch the lintel as I enter. As soon as I see that the Alphas have been joined by various Pack lawyers, I heave a sigh and touch it again.

The air inside is damp and warm with the breath of so many wolves tightly crammed together, and Evie signals for the windows to be opened.

A Pack without leadership tends to revert quickly to pure, feral id, so Evie keeps a tight schedule. Josi begins talking immediately about the helicopter incursion over Great North airspace. Airplanes must fly higher, but not helicopters. They are allowed to fly low over any "unimproved" land.

The lawyers are going to try to claim that the helicopters are disturbing the "Great North Kennel," an invention meant to disguise our inordinately large consumption of cheese chews, peanut butter toothpaste, and skunk spray, but the "kennel" is small because more than twenty-five "dogs" will necessitate an inspection by state authorities.

Our lawyers assure Evie that they are doing everything they can. Money will be spent, and favors called in. Humans will be slapped with lawsuits—as soon as they can track down which human is responsible.

Elijah Sorensson, the 9th's Alpha and the lawyer in charge of the trust meant to protect us, seems distracted. He cradles his cell phone in his big palm. It must have buzzed, because he jumps, his massive hand trembling around the little thing, but after a quick thumb swipe, he covers it again with a murmured "sorry."

Several of the Alpha pairs exchange glances. Lorcan smiles at me conspiratorially, meaning, I suppose, he's forgotten about the worms.

"He does that all the time. Checks his phone," Lorcan whispers. "Apparently he's hoping the human will come back."

Lorcan doesn't like the 9th's Alpha. Something about a wasp's nest when the 9th and the 12th were assigned to clean the Boathouse for Silver's lying-in. But as much as I believe we should have killed the human, I take no pleasure in another wolf's distress. Elijah is thinner now. One bootlace has broken, and rather than fixing it or replacing it, he ties it in an awkward knot low on his ankle.

He has always been a hard worker and is a capable Alpha, but his discipline is slipping. And for a *human*.

"I'm thirsty," Lorcan whispers, looking around for Arthur, who is standing ready in the corner, his head bowed, but his eyes searching. "Do you want something?"

"*Gestille*, Alpha." Be still, Alpha. I put my hand on his leg, my fingers tightening.

Elijah presses the phone to his chest as if his heart is listening for some reassuring noise.

All this for someone who could never be part of the Pack. My eyes flick to the window. It's hemmed in by trees, but beyond the woods and waterways and open spaces and bogs and low slopes is the western edge of our land and a wolf who is in the same predicament.

Our lands, Josi says, lie between two rich shale producers. One of those producers is eager to start exploring for gas here. Others are looking for a route to pipe the gas in the shale of Quebec to points south. Hence the helicopters.

In the end, there are a few questions fielded by the lawyers. When they are done, I stand silently grasping the hilt of my sheathed seax until Evie nods toward me.

I tell the Pack that I was on Westdæl, almost parallel with the helicopter, and could see wolves running under the leafless hardwoods, even from there. If the helicopters come again, I tell them, they must curl around the roots of the nearest tree, even if it is bare, and stay absolutely still, because *westends* in the air respond to movement.

I sit back down, my forearms on my thighs, my fingers curled over my knees.

"The Pack will follow the advice of the 12th's Alpha," Evie says, then grimaces slightly. She's made this slip before, calling me Alpha, and while I'm glad the Pack will do what I need them to, I now have to deal with Lorcan, who is very jealous of his dignity.

He growls deep in his throat. He folds his arms across his chest, casting around to see how that slip has played among the other Alphas.

Aside from that momentary grimace, Evie wastes no time on Lorcan's wounded pride. She wants the entire perimeter covered and has posted a roster in her office. Every echelon must volunteer a wolf—and not just any wolf but a Homelands wolf, one who knows the territory well.

The Alpha starts as she always does with the 1st. Each echelon volunteers one of their own without hesitation, but then it comes to the 12th, and Lorcan angrily volunteers…me.

Evie takes a deep breath and leans against the table. I can see she is not happy with his choice, but for her to question his decision is to question his leadership, which she can do only if she is prepared to both fight him and deal with the chaos when she wins.

Chapter 10

"NU IS SEO MÆL FOR US LEORNIAN ÞINE LAGA AND SIDA."

After all these years, I still find it unnerving that these wolves can dare be so loud.

Through the windows come the sounds of pups and juveniles responding to Victor's call to the law with words or whistles or high-pitched howls, depending on what shape they're in.

It's a signal that our meeting is at an end and the Alphas must go back to the business of taking care of their own.

I head to the Great Hall to sign up for perimeter watch, threading through the pups and juveniles emerging from the woods to join their Deemer at the stairs leading up to the porch.

Nils chases Nyala up the steps, first trying to wrestle something from her jaws, then grabbing hold of her tail. Victor sends them away. They won't take the law until after their first kill, which will be a year at least.

In the coldest months, his pupils gather around Victor near the huge fireplace and learn the laws and the Old Tongue. It's warmer now and the sun is up later, so to get up the stairs, I have to weave my way through the tussling crowd of fighting pups and jealous preteens, still so desperately uncomfortable in skin.

"Nu is seo mæl for us leornian þine laga and sida," he shouts again.

Now is time for us to study your laws and…sida? I must remember to ask Victor how he would translate *sida*. Later, when he is not preoccupied. As long as I have been here, there are still words that I can't translate. Like *sida*.

The door to Evie's office is closed. I knock with one hand, touching the lintel with the other.

Querulous barks answer, and over them, a voice that is not Evie's says, "Come in, but be careful." Through the crack of the door, a fuzzy black head sticks out. I push his snout with my toe, then enter and shut the door quickly behind me, making sure that none of the tiny nurslings sniffing around my ankles escape or catch their wagging tails in the door. All four of them have gathered, heads bent to the side, waiting expectantly for me to pick them up and mark them.

"There's a roster for the perimeter wolves?"

Quicksilver points to the Alpha's desk and the corkboard above it. I lean over, pulling out the worn wooden tack with a number on it that was probably left over from some ancient plan of Homelands, before everything was digitized.

Tiny pin-sharp claws puncture my jeans on either side of my calf. I shake them off.

"John, come here."

John Tiberiusson may not understand the words, but he responds to his mother's voice and pads over to where she sits surrounded by papers. Clambering over one pile, he slips and sprawls flat. Silver reaches for him distractedly, rubbing her cheek into his tiny muzzle, first one side, then the other. Then she holds him in her lap, stroking his belly while she sorts through papers that smell like almond and old paste.

"What are you doing?"

"The Alpha needs new copies of things we lost in the fire. Just some of the important documents from the safe."

The fire that destroyed our Great Hall. That almost destroyed our pups. The fire that was brought by the Shifters who invaded Homelands, led here by Quicksilver's mate, the half-Shifter, half-Pack Tiberius.

My guess is that the Alpha means to protect the runt. She is still recovering from her lying-in, and the four pups, whose eyes and ears are now open, are still too blind, too deaf, and too clumsy to avoid the careless crowds of enormous wolves now wandering Homelands.

I look toward the roster. I am not sure how I feel about the second window that was installed in the Alpha's office. The one that looks north toward Westdæl. It is a change, and like all wolves, I have learned to mistrust change.

"Do you have a pen?"

Silver pulls one from the collar of her shirt and throws it to me.

"Theo!" The runt's runt is teething on the handle of the Alpha's desk. Silver fishes into a box next to her for a cheese chew that she tosses to the little black dot. The three pups on the floor wobble and stumble for it, while John torques and struggles to get away from his mother.

Nudging the tussling pups away with my toe, I lean over the Alpha's desk, looking at the roster. Most of the segments of the perimeter closest to Home Pond have already been claimed.

"Be careful of that," Silver says.

"What?"

"The letter. It's from the Alpha."

In the middle of the big, old desk, recently refinished

and still smelling of linseed oil, is an older and deeply creased piece of paper. I lean over, my hands behind my back, careful not to touch it. There are only two letters in signature at the foot of the page.

A. M.

When Silver says Alpha, she means not Evie Kitwanasdottir, but Ælfrida Mechtildsdottir, the Great North's first Alpha. The one who forced her obstinate Pack from Mercia to the wild vastness of North America. She struck out from the dying Forest of Dean with a sad group of thirty adults, but before she'd even left the Old World, she had added a dozen or so pups from the butchered Pack Wessex.

She and her Deemer, an injured runt from Pack Wessex, rewrote the Old Laws so that new wolves could add their strength to the Pack. So that wolves would learn to use the laws of men to protect themselves.

Wolves had originally laughed at what they called Ælfrida's Folly, but within fifty years, survivors of more than one decimated Pack had dragged their broken bodies across Europe and the Atlantic to what was now called the Great North.

Well, she might have been a legendary Alpha, but her penmanship was crap.

"Can you read it?"

"Mmm," Silver says, struggling to get up from the floor. I do not offer help. She would not appreciate it. A runt whose hind leg is dislocated when she is wild, Silver knows better than anyone that we do not coddle weakness.

"I've spent the past weeks studying her handwriting," she says and hunches over the page.

"'We are nothing if not'... Ælfrida writes *anwend-edlic*, so 'mutable,' I suppose, is best. 'We understand the miracle of change and must not fear it in ourselves or in our laws. I do not care to know the many pedants who will be able to repeat these laws verbatim; I was present at their creation. Instead, I would fervently pray to meet the lawmaker with the strength of marrow to change what we got wrong.' Signed 'A. M.'"

I frown first at the paper, then at the runt reading it. The Alpha does not need this letter for any legal purpose. It has nothing to do with the land or the Great North LLC. No, its only possible purpose is as a shot across the bow of the Deemer.

"How old are you, Quicksilver?"

"Almost 280 moons."

As I thought. "You were born to a powerful pack at a time of peace. So you think peace is your birthright. It isn't. Terror is our birthright. Fighting for our lives...*that* is our birthright. This peace of yours is a fool's idyll." There is a marbleized tin, beige and dark blue, on the Alpha's desk. Kusmi chai, it says. Evie uses it to hold the prepaid cards we have always used for Offland shopping trips. When I open it, my nose takes in the lingering hints of cinnamon and cardamom and clove and black tea. It reminds me of a long-ago smell from my faraway home, though how Vrangelya came to have something so luxurious, I cannot begin to guess.

I close it again. "You have no idea how little it takes for Pack to turn on one another, and once that happens, they are all dead. There is a reason we start every Iron Table saying 'In our laws we are protected.' The protection we need is not just from outsiders; it is from our own most vicious selves."

Silver rubs her palms together slowly. Like with all Pack, her skin bears the marks of her wild life—the scars of hunting, of running through the harsh land with nothing but fur and claws for protection. But when she holds up her right hand, she spreads her fingers, displaying the upward-pointing arrow, a rarer, deliberate marking.

I wasn't there, but I heard about the fiasco of her first visit Offland this past fall. Silver went to Plattsburgh with Tiberius. It was a routine supply run—groceries, bookstore, and pet store to stock up on the all-important cheese chews and peanut-butter toothpaste—but Offland proved to be too oppressive for Silver's wild, and she changed. In the car. In Plattsburgh.

Any *westend* looking through the window could have seen her little soft mouth and tame nose contort and lengthen and turn into a ripped gash and a long muzzle. Only Tiberius's lead-footed driving and pure dumb luck prevented someone from seeing this transformation that would have doomed the Great North.

As punishment and reminder, Silver was made to take the stone and was branded with the rune of Tiw. The rune of the law.

"I *know* the law requires restraint, Alpha. It is written on my skin."

I manage to stop my hand before it goes to the ridges on my stomach. What is it about Pack that we must always write our reminders in the flesh?

"But," she says, "it cannot only be restraint. Our law is also a living thing that must grow and breathe. That is what Gran Sigeburg taught and what Ælfrida knew.

Laws that cannot bend will break. For Victor, the law is dead, petrified and unchanging. He will use it against Tiberius. Against Evie for accepting him into the Pack. Against the human who saved Theo's life. This is not about protecting the Pack. This is about protecting the Old Ways, which is *not the same thing*."

One of her pups starts to mewl at her, and Silver picks her up, giving her a big openmouthed kiss. "He is *wroht-georn*," she says. Strife-eager. "You say that fighting for our lives is our birthright. I know that. But since the Deemer is protected from challenges by the law, I have no choice but to fight for what I love using the law. And"— her upper lip curls back from her teeth—"I *will* win."

The runt is not like the rest of us. Ripped from her dead dam's belly before she was fully formed, her hair stays a wolf's color even in skin and her eyeteeth remain those of a wolf. It is part of what gives her a fierceness that is completely out of keeping with her size and status. But only part. There are other wolves who are far stronger, but their power is entirely superficial. They are not, as wolves say, strong of marrow.

Silver is nothing but marrow.

I tap the desk near Ælfrida's letter with my fingertip. "Do you know Arthur Graysson?"

"The 12th's *nidling*? Not well."

"I would have him help you."

"I don't need help."

"I didn't say you did. But I would have him help you nonetheless. I would have you teach him…something."

I look out the window toward Westdæl.

"One more thing…"

"Yes?"

"How would you translate *sida*?"

"That which is known, familiar. Custom, I suppose." She frowns slightly. "Gran Sigeburg always told me to treat *sida* with respect and with caution at the same time. Never to acquiesce to something simply because it is known, because it is custom."

From the Alpha's window, I can see the southernmost tip of Westdæl.

"John brought me to Homelands, even though *sida* demanded I be left to die because I was too weak."

Theo, the tiny runt, drags his prized cheese chew away from his bigger siblings.

"You too. Gran Sigeburg said when you came, you were *Wearg* and had the mark of an outlaw." She lays her hand across her sternum in case I'd forgotten. "According to *sida*, you should never have been allowed into the Pack. You were too dangerous. But Nils refused to follow custom without knowing what someone barely more than a pup had done to be clawed."

I trace my finger across the perimeter roster to the empty square that stands at the intersection of the 12th Echelon and Westdæl, that most distant corner of Homelands and scrawl my rank there.

"Gran Sigeburg," Silver continues, "said that the reason we carve only a name and the date of the last hunt on the stones in the *Gemyndstow* is because law and hierarchy are things of life. In death, she said, you stand before the moon not as part of a pack, but as a lone wolf, and as a lone wolf, you answer for what you have done."

When I leave, I touch the lintel again.

Chapter 11

"Where are you going, Shielder?"

I pop the last of the honey oatcake into my mouth, then brush the crumbs from my naked breasts.

"Westdæl. Perimeter watch."

"Perimeter watch?" Lorcan repeats again. By the change of the light in his eyes, I can tell that my Alpha has forgotten his peevish outburst. "Why so far away?"

"It was available." Which is true as far as it goes. I take another cup of coffee, the last I'll have for a while.

"Oh, and, Arthur, you will be helping Quicksilver Nilsdottir."

"Arthur?" Both Arthur and Lorcan look toward the table where the 14th sits. Two of Silver's pups are sleeping on Tiberius's huge lap. Another is snuffling around at the butter and crumbs in Eudemos's beard. The fourth is gnawing on Kayla's finger. When their eyes and ears and muscles are strong enough, they will join the other pups on the floor. Then they will belong to the Pack as a whole, but for now, they are coddled by their parents and their echelon.

"After breakfast, you will report to the Theta." I look at him over the rim of my cup. "And, Arthur?"

"Yes, Shielder?"

"Learn something."

Both Arthur and Lorcan look at me quizzically but say nothing.

I'd originally planned to tell one of the wolves in the 12th that I trust to call me if there was trouble, but I didn't, because Lorcan needs to learn something too.

I believe without a doubt that Lorcan would sacrifice his life to save the 12th. I don't believe he will sacrifice one jot of his popularity to lead it.

The sky is dark again as it will be more and more often now.

The wolves of Vrangelya talked—when they bothered with words—of two seasons: damn cold and not so damn cold. "It's damn cold today," they'd say for much of the year. Then one morning they'd walk out and it'd be "not so damn cold today."

The Great North talks of five seasons: summer, fall, winter, mud, and blackfly.

Mud season will be starting with a vengeance now. I can tell from the leaden color of the sky and the heaviness of the air and the cracking of ice and the thawing of earth. Soon it will rain: fine drops at first, then fat drops as the temperature warms up. That rain will mix with snowmelt, and because the substrata are still frozen, anything that is not literally rooted by vegetation will turn into muck.

It rained at home, the first time I heard about the Great North. I remember, because rain was so rare, at least in my memory. It was coupled with a visitor, another rarity. Like all Pack, we were very suspicious and watched this new wolf from a distance, though it didn't take long to ascertain that he was no kind of threat. So the adults all changed—that is where we got the Kusmi chai. We got it from the visitor—because the Alpha, Illarion, gave the visitor permission to hunt our land as our guest as long as he shared the fire afterward for *æfenspræc*, evening talk, so that we could learn whatever news he had of the world beyond our island.

The news was as it had been for years.

"They especially like to hunt the pups," he said in that pointedly cruel way disillusioned adults do when they think they see innocence. "Their heads are easier to carry, and the government pays out the bounty just the same."

Mitya and I stayed away, busy with a game of lemming toss. He hadn't heard the stranger, and I didn't want him to.

But then there was a change, and the stranger stopped talking about where he had been and started talking about where he was going, and that I wanted to hear. I wanted to hear about a better place, a place one actually wanted to go.

I nipped at Mitya to move closer. East, the stranger said. Across the vastness of North America, what we Vrangelya wolves in our isolation still called Vinland, to a spot near the eastern edge called the Great North.

In the Old Tongue, he called it *Deore Norþ*. I always wondered why he didn't use a more common word for great, like *Micel*—Great and Vast—or *Mægenrof*—Great and Powerful—but instead called it *Deore*, which does mean great, but also precious, beloved.

We all listened to him describe this land of no little airplanes that shot at you and many, many trees that were good for hiding. Of deer and black bear that were easier to hunt than our own musk ox and polar bears. And raccoons that were like lemmings but had real flesh on them.

And this land, this perfect land, he said, was owned by the Pack, and they had signs all around telling the humans to keep out. He said. And the humans did. They stayed away.

He said.

When he was done, the Pack fell silent. The pups looked to our Alpha for some kind of confirmation. There would be none, because it was his turn to disillusion us. He'd heard tales of the Great North before, he said with a hard laugh. We would all reach it soon enough. When the *westends* cut off our heads.

The pups—actually the nonadults: Vrangelya wasn't large enough to be divided into echelons, just adults and nonadults—turned on Mitya the way they always did, because despair makes wolves cruel.

It ended the way it always did, with my claws stained with other wolves' blood and my mouth full of other wolves' skin.

After that, Mitya and I pretended sometimes that we lived in this precious land protected by signs that read WESTENDAS, AGAP ONWEG—Humans, Go Away—on a land thick with sheltering trees rather than rusted barrels oozing oil. Where we wouldn't have to listen for the drunk voices of hunters warning us that we had to change into skin if we had time or hide if we didn't. Where we wouldn't have to run desperately from the strafing of their malevolent buzzing planes. We imagined how it would feel not to be hungry. And I practiced hunting for deer so that when we got there, when I made my first kill, there would be a lung for each of us and Mitya would have the heart.

I'd always thought that as long as I was strong enough

and ferocious enough for two wolves, I could keep my gentle, dreamy Mitya with me always.

What a child.

Chapter 12

IT DOESN'T RAIN UNDER THE PINES, EXCEPT FOR THE OCCA-sional bead that rolls down collecting more and more water until finally it lands on my nose in a heavy, balsam-scented plop.

Something is splashing nearby. It isn't regular enough to be rain. Too loud to be an animal drinking. Could be weasel. Weasels like playing in the water, and I like eating weasel. The Great North doesn't like their musky umami, preferring deer, which, let's face it, tastes like chicken.

Keeping low and quiet, I follow the sound to a rock pond carved into the hardpan fed by runlets carrying melt-off.

It's not a weasel.

The wounded wolf sits up, his hair glowing gold in the low sun. He squeezes out the small towel from his backpack and scrubs his skin in the rain and icy water. As he bends to the side, the ropy muscles under his skin coil even with the little effort of dipping the towel back in the water. He gingerly wipes away blood and dirt from his leg stretched out straight in front of him.

The olive canvas backpack is slung across a ragged tree trunk.

He freezes, then turns his head toward me, his eyes half-closed against the setting sun.

"Where did you come from?" he asks. "I didn't think there were wolves left in New York." His voice is odd, cracked and dry as a heel of week-old rye. That part's not odd. It's the mark of a wanderer, of someone who hasn't talked for a long time. What's odd is the wolfish depth and resonance. As if no one told him that while wolves sing with the lungs, in skin, we must speak with the mouth.

"Don't worry," he continues, holding his hand out to me. I eye it warily, unsure what, exactly, he expects me to do with it. "I would never hurt you. I know what it's like to be you." He looks down at his body. "Well, not now, obviously, but sometimes. When the moon is full."

I take a step backward. I am pretty sure this moon-mad fool thinks I'm an *æcewulf*. A real wolf. A forever wolf.

I could play this game. I could just walk away. If he's well enough to find his way here, he'll find his way down to the Outer Woods and out of Homelands.

He slides his palm closer to my nose. I would bite it, but it smells like mint and chocolate. What wolf eats chocolate?

"So here we are. New York's only wolf and the world's last werewolf."

Oh, for the love of…

Like some shopworn carnival barker, he adds a lackluster "Ta-da."

I should just ignore it, but I can't. Werewolf. Manwolf. Of course humans would give themselves pride of place. With an exasperated huff, I throw myself down, tightening the muscles at my hips until I feel the change take hold. The last thing I smell is the damp moss. The last thing I see is the final arc of the sun, shining gold breaking through the single gap in the gray clouds.

The last thing I hear is a shocked intake of breath followed by silence. Not real silence; it's never really silent. Just muffled and milky, like the empty canvas of my changing eyes.

Muscles loosen, becoming rubbery and useless before tightening again as they pull against lengthening limbs and a torso that stretches, becoming broader and shallower. My heart stops galloping and settles into a trot, and my breathing slows too.

Then I feel. Something cold against my skin. My nerves may still be misaligned, but they fire in succession, registering not pressure or pain, just an overlapping softness, almost like liquid against my hip. The liquid moves around my helpless changing body: hip to waist to breast. From left to right, it pours softly across my scarred torso. Breathing hard in my shallow human-shaped lungs, I coil my shoulder muscle and try to aim my arm at him, which is a mistake because all it does is unbalance me, forcing my face and eye into the ground.

Wolves aren't prudish; we spend too much time naked for that. But except for the Iron Moon when we are all changing and all blind together, we give one another a little space as we phase. It takes a long time, and most of that is spent in a monstrous state when we are neither in skin nor wild, when our jaws flatten, but our teeth are still sharp, when our pointed ears migrate down the sides of our skulls. When our shoulders pull back away from the still deep and narrow chests. When fur recedes, leaving naked muzzles.

I can't tell him to go away because my tongue is too long and thin and the roof of my mouth is too high and narrow. I can just make him out now, crouching next to me, bone-pale and naked except for underwear soaked by water dripping from his moon-colored hair.

He is bleached out except for the blue and green of his harlequin eyes and the blood of his reopened wound.

I don't know where the makeshift bandage has gone.

Finally, my ears pop. Not that it matters, because he's speechless.

"*Rangrawalra!*" I snap. I pop my lips twice and try again. "*Yr nodda wurwolv!*"

I get up to my knees and wiggle my tongue, then try one last time. Slowly and carefully. "You. Are. Not. A. Werewolf."

"I am human *now*," he says urgently. "But when the moon is full—"

"Stop. Just…stop. I know what you *are* and it is not a werewolf. Werewolves are made up by humans. You and I? We are Pack. Wolves, if you prefer. Never werewolves and never, *ever* human."

He goes quiet for a minute, one hand to the back of his neck, the other at his rib cage. "But…you have…" He bends his fingers into stiff claws and draws them from his right nipple down to his left hip, mirroring the path of the four claw marks across my body. "And I have these." He pulls his hair to the side and stretches out his neck. "They feel like bite—"

"It's not something you catch, like rabies. We are *born*, not *made*. Those on your neck? Those are carry marks. Sometimes when an adult carries a pup, they can be a little…rough." Wolves' jaws become like pincers if they are frightened or angry or running. My fingers press at the tiny knots of thicker tissue hidden under my skin. My Pack was always frightened and angry and running.

He presses his fingers into the back of his neck. "I had a dream once, at least I thought it was a dream, but now

I'm wondering… A wolf carried me in her teeth. I don't know how I knew it was a 'her.' Just a dream thing, I suppose. Anyway, she carried me and then put me down in the middle of…nothing. Endless white and cold. And then she leaves. In my dream, I try to follow, but she was fast and the snow was higher than I was. My legs…" He stops, clearing his throat. "My legs were too short."

Then he looks at me, his eyes focused again. "What do you think?"

"Are you asking me if it was a dream?"

"I guess."

I am familiar enough with the workings of desperate packs to imagine what happened. The white pup eventually opens his eyes for the first time, revealing one the blue of heaven, one the green of earth. There follows a flurry of superstitious whispering, then some wolf—the Alpha if it was a well-led pack, some lower wolf if it was not—is tasked with getting rid of the cursed thing.

I imagine the pup going limp as they always do, as the wolf takes him somewhere far, where the Pack will not need to know whether their problem has been solved by predators or the elements or the despair of loneliness.

"Yes," I lie. "It sounds like a dream."

The imagining is easy. The unimagining is harder.

Chapter 13

HE STARES AT THE BLOOD WELLING UP FROM THE straight line sliced in his thigh.

"I remember now. You stabbed me."

"I didn't stab you. It was surgery. With a knife. I needed to clean you out. We are strong, but you were dying."

The blood mixed with water has turned his knee pink.

"How did you know what I am?"

I wonder where the bandage has gone.

"Your smell. Humans smell like steel and carrion. Wolves smell wild."

He holds his wrist to his nose.

"You can't really smell it on yourself. It's easier to smell on other wolves." He leans toward me, but there are limits to my tolerance for this wolf's curiosity.

Jumping up, I rummage through the worn canvas backpack for his spare clothes. Then I stand, my arms crossed, while he struggles first into his pants and then his shirt.

The sun slips down behind the serrated silhouette of the mountains to the west. On most nights, this would be the time when the Great North's Alpha would start the *æfensang*, evening song, but the helicopter intrusions into Homelands have made the Pack afraid, and frightened Packs are silent.

"Do you think you could…?"

"What?"

"Help?" His arm is contorted, reaching for the hem of the dark Henley stuck to the damp skin above his shoulder blades.

I watch him straining for the bunched fabric. More proof, if I needed it, that this wolf has never been part of a Pack. Even in the Great North, a wolf who asked for help would likely be challenged. In Vrangelya, they'd be dead.

He looks at me expectantly with those different-colored eyes, the trick of genetics that guarantees he will never belong to a Pack. He will never be challenged for *cunnan-riht*, fucking rights. He will never fight for rank in a hierarchy. He will never be set upon by vicious dominants looking for a scapegoat. So what does it matter what other wolves might think? There are no other wolves; there's only me.

And what do I think? After Vrangelya's end, I spent a year wandering alone, looking for the Great North, and it nearly killed me. This wolf has survived years, maybe decades, on his own.

The Great North may have been weakened by peace, but this wolf has never known it.

I pluck at the shirt, gingerly extricating it, but as it starts to come down, I notice one other scar, made by a bullet like the one at his shoulder. An exit wound. It's not the exit wound itself that's odd. What's odd is that the entrance wound and exit wound are aligned. If I put a dowel through the front hole, it would come out the back.

Now, if he had taken the bullet wild, the changes to his chest, the way it grows wider and shallower when he shifts from four legs to two, would mean that the scars would not line up when he was in skin. One would be at his nipple, the other under his armpit, an impossible trajectory for a human but not uncommon for wolves who have been shot wild and survived long enough to change.

Without thinking, my hand goes to the same spot below my shoulder.

He looks at me. Not like the wolves of the Great North, whose eyes always cling to the safety of my clavicle, but into my eyes. At least until his gaze drops pointedly to the scars of my waist, following the curving track of four claws that swipe from my left hip bone to my right breast. He sees the hard ridges and the soft flesh in between. His fingers go stiff, kinked, as though trying to imagine the feeling of the claws tearing through flesh.

When he looks back into my eyes, I see the same response I know he sees in mine.

Don't ask.

"My name's Frank Carter," he says, pulling tighter on white ties at his waistband.

I say nothing.

"Generally, one says 'Nice to meet you, Frank. My name is…'"

"The Alpha Shielder of the 12th Echelon of the Great North."

"Yeah, I don't think that's your name."

"Frank Carter's not your name either."

He looks at me sideways. "And what makes you say that?"

"Wolves identify each other by scent. Any other identification, the kind humans need, is faked. But the Pack makes good fakes. Not the kind with half-drunk serifs."

"The Pack?"

"Yes, the Pack."

"How big's the Pack?"

"Big enough and powerful, and like all wolf packs, very territorial. I have not told them you are here, because you need some time to heal, but if they find out, you will be dead and I will be punished—and our punishments are painful."

He holds out one hand to me. This time, I help without being asked, but as soon as he stumbles upright, he puts his arm around my shoulders.

"What?" He looks at me with his eyebrows raised.

"I'm not going to make it back up by myself."

"How did you *think* you were going to get back up?"

"I didn't. I thought I was going to wash up, keep heading down until I got some reception, call my manager, tell him I was sick, and see if he would take me back. When he said no, I'd move on a little sooner than I'd expected."

"And now?" I say, distracted by the hand settled somewhere between my left breast and my left bicep.

He settles his weight against me, and not just the weight of his arm but his entire body. His skin is warm. Or not really. It's just less cold than mine. When he leans on me, it feels uncomfortably close. Certainly closer than Lorcan, who touches me as little as possible even when he covers me. Teeth. Cock. Occasional tickle of chest hair. Nothing else.

A cardinal calls. *Whip whip chupchupchupchup.*

Chew chew chew chew chew comes the answer.

"Do you know what an endling is?" the wolf asks.

I shake my head, trying to remember when I took his hand in mine and wrapped my free arm around his waist.

"It's the last of its kind. There always has to be one. The one who calls but is never answered. That's what I thought I was. The endling werewolf. I know, not werewolf, but still the last." He smiles faintly. "Then you answered."

He didn't call and I didn't answer. I just happened to be the wrong wolf in the wrong place at the wrong time. I will patch him up, but then I will send him away and I will guard this land to make sure that nothing and no one ever gets in again.

"D'you smell that?" His eyes swim, too tired to focus. "Smells like mmm." I didn't catch that last part. "I wasn' paying attention. What rabbid dozn run when a wolf comes?"

I pull him tighter and drag him those last feet until he can crawl into the cave and collapse onto the open sleeping bag. Arranging his body as best I can, I zip the sleeping bag around him. At the top, I pluck his hair away so it won't get caught between the teeth.

"Eyulf," he says. "That's all. Just Eyulf."

I look at the white strand between my fingers. The cardinals are still at it in the woods lower down. *Whip whip chupchupchupchup*. I've only bothered with my rank and echelon. *Chew chew chew chew chew*. But now it doesn't really seem like an answer.

Silently, I mouth the two syllables of a name I haven't said since I first came to the Great North. When I'd told Nils and Alexandra my name was Varya Timursdottir, even though I'd lost the right to my Pack name.

"Varya. That's all. Just Varya."

"Varya," he murmurs. The sound of that name and the smell of cold peel my nerves bare.

I sit for a moment until his breathing slows and his eyes flit around under the fine translucent skin, and I wonder at the cruel irony that led him to be named "lucky wolf."

Chapter 14

THERE IS ONE THING I AM SURE OF WHEN I WAKE UP TO the hazy purple-gray of early morning. Based on his increasingly incoherent ramblings about rabbits, Eyulf was clearly able to scent the Pack when he was caught.

No one sets a trap near Homelands.

I circle the peak of Westdæl, my nose to the ground, searching for any smell—blood, rust, iron, sepsis—that might indicate which way he came. If it had only just rained, the scent might be stronger and closer to the earth, but days of rain have washed it away.

At the very bottom, where the westernmost border of the Great North's territory meets up with human land, there is a line of the Pack's inevitable signs. They aren't the rough WESTENDAS, AGAÞ ONWEG I'd imagined when I was young. Instead, they are bright-yellow plastic and read:

POSTED
PRIVATE PROPERTY
HUNTING, FISHING, TRAPPING, OR TRESPASSING
FOR ANY PURPOSE IS STRICTLY FORBIDDEN.
VIOLATORS WILL BE PROSECUTED TO
THE FULL EXTENT OF THE LAW.

Then they give the name and cell of not one but two Pack lawyers: ELIJAH SORENSSON (JD, LLM) AND JOSI DIANASDOTTIR (JD)

In most parts of Homelands, it's not the lawyers who discourage interlopers; it's the land itself. The Great North clears no deadfall and maintains no paths and marks no hazards and never cuts back its witch hobble. This land is, as the law says, entirely "unimproved."

I can't find any sign of Eyulf's passing or a trap near the boundary with Westdæl, nothing along the empty and exposed length of the Gin. I head farther east along the border of Norþdæl, where I meet up with two wolves from the 7th and 8th assigned to patrol the precious sanctuary of the High Pines.

Their eyes do not meet mine, and they twist in the air, quickly heading back the way they came. I watch as they disappear into the firs, their tails tucked firmly between their legs. As soon as they're gone, I continue my search all the way to the border and look to the lands that *westends* think are wild.

There the deer have become bold, eating away the vegetation and making the land more comfortably accessible for things on two legs and too uncomfortably exposed for things with four. It's a very different place without wolves. Fewer plants, fewer animals. More packaging. Pringles, primarily.

But no traps.

I head all the way to Endeberg, the final mountain in this northern range—and still nothing. Then I head back, nose to the ground.

The Arctic wolf sits on a stone, his leg stretched out in front of him. He has a sturdy branch with a Y at the top propped beside him, the notebook on his lap.

"I know where the trap is. If that's what you're looking for."

He closes his notebook and puts a pencil back in the metal box. It rattles as he drops it into his backpack.

"It's not far."

I cock my head to the side.

He slings the backpack over his shoulders and fits the branch under his arm like a makeshift crutch. Then he starts hobbling, not west and north, the areas nearest to the humans, but rather to the south and east.

With each step deeper into Homelands, my fury rises, until unable to stand his slow progress, I swirl around on my hind legs and shoot off in the direction he's headed.

"Wait, Varya!"

I can't *wait*. It's one thing if traps are laid Offland, or even in Westdæl, where Pack rarely go. But he pointed toward the interconnected waters of Clear Pond and Beaver Pond, and those are frequented by wolves—and even juveniles and pups sometimes. Maybe not so much now, because the water is mostly frozen, but very soon they will be good hunting grounds for the beavers and rabbits and ground squirrels that our young favor.

As I clear the ridge, the ember in my chest bursts into flames. A silent coyote circles the ice, scraping at the steel jaws that hold his bleeding mate.

Someone has dared to set a trap in Homelands.

With a choked howl, I run down the hill. One way or the other, I will deal with this. Either with fingers if there's a chance she can survive, or with jaws if she needs to be freed in another, more final way. Her mate looks helplessly toward me and flees to the camouflage of a nearby buttonbush, while she crouches low, as far from the iron jaws as she can get.

Now I'm close enough, and I throw myself on the

ground, already leaning into my hips. I don't know that she will survive, but if she doesn't, her nurslings will die too. During the seemingly endless span of the change, I hear nothing but the sound of my pulse raging at the *westend* who dared ignore our signs, dared walk a half mile in, dared to set a trap.

And dared to do it twice, because the trap Eyulf tripped has been reset.

My change isn't entirely finished when I run the rest of the way down the slope. Or not run, really. Careen, my bare feet rolling on loose stone and sliding down moss-covered rock, blinking and popping my ears until I finally tumble over a chunk of gneiss tossed here by some unfeeling glacier solely to trip me into the snow-covered edge of Beaver Pond.

"*Varya, stop!*" Eyulf screams, scuttling desperately down the hillside with one leg and his makeshift crutch. It's a plea made as loud as his hollowed-out voice will allow. But it's not the volume that stops me. It's that the two words have summoned a memory to the top of a mountain made of them. A little bird flittering on the icy ground of another land. Of another voice in another language.

Opstand, Varya!

Stop, Varya.

"*Westends* will waste a little life," Yefim had said, "to take a bigger one." I remember watching the little bird with a red cap that I now know was a redpoll flittering just out of my reach. Taunting me with my hunger.

A few weeks later, another bigger bird flittered just out of reach of our starving Omega dying in a larger trap. Illarion did what was needed and killed him.

What rabbit doesn't run when a wolf comes?

One that's trapped.

The trap holding the coyote is not large enough or powerful enough to have mangled the wanderer's leg. It was about the right size to catch and mangle a rabbit.

I back away, careful to step only into my naked footprints.

There are sticks everywhere. This isn't called Beaver Pond for nothing. I tear one that looks good and strong from a frozen pile of them and begin poking the ground with it.

Most of the earth is still icy hard, though I know the qualities of ice well enough to identify the thin ice above the fresh water runoff. I move forward slowly, pushing at all the likely places. Then at the less-likely places. But it is an unlikely place, a patch of snow dotted with dried sedge that erupts with a loud crack.

Snow, dirt, and grass fly into the air. The stick shatters in teethed jaws that even I know are not legal.

A low rumble moves through my human chest, enraged that someone would try to do to the Great North what had been done to Vrangelya. This trapper took great pains. They carved out a depression and drilled a hole into frozen ground. They set spike and chain. They covered the tray with plastic and then buried the whole thing in dirt and a neat covering of white snow and then...then they carefully stuck in pieces of grass.

And they did it here. *In the Deore Norþ*.

The coyote struggles to her remaining three legs, moving as far from me as the trap will allow. She is dehydrated and cold and desperate to get back to her young litter. Traps are so indifferent that way. Young, old, or nursing.

"What are you going to do?" Eyulf asks, breathless when he finally arrives at the edge of the pond.

"Free her. Be careful. The ice is thin there."

"I can see. It may be kinder to kill—"

"She's got a mate waiting"—I lift my chin toward the male waiting anxiously behind the spare gathering of buttonbush still dotted with dark seeds—"and pups somewhere. There is a chance she won't die."

I'm glad to see her fighting, snapping at my hand with her little jaws until I wrap my fingers around them. I ignore the scrabbling of her claws against my bare skin as I force open the trap, releasing her leg.

"*Astille, guðling*," I whisper. Hush, little warrior.

My arms wrapped tight around her struggling body, I take her toward the gray ice, where snowmelt from Westdæl still runs clear before joining the murky beaver water and becoming undrinkable. Slamming into it with my bare heel, I squat down while she scrapes with her hind legs at my torso. At first, she rejects the frigid water cupped in my hand. I suppose it does, after all, smell like wolf. Finally, thirst overcomes her, and her soft tongue laps against my palm.

Scoop by scoop, I dribble the water into another creature's mouth. Not too much: it's too cold and she needs food too. By the third, she has drawn closer to my body, clinging to the heat of my body. Her muscles relax, her broken foreleg dangling.

When I set her down, she doesn't snarl or bite or run the straight shot to her mate. Instead, she hobbles slowly toward the buttonbush, even stopping to look back along the length of her flanks.

That's not good.

We never say that we are "human," only that we are "in skin." It is a tacit acknowledgment that we are, in essence, wild and that the layer covering our true natures is thin and superficial. I may have helped her, but I cannot allow her to go on believing that things that look like me or smell like me are safe.

So I lunge. Even with my pathetic flat teeth, my bite hurts, sending her racing for her mate as fast as she can.

But now, because I bit her with those pathetic flat teeth, I have tongue bunnies.

"What'd you do that for?"

Sticking out my tongue, I carefully pick away the long hairs, while the coyote's anxious mate parallels her, smelling her, nosing her leg and the spot on her shoulder where a creature that smells like a wolf and acts like a wolf but doesn't look like a wolf bit her.

"It is against the law to tame prey. To take away their fear and then kill them is a crime."

There's a snorted laugh as he carefully braces himself against the big rock. "Really? And what law would that be?"

"The only law that counts here." I take the chain of the smaller trap in two hands and pull. "Pack law." It comes out, the chain clotted with frosty mud. I drop it and turn to the larger trap.

There's a hole drilled next to it that stinks of frozen deer chum. I wrap the chain around my hand. Predictably, whoever set these drilled the chain of the bigger trap deep. The frigid metal cuts into my skin.

Settling my bare feet firmly on either side of the
ground, I wrap the chain once more around my hands
and bend my knees. Extending my legs, I haul the thing
inch by inch out of this frozen land and then drag both
traps to the rock.

"Watch out."

As soon as he hops away, I swing the chains and
the traps and slam them again and again against the
rock. Stone chips fly, and the metal bends and finally
breaks. In the end, they are both warped and broken
like picked-over carcasses scattered around my makeshift anvil.

The Pack calls. Maybe I shouldn't have thrashed at
the traps so hard, because now the wolves are worried.
They call from the direction of Home Pond, asking
questions that I can't answer at this distance in this form.
Then their calls move closer.

"They're coming," I whisper to Eyulf. "You have
to go."

"Go? Why? Why should I have to go?"

"*I told you*. Packs are very territorial." I push the stick
toward him, but he refuses to take it. "They do not toler-
ate strangers."

"Like you? Pox are vehrrreee tehrrrritohrrial," he
says, his voice rolling deep across his tongue. "You're
not from here. How come you're a stranger who belongs
here and I'm a stranger who doesn't?"

That's it, isn't it? But I don't have time to explain
why there will never be a place for him in the few minutes before wolves come and see the Bone Wolf, the
harbinger of the beginning of the end and...

"If you go now, I will find you and I will tell you why

it has to be this way. But if *they* see you, they will hunt you down and you will die."

With a truncated howl, the approaching wolves tell Home Pond that they are nearing the place of the worrisome noise.

"*You've got to hide*," I hiss. "*Go now, and I will find you.*"

It takes too long for him to scrabble up, and he only just finds the tree line when the two wolves, flashes of gray and tawny brown, emerge from the woods near the eastern edge of Beaver Pond. After a quick conspiratorial glance, they drop their heads, tuck in their tails, and lower their eyes as they lope around the pond.

I stay silent. They can tell everything they need to already. Two traps. Coyote caught. Shredded metal. By not saying anything, I do not have to lie. I do not tell them that the reason I strayed so far from my perimeter detail was because this is the second time these traps have captured a living creature.

One of the wolves sniffs the air near me, scenting the sticky blood freed by the hard, icy chain. I do not look at him but stand, my legs stiff, my hands clasped behind my back. Wolves should never see their dominants in distress. It makes them anxious.

The two wolves rub muzzles against the remains of the traps, gathering the scent. They mark the area in the way of wolves before backing away at a low crouch until, at a respectful distance, they whip around and run for Home Pond.

Other wolves will smell the news they bring and come. Wolves with work gloves who will take the pieces of metal back where they will warm up, and the Pack's best trackers will see if they can identify the *westend* through the gloves I already know they wore.

If they find the culprit, the Great North will hunt them down, not with jaws and claws but with writs and torts and whatever legal mumbo jumbo comes from an army of lawyers with way too much time on their hands.

Chapter 15

THE WOLVES SHOWED NO SIGN THAT THEY NOTICED Eyulf, passing by his trail without a single twitch of a nostril. Missing the scent that snaps at me like a north wind in winter, pulling me almost in a trance to a rocky promontory midway up Westdæl that gives out over the Gin and the vastness of the High Pines.

Eyulf leans back, his arms straight, his head bent to the side, staring into the distance. He doesn't look at me but knows I'm there.

"I've been to a lot of places that are called wilderness. None are like this."

He points with his chin toward the lower slopes of Norþdæl. "See? They're almost ready. Must be beautiful in the spring."

It takes me a minute to figure out what he means by "almost ready" before I realize that he's looking at the hardwoods that have taken on a dusky-purple tint like a watercolor wash. It's one of the first signs of spring, but it hasn't spread Offland yet. Those trees are shorter, the branches sparser, the spaces in between wider. And because deer are in the mood to eat anything remotely tender, the trees have been denuded of the tiny mauve buds.

"And the place you come from, is it like this?" he asks.

I feel the itch at the back of my neck, a prickling that if I were wild would mean my hackles were raised at being asked something so personal.

"It is—was—colder," I hear myself saying. "Barer. Though…for a couple of weeks, it was covered with flowers."

"What kind?"

"Of flowers?" My mind pokes around the oubliette of my heart where all my memories are stored, trying to find a name for those rare bright spots against the gray scrub. Nothing. Not that I've forgotten; I just never knew. "They were low, mostly. Yellow, purple, and white. Mostly. But I don't know what they were called."

"Pity."

Pity?

"They say," he says, still staring across the shielding expanse of gray and pine, "that the colder the land, the more passionate the thaw."

At that moment, the peach-and-gold line of the sun gives way to lavender, and Evie starts evening song. *Æfensang*. It begins as it always does, with the Alpha howl moving through the lower registers, strong and secure and open. It is meant to reassure and bind her wolves. Anyone who is wild joins in—higher, more staccato—weaving their voices around the deep power of their Alpha's call.

After a rough intake of breath, Eyulf closes his eyes and lets the sound envelop him. I did the same thing my first evening at the Great North. We'd never sung in Vrangelya. Why would the hunted call out to the hunters?

I was sitting in the medical station that first evening, waiting to be checked for fleas, when the unabashed, unafraid cry rolled through the cool, early evening air. I did exactly the same thing as this wolf: closed my eyes and let wave after thrilling wave wash over me and lick me clean.

It was then that I knew why they called it *Deore Norþ*, and I also knew that I would do anything to make sure that there was a place left in the world for wolf song. I knew I would pit my hard body and my harder will against anyone who would dare do here what had been done in Vrangelya.

> *Wulf sang ahóf, holtes gehléða...*
> The wolf raised up his song, the companion of the forest...

Only Evie fully understands the warp and weft of the chorus of voices. Only our Alpha can truly read in it the mood of Homelands. By picking apart the harmonies, she knows where her wolves are and that they are safe. She calls again to make sure she hasn't missed anyone.

She doesn't worry about those who are in skin. We are safe enough. I let the sound embrace me and remind me—in a way that nothing else can—what it is that I am responsible for, something so much larger and more important than myself.

Eventually, Evie stops, followed by the rest of the Pack. Except for the high-pitched sound of the pups in the barely audible distance, who are too caught up in the joy of communion to notice that it has ended. Then with a final *roo-oop*, they fall silent too.

The still wolf next to me sighs. "So that was the Pack?"

"Yes."

He raises his hip slightly and hooks his finger, retrieving something from his pocket. "You going to tell me why?"

I don't remember the last time I bothered with *why*. The last time I've bothered with more than a few barked words—plus or minus the Alpha stare. I dig back, looking for a why that will explain things to this wolf who knows nothing about who we are until I wind up near the beginning, when humans decided that the uncultivated woods and the unclaimable mountains and the untamable wild were not magic as they had once been but evil. And that wolves were the perfect symbol of everything incomprehensible and uncontrollable both in nature and in themselves. Something that must be destroyed.

So many of our stories came from this dark time as we tried to make sense of what was happening to us.

He is quiet for a long time after I'm finished, sitting with his nose against his fisted hand.

"And in what part of your fairy tale does hell's all-seeing immortal guardian wolf go 'Ooo, bunny' and desert his post?"

"It's not about *reason*. Packs are always teetering on the edge of extinction, so they're suspicious of everything. What they believe, what they *know*, is that the smallest thing can push them over the edge."

"But you don't believe it?" he asks, putting his palm to his cheek.

"No."

"And why is that?"

"Because—" A stick falls on my head from a saw-whet building a nest in the branches above. "Because I have seen the monsters who will end us, and they're nothing like you." I start to disentangle the twig from my hair. "What do you have in your hand?"

"This?" He unfurls his fingers from a small, dark-gray

ball. At first, I think it's an owl pellet, but then I realize what it is.

"*Is that mine?*"

"I like the way it smells," he says, and then pushed by some primal instinct, rubs his cheek into the felted mass of dark-gray fur.

I lunge, but he's got long arms and his reflexes are scary fast and there's nothing but air in my hands, my body falling on top of him, uncomfortably aware of every steel-sinewed inch.

Scrabbling backward, I rub the underside of my arm.

"What is *wrong* with you? You were shedding. It's not like you need it anymore."

"What's wrong with me? What is wrong with *you*?" I snap, feeling a rising wave of panic. "You can't rub your face with *my* fur. You don't… You can't mark *yourself*. It has to be offered. It *has* to be offered." I put my hand up, protecting the back of my jaw, where the scent is strongest. "Wolves who mark each other *belong* to each other. They are responsible for each other. I belong to the *Pack. They* are my responsibility. I will *never* belong to a wolf again."

He strokes the fur in his hand, then lifting his hips, he sticks his finger into his pocket, pushing that piece of my wild deep inside.

"Again?" he asks quietly.

He can find his own way.

―⁓―

River-rounded stones slip under my feet, and I steady myself on the trunk nearby. I mark it in mind, because it's just the kind of place where ungulates will easily lose their footing. A place to herd deer and bring a quick end to a hunt.

"Varya!"

Crows caw overhead. The grans say to pay attention to crows, because they bring news from Offland, if you know how to read it.

"Varya!"

I've always paid closest attention to the practical things, but I squirrel away the other things, too, such as the names the Pack insisted we know in order to acknowledge that every living thing has a place in Homelands.

"*Varya!*"

Maybe I don't know the names of any of the flowers of Vrangelya, but I know everyone here. I know that soon the ground will be covered with white-and-yellow bloodroot. Tiny explosive trout lily. Mounds of green-framed white trillium. Rue anemone in the palest pink. All blooming in the short frame between the thawing of the ground and the leaf-out that will block the sun.

"*Varya!*"

It's what happens in spring when all of Homelands calls out:

Look at me.

Listen to me.

Love me.

Make life with me.

"*VARYA!*"

"Stop yelling. Someone is going to hear you."

He collapses against a tree, holding his leg, breath leaking out between gritted teeth.

"I want to clarify something," I say coolly. "Just

because I agreed to tell you about *wolves* does not mean I agreed to tell you about *me*."

His sweats are streaked with mud and the brighter green of moss from more than one fall.

"You should be more careful. What happened to your stick?"

"It slid down the hill. I couldn't go back and get it."

Drops of bright blood have started to soak through the leg of his pants.

"You've opened it up again. Come. I'll change your bandage."

This time, I'm ready for the weight of his arm across my shoulder. What I'm not ready for is the way the wind picks up from the north and blows the wolf's white hair across his face and onto mine. I smell the electric sharpness of his skin, combining with the hard, icy fragrance he stole from my fur.

Exhaling sharply, I clear away the combined scent of two wolves belonging.

Chapter 16

"Can I ask you a question?" Eyulf says.

I peel off the blood-soaked bandage.

"Does that mean no?"

"Wolves don't waste time on rhetoric. Either ask a question, or don't ask a question. It's 'May I,' by the way." I hold out my hand for the antibiotic. "Take the lid off."

"You really have no sense of humor, do you?" he says, unscrewing the top.

"No. Put your fingers here." I wrap the top layer of gauze tight around both leg and fingers. This way, when he pulls his fingers out, it will stay tight, but not like a tourniquet. "You had a question?"

He raises his eyebrows and opens his mouth, then closes it again.

"I change during the full moon—"

"You change during the *Iron* Moon. Humans call it the full moon. Wolves call it the Iron Moon."

"I change during the Iron Moon." He pauses, listening to the sound of the words on his tongue. "But I don't go back and forth like you do. Like you're changing socks."

"It's not at all like changing socks. And I'm done with the antibiotic. They call those changes *sawolþearf*, soul-needed." Or that's the way Nils explained it when he showed me around Home Pond. Some wolves were in skin, but so many, *so* many, were wild. They'd run up to Nils, huge heads lowered, when he introduced me.

Then they snuffled around with their wet noses, while I stayed frozen stiff so that I wouldn't throw myself sobbing onto their rough, warm, richly fragrant fur.

"*Forhwi*?" I'd asked Nils. Why? Why would they risk so much to be wild?

"*Hit biþ sawolþearf*," he'd said, not understanding my terror. *It is soul-needed*.

"Soul-needed?" Eyulf laughs bitterly. "I'd really like to know what it was about the West Fargo truck stop or the basement of a Pick 'n Save or the bathroom of an Earls that made my 'soul' decide it needed to be a wolf."

"Your soul didn't decide anything. *You* triggered it."

"No I didn't. I didn't *do* anything."

"Turning into a wolf is not like changing socks, and it isn't arbitrary either." I hold out my hand for the gauze. "Did anyone ever see you?"

"No. Didn't happen that often." He looks at his all-too-human fingers. "Just often enough to remind me that I'm not fit for human company."

I roll the last of the bandages into a neat column and put it away. It used to be safer: one sighting of a wolf changing would be discussed, then discredited and finally dismissed as folklore. Now humans film everything, and that one sighting could be seen by millions overnight.

It isn't good for this wanderer to be a monster in both worlds, belonging to none, but it's worse for the Pack if the wanderer can't control his change.

"You have a trigger, and we're going to find it. Mine is here." I push my thumb deep into the lower part of my hip. "But they can be almost anywhere. Do you remember anything about what you were doing when it happened?"

"Not really."

"'Not really' doesn't mean 'no.'"

"It means I only remember one time. The other times, I wasn't doing anything, and next thing I know, I'm a fucking wolf."

"'Fucking'? You sound just like a human."

"You don't say 'fuck'?"

"Of course I do: I fuck, you fuck, he/she fucks, we fuck, they fuck. But a fucking wolf is a wolf who is fucking."

"Strangely enough, that's exactly what I was doing the one time I do remember. At least trying to. Until I changed." He pulls his backpack to him, looking distractedly through it.

"Human?"

"*No*, I changed into a wolf."

"I know *that*. Were you fucking a human?"

"Jesus, of course she was human. What else am I going to meet?" He opens the front pocket wide. It still smells of sharply industrial chocolate and mint. "And you don't have to make that face."

"I'm not making a face." I nod toward his bag. "What are you looking for?"

"Yes, you are making a face, and food. I wasn't expecting to be here this long."

I open the big bag I brought from Home Pond. I am not particular about what I eat, so I didn't pay much attention to what I got from the larders, and Eyulf's face falls when he opens the containers of freeze-dried egg yolks, chia seeds, and dehydrated tofu skins.

"So what exactly happened when you fucked the human?" I start searching through boxes, trying to remember what kinds of things are actually popular.

He chokes on one of Gran Tito's soy chips.

"Let's make a deal," he says, desperately swigging water to wash down the masticated soy chips turning to concrete in his mouth. "I will try, I mean really try, to stop using 'fucking' to mean general shittiness if you will stop using it to mean sex."

"Fine." *Ah, cheese chews.* "Do you want one?" He shakes his head. "What exactly happened when you sexed the human?"

"It's like talking to a fucking alien," he says, even though I *had* said *sexed* as per our agreement.

He seems to have misunderstood. All I needed to know was what muscles he was using when he sexed the human, but he starts going into unnecessary detail, and because my teeth are soldered shut around the hardness of the cheese chew, I can't stop him.

Then I realize that I am content with my cheese chew and listening to this wolf who smells cold and belongs to nobody but me talk in his too-wild voice about things that are not strictly necessary but are a testament to his resilience.

I eventually disengage my jaws enough to correct him but don't bother.

He seemed to have spent most of his time in the lower reaches of Canada and the Upper Midwest, and sometime in his wandering, he came to the Upper Peninsula. He isn't sure exactly when, but it was before he started keeping notebooks to help him remember.

The UP was unpopulated enough for his wild, but as he was wandering, he came across a bar advertising for help, if you call a hastily scrawled memo on a piece of paper ripped from a spiral notebook advertising. The

bar was called The Last Place on Earth, which sounded
about right to him, so he applied, and because he could
carry two half-barrel kegs up from the basement at the
same time, he was hired. The boss set him up with a man
who would "process" his ID for fifty dollars. Eyulf gave
the name of a guy he'd met at the Greyhound station in
Iron River.

Then the summer came around and Lorianne, the
boss's daughter, came with it. She started working at
The Last Place on Earth. Mostly at the register. She was,
he said, a tease. Not mean—she liked his hair loose and
would pull off the hat he wore to keep his hair back,
that kind of thing. This teasing bothered her boyfriend,
a young man who was built like a boulder, so everyone
called him Bob the Boulder, though his name was Jonah.
He did not like Eyulf because Lorianne did, and because
Eyulf refused to buy the meat pasties his mother made.
They made him ill, Eyulf said.

"I have a sensitive stomach," he explained.

"You don't have a sensitive stomach. We can survive
eating almost anything, but carrion—and especially carrion pastries—cause bloat."

"It's pasties, by the way. Carrion pasties." He looks
skeptically at the rough brown log pinched between his
fingers. "And what *is* this?"

"Date bar."

"That's shockingly normal." He pops it into his
mouth. "Anyway, one Thursday—they had pasties
and karaoke every Thursday, that's how I know it was
Thursday—Lorianne had a fight with Bob. She got up
onstage and started singing some song about touching
herself, and she looked at me. I wasn't doing anything.

I was standing near the wait station, like I was supposed to until each set was done. So's not to distract people from the singing when I cleared plates.

"But she's singing and leaning toward me and staring right at me and kind of rubbing her hands around her hips and everything."

"She was flagging you," I add helpfully. "Showing you she was receptive."

He sucks in his lips for a moment, then releases them. They look fuller at that moment and a little redder, and I think to myself that I would bite his mouth. Which is not an impulse I've ever had before.

"Yeah, well, the Boulder snuck up behind me, and because I was, I guess you'd say distracted, I wasn't ready. I'd learned that humans are very fragile, so when I got into fights, I needed to be careful. But," he says again, "I wasn't ready, so when he wrapped his arm around my neck, I pulled it out."

"Did he exsanguinate?"

"Exsanguinate?"

"Bleed out? Was there carpeting?" Humans use carpeting, but wolves know it collects fur and bloodstains.

"*No.* I didn't tear it *off.* I just pulled it out of the socket. Jesus, Varya. Some guy popped it back in, though Bob went to the hospital for… I don't know why. I didn't get blamed or anything," he says, licking cashew butter from his finger. "Everyone saw. But suddenly Lorianne was teasing me more and smelled different. That night, she came back after everyone had gone. I always stayed late to clean up. Restock. She turns on the music and starts touching me and moving against me, and then she rubs against me and…and did I say nobody was there?"

"Yes."

There's no one here either. No one anywhere near Westdæl. No wolves can hear him, but his voice becomes hushed and he leans closer. His breath smells like the sweetness of dates and the earthiness of almonds. "She unbuttons my shirt. Then she unbuttons my jeans, and her lips go further down. And then…" He circles his hand through the air. I think he means "and so on" or something, but the "so on" makes no sense.

"Then?"

"You know. With her mouth?" He looks at me expectantly.

Thoughts ping around in my head like a swarm of mayflies.

"She puts her mouth on your cock?"

He chuffs in exasperation. "Have you never done… anything?"

"If you're talking about sex, I sex all the time. It is our responsibility to grow the Pack. But you can't grow the Pack with your mouth."

Even as I say it, I imagine the human's mouth on Eyulf's body, the body that I've held hot and naked and dying between my legs. It makes me angry. I have forgotten the point of the story.

"That's when I kind of clenched up." *There it is. There's the point of the story.* "My feet started to change, and I…collapsed. Took two cases of beer with me as I went. I think that's what got to Lorianne. I heard her scream that her father would kill her. The door slammed, and then I didn't hear anything."

I watch him spread cashew butter on a soy chip, which will keep him quiet for a while. Stop him from distracting me with the biting of his lips and the tonguing of his cock and let me think about where his trigger must be.

If he was lucky, it would be in his lower back or his hips, but this wolf has no luck at all so it's probably in his pelvic girdle. That would explain why he thinks he didn't do anything. Those are tricky to control and a yawn, a stretch, or a suppressed sneeze can trigger the change, until he learns how to really control it.

"Lift your shirt."

His mouth is glued shut with cashew butter and soy chips, so he only manages to raise his eyebrows and one questioning hand.

"If I'm going to help you learn how to control your change, I need to find what causes it. So, I'm going to touch you, and you are going to tell me what feels right."

He takes a big swig of water. "What do you mean, 'right'?"

"I can't explain it exactly, but you will know. It will feel…it will feel like I've touched more than your body. It will feel like I've touched your soul."

His lips open slightly, but after a few moments of silence, he takes another drink and props the bottle on the ground. Standing, he crosses his arms in front of him and starts to pull off his shirt. His hair catches on the collar and spills down across his back and across his wide shoulders.

He stretches his arms to either side.

"So touch me."

Chapter 17

WHAT DOES THE COLD TASTE LIKE? DOES IT TASTE LIKE ice? Like stone? Like lichen? What does it feel like? Smooth, suede skin stretched tight across his muscle-banded belly interrupted by a line of dark hair. Is that soft like an undercoat or rough like guard hairs?

I have forgotten the point of this story.

"Varya?" he asks, looking at me over his shoulder.

Right, there's the point of the story.

"Pull your waistband down a little."

He doesn't hesitate, just lowers his arms and pulls the waistband low on his pelvis. The muscles flow and coil, begging to be touched, but I am careful to keep my palms pressed tightly into my thighs.

Then with just two fingers held stiffly out, I press against one of the notches on either side of his spine. Slowly I work my way down and to the side, pressing again and again until I've traced a belt across his lower back. He sucks in a deep breath, his back suddenly stiff.

"Do you feel something?"

"Yes," he says with a hiss. "Has nothing to do with my soul, but yes, I feel something."

I keep going, tracing the top of his hip, my head down, grateful for the black veil of my hair covering my face.

I dig in slightly under the pelvic ridge, and he shivers. "Do it again?" he says. "Yes," he exhales sharply. "I think…that's it."

"What does it feel like?"

"It feels like…it feels like if I had a cliff to jump from, I could fly."

Which is about right. It's too hard to explain exactly. The way it feels when your senses spread out on fragrant updrafts of juniper and deer and moss. Held aloft by the rustlings of aspen and the chattering of squirrels and the nattering of chickadees. Caught by the sun reflected from spiderwebs and the shadows cast by leaves.

Turns out to be hard to explain inexactly too.

Pushing my hair back, I wrap my arms in front of me, my hands imprisoned between elbows and ribs.

"Your trigger is in your pelvic girdle. It's a tricky place, but not impossible. Once you've healed enough, I'll help you learn how to change."

"When my soul needs it?"

"Yes. When your soul needs it."

***

I finally caught a weasel.

I take it to the little promontory so that I can enjoy my weasel while keeping an eye on this corner of the territory that has been given to me to guard.

The moon breaks briefly from between the clouds. My mind automatically calculates the number of days until the Iron Moon. The Pack doesn't know what it's like to wander Offland, but I do. In the year when I searched for the Great North, I had a calendar. It was red and said Scotiabank. Days were marked with tiny circles in the corners that filled up and emptied out as the month went on. As soon as the new moon passed, I consulted it with the compulsion of a grooming rat, terrified that somehow my calculations were wrong or I'd been thrown off by the inevitable cloud cover.

A weasel leg cracks between my back teeth.

I could give Eyulf one moon. What's the harm in one moon when he doesn't have to be afraid? One moon when no one is going to shoot at him? Make sure he is controlling his change? Besides, the Great North doesn't much like Westdæl anyway, and if I mark it, the threat of my own grim self should be enough to convince any interlopers to stay away.

One moon.

A crow flies to the tree above me, careful to keep a respectful distance. Still, I put my paw protectively over my weasel while I chew on the particularly flavorful skin behind the jaw, but the crow doesn't seem to be interested. With a flurry of wings, he heads up to a higher branch. Crows cache things around Homelands. Not shiny baubles like humans think, just food.

I'd almost forgotten about him when something drops to the ground. My weasel done, I sniff around to see what it is.

Pizza.

Pay attention to crows, the grans say. *They bring news from Offland. If you know how to read it.*

Pizza?

Hikers bring all sorts of things into the parks that surround Homelands: sandwiches, trail mix, pretzels, little plastic packs with tuna fish.

Under the crow's watchful eye, I nose the remnants of a pepperoni slice, sorting through the mixed scents that signal close encounters with the world of commercial ovens and deliverymen.

When the clouds part, the moon picks out what looks like an oily gray pillar far to the north. Jumping down, I run toward the Gin, scrabbling awkwardly up the loose hillside, trying to see into the dark distance. The wind shifts, bringing with it the tang of smoke. It is nowhere near our territory, but when fire starts on sodden ground and crows eat pizza, wolves must be watchful.

Instead of going back to Westdæl, I run through the High Pines all the way up to the peaks until I find a spot with a clear view toward the plume of smoke. Then I settle in: alert, my legs straight, my eyes forward, my ears swiveling, my nose searching.

Only when the smoke dissipates in the early morning do I knead at the soft floor and curl into a loose ball in the slightly musty, balsam-scented bed.

The next morning when I head back for Westdæl, Eyulf is gone.

As soon as I look into the eye-shaped cave, I can tell it's empty, or not empty, because everything that belongs to the Pack is there: food, clothes, sleeping bag. Only Eyulf and his canvas backpack are gone.

I should feel relieved. Now I don't have to think about letting him stay for a little longer. I'd done what I'd set out to do. I helped him until he was well enough to leave Homelands, and he did. Now, no one will know about my Arctic wolf, and when the time comes for me to return, I can just stuff everything back into the backpack and cart it to Home Pond. The wolves of whatever echelon is on laundry duty will clean the clothes and the sleeping bag. They will recognize the scent of Ronan, who is one of theirs. But not of Eyulf, who is one of mine.

Then because wolves are not sentimental or wasteful, they will wash everything and hang it out to dry, and in the end, the items will be put clean into dry storage, and there will be no trace left of either Ronan or Eyulf.

I *should* feel relieved but I don't. This is another loss. Smaller, maybe, but every one chips away at my edges and makes me feel like an increasingly outlandish puzzle piece that fits exactly nowhere.

Eyulf's mineral smell leads me to the border of our land, where the dark chaos of the Outer Woods overlooks the cleared paths and rusticated signs, giving the destinations and the distances, including "Wolf Hill— 2.8 miles."

It's called Wolf Hill because, a century ago or more, one of our wolves wandered Offland and got shot there. It is a reminder of why it is not only stupid to be wild in the land of humans, but also *felasynnig*—immoral and illegal—because it endangers both the individual wolf and the whole Pack.

While I would still be punished for disobeying the Alpha, going Offland in skin presents negligible dangers to the Pack, so with a quick twist, I turn back to the cave and clothes that will permit me to walk unnoticed into the land of humans.

Chapter 18

NOT ENTIRELY UNNOTICED. A HIKER DECKED OUT IN layers of fleece and waterproof nylon and thick boots with layers of socks poking up over the top looks askance at the running pants and tank top before his eyes stop at my feet. I wiggle my toes in the icy mud, daring him to say something, but even this *westend* understands an Alpha stare, and lowering his eyes, he closes his mouth and shuffles off.

There's a reason I don't go Offland much. I broke a human's cheek for what I now realize was a relatively small insult to a female of my echelon. The Pack paid him compensation, but from then on, I stayed in the car. Armed with a good fake ID, I sat there with my foot itching to hit the gas and take my wolves back.

"Were you looking for me?" Eyulf asks. I shield my eyes from the midday sun and the strong, slim silhouette on the granite seat above me, pencil in hand.

I gesture him to move to the side and start my run across the empty trail. My bare feet hit a stump, propelling me up toward the rock. I hold the edge and, with a twist of my hips, throw my legs across to the top.

My hand shoots out before the pencil has a chance to roll down the sloping back.

"You could have just come up the other way," he says, not bothering to look at me.

I know I could have. I knew it as soon as I saw him

there, his injured leg hanging over the insurmountable ledge. But I also knew as soon as I breathed the sigh of relief that I wouldn't.

"What are you doing here?"

"You'll see when I'm finished." He angles his back to me and looks at his phone, precariously balanced on his thigh. "Pass me the periwinkle?"

Periwinkle?

"What's a periwinkle?"

"It's a color. It's a kind of blue." There are many kinds of blue in his metal case. Here's Phthalo. Prussian. Turquoise. "Just hand me the box…"

I pass it to him, and he picks out a color partway between blue and purple. "Periwinkle," he says, holding it up. "So now you know."

Well, that's certainly useless. Periwinkle. There is no periwinkle here, just dingy snow, churned up by boots, beige winter-dead plants and gray rock and the darker forests of Homelands looming beyond the big bright-yellow signs.

Another hiker comes by and looks at me. Again, he opens his mouth. Again, he looks into my eyes. Again, he sees something he doesn't want to deal with and shuts his mouth.

"If you wanted to blend in," Eyulf says, "you should've at least worn shoes." He passes me his spiral-bound drawing pad opened to one page. "Here."

The page is divided into six panels, each one with a single flower. Or single cluster of flowers. The detail makes them impossible to mistake. In my heart, I rec-ognize them all, and if I didn't know their names, I do now.

A delicate yellow cup on a fine bent stem emerging from a bed of ragged leaves. *Arctic Poppy*, it says.

A low clutch, pale blue and purple with a magenta throat above jade-colored compound leaves. *Boreal Jacob's Ladder*, it says.

A mouse-eye view of white balls of fur up close and rolling down hill after hill. *Arctic Cottongrass*, it says.

A small gathering of vivid blue trumpets hugging the ground. *Gentian*, it says.

A hillock of bright-yellow flowers surrounded by tiny green leaves. *Saxifrage*, it says.

The last is the most beautiful of them all: a cluster of minute flowers, each with a yellow center surrounded by perfect overlapping petals of sky blue.

And periwinkle.

Forget-Me-Not.

It says.

"I know you could have found these yourself, but I didn't think you would."

Staring at the page in my hands, I can almost feel the icy winds of Vrangelya that forced everything there to hug the rocks that passed for the soil of home.

"How did you…?"

He picks up his phone and turns it off. "You said you came from an island in the Arctic. From your name and your accent, I figured it was in Russia." He snaps his pencil case closed. "Then it was just a question of walking until I got reception." The case slides into his bag.

I just keep staring, unfocused, at the notebook.

"Do you miss it?"

"What?"

"Your home."

"This is my home. That is—" That is what? My birthplace. The forge that tempered me, mind and body. My reminder of how quickly things can fall apart and how quickly a heart can dry to the consistency of beef jerky. "Gone. It's gone. But I'm glad to have this. I mean, I would be glad to have this. Can I?"

"I made it for you," he says and begins to slide down the gentle slope of the back of his granite perch. Then he limps around front. "But maybe you can wait? Until I leave?"

"Yes." I wait while he retrieves his stick and tucks it under his arm, then we silently walk back toward Homelands.

The wind slips under one of the signs, making it heave, then collapse against the pole with a bang. Eyulf stops, his eyes closed, breathing in, his mouth barely open. He sucks in breath after breath, too fast and too deep. I put my hand at his back.

Then he sighs, and we keep moving.

I did the same thing that first time I crossed the boundary and smelled the thick crisscrossing scent of wolves who were nowhere and everywhere, who had marked the perimeter, the browse lines, favored watering places, and unstable bluffs. Of wolves who had turned and twisted in the earth, leaving that peculiar muddled scent of two wolves announcing to the Pack that they are together.

It was the freedom to be wild, and after so many months of wandering frightened and alone, hiding from moon to moon, to realize that the *Deore Norþ* wasn't a place that wolves went when they died. It was a place where wolves *lived*.

I threw myself into the promise of those markings. I dug, trying to find the end to it, but I couldn't. Just layer after layer of wolf. I lay in the trough I'd made and rolled around in it, nearly sick with the need for it.

That's how they found me. A perimeter wolf discovered me squirming in a damp hollow at the border. She tried to take me in her jaws, but however young my body was, my soul was too old. Having traversed and survived half the world, I was ready to match my experience against any wolf here. I would not be carried the last miles like a pup.

Nils took a look at me leaning into my front legs, ready to fight or flee. Not that I was going to do either; it was just the way I was. In a constant state of readiness.

He said something to his mate, Alexandra, in the tongue I now speak but didn't then. Then he spoke to me in the Old Tongue, and because it had been so long since I'd heard it, I mewled from the perfect cadenced beauty of it.

"*Þu þearft bæþes, wulfling.*"

You need a bath, little wolf.

Jean—she hadn't moved to the Great Hall and wasn't yet a gran—marched me to the Bathhouse and told me to change. But I just couldn't let them see me naked. Exposed. They would see the mark that every wolf knew meant I was a lawbreaker and an anathema. *Wearg.* I hadn't found another pack, and I had no confidence that I would. Even if I did, I would never find another land so deeply marked with wolf.

I became, I think, a little unhinged: running and scratching and snarling until finally Alexandra came. She was a towering wolf. Amazing that her one offspring should be so small. She leapt at me with her long arms. I bit at her and fought, and she dunked me in the cold bath and held me down and scrubbed hard until she felt my belly under my fur. In her hesitation, I knew she'd discovered what I'd been so desperate to hide.

She kept washing, more gently now, because the fight was lost and I'd gone limp. When I was all clean, she told the wolves in the Bathhouse to leave. Then she gave me a little pile of clothes and privacy.

I remember those clothes. Brown corduroys with bald spots on the fronts of the thighs and knees. A yellow striped shirt dotted with a dozen watchful blue eyes. I saw them on subsequent generations of pups, though I presume they're gone now, like everything else lost in the fire.

Alexandra combed my hair with a lice comb, while the Alpha asked how I, a child, had come to be marked as *Wearg*. I told him. I didn't embellish, but I didn't leave out the important facts. I told him what had been happening to our Pack and what had been happening to me. He looked to his mate and said something in this new tongue. She responded with a sad smile. Then he bent over, cupping my little face in his big hands and marked me.

Alexandra marked me too. Not long after that, Nils was shot ripping his unborn pups from his dead mate's womb. He ran toward Homelands, but by the time the Pack located him, only the minuscule silver runt was still alive.

"When wolves mate," I tell Eyulf, even though he didn't ask, "they are braided—bound—with the land and the Pack as well as their mates. So it's a thing. That feeling for the land."

"And you? Are you braided?"

Lorcan has asked me more often recently to go through with it. I've done my best to avoid answering.

"Varya?" Eyulf asks. His hand touches my arm and then slides down to my hand.

"No," I say, staring at his cool fingers loosely coiled around mine.

He lets go.

"I'm glad," he says.

I miss his fingers.

Chapter 19

THE FOOD THAT I BROUGHT BACK FROM HOME POND is almost gone. Even the dehydrated tofu skins and freeze-dried eggs. If he wants to eat, he's going to have to hunt, and if he wants to hunt, he's going to have to change.

But first, I need to make sure that he's healed enough. That his skin won't tear and his veins won't rupture during the stretching and torquing that comes with turning from a hairless biped into a wolf.

It's hard to judge the texture of a scar or the sponginess of the tissue through denim. "You need to take those off."

"Off?"

I push a little harder.

"Off. They're too thick, and I can't feel through the—"

He makes a half-hearted attempt to pull up the cuff, but he already knows it's too narrow. After an exasperated grunt, he asks me to toss him the towel.

"I have seen naked males before. Many. Hundr—"

"I'm happy for you," he snaps, grabbing the towel himself and wrapping it around his waist. "But you haven't seen *me*."

I have. But then he was a dying stranger and now, even though I've only known him for a short while, I understand him better than any of the Great North. Is it because he's an Arctic wolf? Or because he's a survivor? Or because he doesn't know that he is supposed to be afraid of me?

Whatever the reason, it feels different somehow.

His back to me, he starts to unzip his jeans and shift them slowly down, all the while clutching at the frankly inadequate bit of terry cloth. Finally, he kicks his pants away and turns, the faded turquoise rectangle covering front and back—but only just—and leaving his wounded leg exposed. That and the sloping hollow above his muscled thigh and below his hip bone. A part of no great importance.

On another body, it would be of no importance whatsoever.

I focus on the still-pink circlet of scars around his leg, pulling the scar tissue gently apart with two fingers to see how elastic it is. Then I push down, softly at first, and gradually harder. If it starts to swell or bruise, the change will tear apart the underlying network of blood vessels.

He jerks.

"That's a bad sign."

"What?"

"Well, it shouldn't hurt that much."

"Doesn't," he says.

"This is not the time to hide what you're feeling. If you change before you're fully healed, you will tear yourself open again. I know what I'm doing."

He leans forward, his arms draped between his legs.

"I'm not sure you do."

Ah. The towel that was barely adequate before is simply laughable now that it is also responsible for covering a thickly engorged cock.

I look up, up, up to his eyes. They've changed, darkened. They are no longer the pale blue of old ice and bright variegated green of forest depths, but the deep blue of late evening and the dark green of rain-drenched fir. His white hair loops forward and then falls over his shoulder. A sharp, green muskiness like rubbed coriander bothers my nose with something warm and dangerous.

I jump away, like a skittish fawn.

"I don't think it'll open up. Remember, your trigger is here." I point without touching toward the place I'd found before. "It's inside, not outside, so you need to tighten those muscles. But take your shirt off first."

"Okay," he says, pulling off his shirt. "Why?"

"Because if by some miracle you get it right, I'll have to cut you out of it, and we don't have that many changes of clothes."

Turning away, I smooth the T-shirt still warm from his body against my chest. Philadelphia Frostbite Regatta, it says. When I glance back, his eyes are closed and a tremor roils through the cut muscles. Parts of him around his pelvis that don't look like they could tighten any more ripple.

Sitting down on a dry trunk, I stare at the lower slopes of Norþdæl, blanketed with wine and gray and dark gold, dotted with dark-green evergreens and occasional skeletal fingers of white birch.

"How are you doing over there?"

"Working on it." He coughs a handful of fake coughs, trying, I suppose, to reproduce whatever caused that earlier change.

"Hey?" he says.

"Yes?"

"I'm going to be able to change back, right?"

"Of course. Once you learn what your trigger is, you'll never forget it."

"Like riding a bike."

I scratch my ear. "It's nothing like riding a bike. You're changing into a wolf. Wolves don't ride bikes."

"It's a… That's not what I… Never mind."

A squirrel squats on his hind legs, eyeing me from a distance. At this moment, from this angle, the daylight moon forms a curved crown above his head. "Except… you do know not to change before the Iron Moon, right?"

"Why?"

The squirrel's whiskered nose twitches, worriedly.

"Because the Iron Moon takes us as she finds us and makes us wilder. If she finds us in skin, she makes us wild. But if she finds us wild, she makes us *æcewulfs*. Real wolves. Forever wolves."

"And you don't change back?"

"That's why they're called *forever* wolves."

He stares down at his feet, clenching and stretching his toes, as though confirming that for now at least, he still looks human. "Is it like when you're a wolf, but you still know who you are? You still remember everything?"

"Nobody knows what they remember or don't, but they're definitely not the same. They're not Pack anymore." Over my shoulder, I see the panic on his face, his hand clinging to the little towel, like the last vestiges of his humanity.

"Don't worry. I won't let that happen to you," I say.

His eyes consider mine for a moment. I nod at him, and he starts again, pressing harder, moving, clenching, roiling, undulating.

The squirrel takes advantage of my distraction and bolts up a nearby tree. High up, he hangs, head down, legs splayed, and chitters at me for invading his territory.

"*Varya!*"

I leap at Eyulf's strangled cry, just managing to catch him as he pitches forward, his feet narrowing, arch elongating, calf muscle tightening.

How did I forget to tell him to lie down?

I stagger to the ground, his body writhing in my arms. His green eye searches blindly, his grotesque mouth mangles a groan before going silent. The towel drops away from his narrowing hips and his clutching fingers. My hair falls forward over him.

Astille, wulf. Þu eart gesund mid me.

Hush, wolf, you are safe with me.

My hands run over his skin, like water.

Chapter 20

I CERTAINLY DON'T REMEMBER ALL THE STEPS I TOOK to end up here, naked and exposed on the promontory, waiting for the change to take hold while the rain beats strangely sharp against my skin.

I watched Eyulf through his change, then took myself off at a discreet distance, because *I know* how we look in this grotesque between stage. I curl myself tight, my arms over my head, and give in to the sense-dulling oblivion of the change that for once doesn't last nearly long enough. Shaking out my fur with a shudder that starts at my head and then dominoes all the way to the tip of my tail.

An owl flutters on his branch, then rearranges his wings. He snaps his beak shut while I head back, watching Eyulf test his wounded leg in his changed body. He is beautiful wild: lithe and strong and long-legged. His head sleek, with long, sharp fangs. His fur is, as I expected, longer than usual and catches each breeze. When he takes a step forward, muscle and bone roll gracefully, except for a slight hitch at the end.

He turns his head, looking along the length of his torso at me. Earth-green and sky-blue eyes and a thin thread of bright blood trickling from the healing ring around his leg are the only colors on the pale canvas of his body.

We turn our heads in unison, leaning into our front legs, eyes scanning the sky for the group of straggling snow geese who are searching for a place to rest. They would never choose Clear Pond, which is too hemmed in by trees, or Home Pond, which is too hemmed in by wolves, so they will head to Beaver Pond. I wouldn't bother with them if Beaver Pond was open, because wolves really only have one chance in the water.

But it's still mostly frozen, which will force the geese into a tighter formation and give us more opportunity. Together, we move around the easy slope at the back of Westdæl.

At the base, we pause behind a still-snowy shock of Labrador tea. I lay my chin across his forehead, then take off. He follows me, even though I had told him clearly to stay put. I have to remind myself that he has never been in this form with someone he might need to communicate with. It is a language I take for granted. I snap at him with bared jaws; that he understands.

The geese drop out of the sky, some of them leaving silty contrails in the gash of open water, but others find themselves on ice where big Arctic paws and long legs are so much more useful than webbed feet and stubby stems. I move along the edges of Beaver Pond until I get close enough to burst toward them.

They begin flapping off, focused only on me and not on the white wolf who jumps out and catches one slowly struggling goose.

Repositioning his jaws, he bites hard and the hunt is over. It is, as wolves like to say, a good kill.

There is an invisible perimeter surrounding an eating wolf. The larger the prey, the tighter it is, because our law requires that we make a death count by eating everything. A buck will be shared; a goose will not.

I stand outside that invisible perimeter, keeping watch.

With one paw, he holds down a wing and immediately starts to tear at the goose. The blood is hot enough to release a tiny breath of steam into the mountain air.

A hawk circles overhead, but I can already tell he is going to be disappointed. Eyulf's dismemberment is slow and deliberate, and he eats everything. The Great North wolves often leave the fleshless ends of a bird's wings, but not this one. He keeps chewing and swallowing until finally the last tip of the last feather disappears down his gullet.

The hawk catches a thermal and drifts away, disgusted.

With a long, luxurious swirl of the tongue, Eyulf cleans his mouth, then wipes his muzzle with his foreleg and shakes out his fur.

He splays his paws out in front of him and leans into his hind legs, shivering his hips like a pup who wants to play. I'm not sure how old he is, but almost as old as I am, and I've been too old to play since…well, since forever.

I head back to the northern slope of Westdæl. I've fulfilled my responsibility to him, and now it's time to fulfill my responsibility to the Great North, running my slice of the perimeter again and again and again until long after the light has left.

But as soon as my back is turned, teeth nip my left flank. With an awkward jump, he just clears my snapping jaws. I move away, my nose to the ground, because *I have responsibilities*.

He jumps, putting his forelegs across my shoulders; I whip around, snarling, my ears horizontal and my tail up. I move in close, muscled chest against muscled chest. He doesn't back away or back down. Instead, he does the unthinkable.

He raises his front paw and *pats my nose*.

No one pats my nose.

I charge after him, but he hides, and as I run past, sharp teeth grab hold of my tail.

And no one nips my tail.

I round on him, but he won't let go and I can't catch him, because he's holding my tail and dancing just out of my way, so I twirl around and around until I leap up and change directions, giving his jaw a little wrench. Then I grab his tail, see how he likes it, but we go around the other way, until I feel giddy and scattered.

He trips—his leg, no doubt—and we start to tumble down the side of Westdæl. I slide to a stop as the land levels out in the emptiness near the Gin, and he rolls to a stop next to me. I jump up and on top of him, snarling as I take his muzzle in my jaws. He slips out and takes mine in his, and we jaw spar.

We tussle hard until he tires and hesitantly taps at my withers, patting me down. I sink onto the ground, my chin on my paws, and then feel his strong body beside mine and feel his head near my shoulders. One paw against mine. After a minute or two, he sighs, the smell of goose blood on his breath.

I should get up, but not quite yet. Wait until my mind stops spinning and my heart settles. Let him relax, panting warm and heavy against my fur.

Listening to the fast, regular-beat heartbeat strangely loud in my ears.

He lifts his head suddenly. There are shadows streaking across the ground. Birds race for tree cover, emptying the sky. If I'd been paying attention *like I was supposed to*, I would have realized immediately that it wasn't a heartbeat.

Thuppathuppathuppathuppa.

Both of us jump up, scrambling to get away from the exposed spaces of the Gin and up toward the forests of Westdæl. I am already at the tree line when I realize that he is still struggling to get up. A white beacon against the loose gray stone.

He tried to do too much, too soon, and while he managed to tumble down Westdæl, gravity is not prepared to allow him to tumble back up.

Racing back, I launch myself from a shelf and slide the rest of the way, my feet skittering on the rocks until I draw up next to him, the sound of the helicopter blades banging loud against my skull.

My teeth clamp tight around the loose skin at his neck, dragging him toward the base of a nearby tree. He curls himself around the base, and I cover his beacon with my dark-gray body.

Alys us fram westendum and fram eallum hiera cræftum.

The helicopter emerges over the Gin, its blades almost perpendicular to the ground, sending loosened leaves and a spray of water into the air around us. I cling to Eyulf, who knows not to move. The only sign of life is a tiny whimper, a searching glance as his green eye meets mine.

I press my muzzle against his.

Alys us fram westendum.

Alys us.

Chapter 21

LEONORA, THE GREAT NORTH'S HUMAN BEHAVIORS teacher, says that humans judge one another by clothes, by apartments, by vacations, by cars. These are the things that signal their status and what echelon they belong to.

Wild or in skin, wolves judge each other by strength in action. By decisiveness. By willingness to sacrifice. Every *thing* we have is shared. Our cabins are assigned and filled with furniture rummaged from the collective stores. Our cars are held in common. Our clothes are passed around and advertise schools we've never gone to, sports we've never played, jobs we've never held.

Even Offlanders, whose position in human society may require their own stuff, do not actually own it. If they have an apartment, they squat there, keeping it pin neat until some Pack financial advisor decides that it is time to sell.

The only thing we truly *own* is the seax, the knife that is the emblem of becoming a full member of the Pack.

Other wolves judge us by the condition of our blades. A wolf with a pitted blade in a dry sheath is falling apart and will be challenged.

So while Eyulf sits at the rock pond, drawing, I search for a likely stone that I can use to sharpen Ronan's knife. It isn't mine, but I cannot abide a dulled blade.

Neither of us much feels like being wild. Even when

the helicopter was gone, it just felt safer, being in skin and clothes.

"The helicopters are new," I say when I finally feel like talking. "Here. They're new here. The Pack's lawyers had always managed to keep them away."

He rolls his thumb across the big box of pencils. "Wolves have lawyers?"

"And accountants and fund managers and engineers and hackers. It takes a lot to protect a place like this."

He looks at me and then back at the black pencil. "Have you ever been shot at from the air?"

"Yes." I need something that's big enough to accommodate the sweep of a blade, small enough to fit my hand.

"You don't ever get used to it," he says.

"No." I need a rock that is water-smoothed, fine-grained, with just the right amount of grit. "But you were shot in skin."

I don't look at him, but I hear the silence when he stops fiddling with his pencils. Then he pulls out an eraser and rubs tight strokes on the page.

"How did you know?"

"I've seen shot wolves, and some who've survived long enough to change back. Their entry and exit wounds don't line up when they're in skin."

Weighing a rock in my hand, I decide it seems about right.

"I guess that makes sense."

I pull the stone smoothly away from me. *One, two, three.* "Why would a human shoot another human?"

He takes out the gold-brown pencil and holds it to the side, rubbing it back and forth against the paper.

"Why would a wolf"—he taps the dull end of the pencil against his torso—"gore another wolf?"

I turn the seax and start again.

"I was shot by my family."

I stop my scraping and stare at the line of the blade. "Family? What do you mean 'family'? Wolves don't have families."

"I did. Lionel and Barbara Hauptstadt, and their daughters, Unity, Charity, and Purity. And Elsa, a white wolf with floppy ears and a sloppy tongue."

"*You mean a dog?*"

Eyulf pushes his stubby black pencil into a sharpener and begins to crank it.

"She ran around on four legs like I did, she barked like I did, she had white fur like I did. As far as I knew, she and I were alike. Wolves didn't raise me. A dog did."

Turns out Lionel was the one who refused to call the new dog Snowball, the girls' preference. In a perverse joke of fate, he named him Eyulf—lucky wolf—instead. Apparently, he hoped a dog named Lucky Wolf would bring more of it—luck—than a dog named Snowball when he went hunting for deer to feed a family that needed it.

Neither the dog nor the name could change the fact that Lionel's aim was piss-poor and he did not have a hunter's nerve.

The Hauptstadts lived in a farmhouse that hadn't had a farm for a while and was instead just a ramshackle building with a tractor rusting in the backyard, the smell of absent cows everywhere, and fallow lands that belonged to the bank.

Barbara, the second half of this broken couple,

worked long hours as a cashier at the Save-On-Foods. The only thing they succeeded in was keeping themselves and their despair from infecting their daughters, who largely raised themselves.

The girls slept in a big room past a parlor that no one had ever used. It had a collection of tiny perfume bottles with stained bottoms, a clock made of corroding metal that no one ever remembered to wind, and an ombré openwork shawl of rust and brown draped over the back of the sofa.

This would, he said, come into play later.

He has a beautiful voice. Deep and wolfish even in skin. I think I could listen to it forever.

What he didn't learn from Elsa, he learned from the girls. He and Elsa slept outside, but in the evening, they gathered in the back room while Unity read to her sisters. He watched Unity's finger trace the markings on the pages. Elsa often fell asleep, though he would paw her awake during the exciting parts.

He was in his second winter at the Hauptstadts before he fully understood the language of humans. It took another year to decipher the meaning of those little markings on the pages. Twice the girls caught him reading—paws on the pages, nose hovering above the words—and laughed and laughed.

That night, he pushed the book he'd been reading toward Elsa, who chewed spittily on the corner but showed no other interest.

He worried about Elsa. Not only was she not much of a reader, but she also wasn't even particularly good at following straightforward directions: Leave the stupid cat alone. Don't eat Daddy's shoe. Stay away from the tractor.

At first, he admired her rebellious spirit, but it wasn't rebelliousness that drew her to the puddle under the tractor. "Don't lick that," Purity had said. "It's poison."

As directions go, that seemed, Eyulf said, "unambiguous," so later, when he went mousing, it didn't occur to him that she would immediately head to the shimmering puddle under the tractor and lap it up.

By the time he returned to her, it was too late. Whatever the poisonous stuff was—antifreeze is my guess—it made her unable to walk, then unable to move. In pain. The girls were sobbing, begging with their parents, but if the parents would not speak openly in front of the girls, they hid nothing from Eyulf. Like the fact that they couldn't afford to take Elsa to the vet.

Do something, his wife had said. *You've got to do something.*

So Lionel got in his truck to drive Elsa away. Put his gun in the gun rack. He didn't stop Eyulf from jumping in beside her, nosing her and nuzzling her jaw. Whining for her to wake up as he had during all those exciting parts she'd slept through. She started to shake uncontrollably, her eyes opened and frightened. Her claws made strange scraping sounds against the metal bed.

They went not to the woods behind the house, but to a farther wood up in the mountains. Lionel took the dog out and put her on the ground. He loaded up his gun and shot, and that piss-poor hunter missed. Shot her in the back but didn't kill her. She opened her eyes and looked at him, a look of such absolute betrayal that Lionel turned tail and ran.

Leaving Eyulf to learn a brutal lesson on the difference between sentiment and love. "Sentiment is what you do for yourself," he says. "Love is what you do for someone else. I loved Elsa, so I killed her."

The girls were devastated. Charity in particular begged her parents to let Eyulf sleep with the girls at night. So for the weeks and months and years that came, Eyulf slept on the floor of their room. Not all nights, but enough.

Enough so that when the unthinkable happened, he was sleeping on the flattened green shag at the foot of their beds.

"I woke up feeling sick. My stomach was churning, my muscles stretching and clenching. It couldn't be the tractor poison, because Lionel had cleaned that up long before. Then my ears started ringing, and even though it was dark, it got darker in a way it never had been before, and I was completely blind.

"Every bone and muscle and tendon felt out of place and rubbery, and when it finally felt solid again, it was all wrong. It was like I was both naked and cocooned. The dark had gotten darker, the quiet, quieter. My nose was almost useless. I kept sniffling and snorting and trying to pop my ears and shake my head.

"And for the first time, I felt really cold. I curled up tight, trying to fluff my tail over my nose, except there was no tail. I tried again to wag it, but when I looked behind me, it was gone. All I saw instead was a skinny naked ass, and I started howling."

If he'd been at Homelands, he would have known what he was. He would have spent his life surrounded by wolves shifting. He would most likely have experimented with it himself at least a few times. He would know what would happen with the Year of First Shoes. The whole Pack would have helped him during the difficult transition from pup to juvenile. The Pack would work together to train him how to wear clothes and hold forks and speak with tongue and mouth, not with chest and throat.

But there was no pack.

"You can imagine," he says with a laugh. "The girls wake up, and all they see is this screaming, naked, white-haired boy. Of course, I didn't know how to walk, so I was careening around on my knuckles and toes, bumping into everything. They started screaming, too, which was really hard on the ears. I scuttled out into the parlor, dragged on the throw from the back of the sofa, because I was cold."

"Then I heard the gun locker being opened upstairs and scurried toward the porch and the stairs, but instead of clearing them with one single jump, I fell. Lionel had thumped to his daughters' room and then back toward the door and off the porch, and meanwhile, my fingers and toes had gotten trapped in the stupid shawl and I tripped into the ditch. I'd only just managed to right myself when the screen door slammed shut.

"Then I hear the *click-clack* of his pump action, and wouldn't you know it? The first time in his life that Lionel Hauptstadt manages to hit something, it's the skinny freak whose penis is caught in the openwork shawl.

"The one fucking time he actually aims true, it's at me," he says.

He laughs. "Hysterical, right?"

I look at the stone in my hand. "It's not funny, and you know it. Don't pretend."

He looks over a gray pencil held sideways, then goes back to his drawing.

"I was shot by a human and survived. You were

gored by a wolf and survived. The difference is I choose not to relive what happened every minute of every day. Torturing myself—"

"*The difference is*, you are not to blame for what happened to you. I am. What I did destroyed everything. If I 'choose' to remind myself, it's so that the same thing doesn't happen to them."

I press the seax to my thumbnail, testing its edge.

"Can I ask you something?"

The blade digs through to the nail bed.

"Why do you always say 'they'?"

"'They'?"

"When you talk about the Pack, you always say 'they,' never 'we.' Like you don't really belong."

Blood beads in a neat line across my thumbnail.

"I am all that is left of...of Pack Vrangelya. If I forget, there is no one to remember that they ever existed."

After drying the blade on the ragged T-shirt, I slip it back into the sheath.

"And me?" he asks. "Will you remember me?"

My finger traces the clumsy α carved into the leather by a wolf who never understood the sacrifices required of an Alpha.

"Yes."

He turns his head to the side, looking at the page. "Do you want to see?"

I move next to him. It's a figure. Not really a figure, but parts of a figure: dark hair escaping from a careless knot, a knife, a stone, water, the tensed muscle of a forearm, brows that are too black and straight above eyes taut with concentration.

A gap between shirt and waistband reveals the tail

end of a scar that looks almost beautiful, a finial decorated with delicate rootlets.

"Where are we?" he asks, holding the black pencil over the corner of the page. "I like to remember."

"Franklin County, New York. That's what the humans call it."

"What do you call it?"

"They… *We* call it Homelands."

So that's what he writes, *Homelands*, then above it he adds *Varya*.

He closes the notebook and stares at the black cover for a long time.

When I get up, I smooth my shirt in place so that nothing is showing.

Chapter 22

IT STARTED WITH THE SMELL OF LOAM, OF TURNED earth hanging in the air, like the scent of blood around a wound.

Faint, almost nothing, but just wrong enough to pull me from Westdæl to the crumbling bottom of the Gin, where I feel a faint rumbling in the earth.

By the time I have picked through the giant broken trees and small streams and slick stones to the upper reaches of the High Pines, I don't feel it anymore, but the warblers and thrushes and flycatchers and kinglets who should have already sorted out their nesting sites and gotten down to the business of filling them are instead fighting inside our border, a sure sign that displaced interlopers are looking for new homes.

The duties of a perimeter wolf are clear. We are to guard the perimeter, not worry about what is going on Offland. Standing next to one of the NO TRESPASSING signs, I lean into my front legs and pivot my ears, trying to discover what the *westends* are doing that would stir things up like this. A pregnant doe struggles up the human side of the mountain. She looks at me warily. I am hungry, but I have other concerns, and we are not allowed to hunt the pregnant or calving. She shifts directions toward the east; I watch her, particularly when she comes to the wolf-marked border. She stops, sucking in the unmistakable scent of predator, but then without a look behind, she lifts her hoof and steps over.

Kinglets may be reluctant to give up their nests, but a little tussling and some redoubled effort and they rebuild. We do not hunt kinglets.

We do hunt deer, and for this doe to keep coming means that whatever is on the other side of the mountain is worse than wolves.

It takes time picking my way down the Offland face of the Norþdæl mountains. The trees are not so dense here, the roots don't run as deep, and the rain turns the earth into mud, making the hardpan that covers large swathes of the descent like a slide. The exposed earth between them is hardly better, and paths carved by hikers turn into rivers.

On this side of the mountain, though, the smell of turned soil is joined by a grinding, whirring sound and a sick, sweet, smoky smell of engines.

Once upon a time, the runoff from Westdæl and the High Pines fed a river running north. But without wolves, the deer lost any sense of proportion. They ate not only trees and bushes, but all the sedges and grasses that edged the river. Without the roots, the soft, damp banks eroded and collapsed. Without banks, the river itself turned into a weedy, meandering slough, though the ancient outline of its course is still visible as a foggy trough that runs along a plateau before it drops to the valley below.

Standing at a high point still covered by trees, I watch monstrous yellow trucks with thick chain-covered tires churn through mud and strip the plateau bare.

One with a single giant claw grabs an ancient white pine and forces it to the ground until it submits with a groan, its baroque tangle of roots suddenly exposed. Then the machine throws this hundred-year-old life to the side where another truck sucks it in, cutting and stripping the trunks, turning them into logs. The third shovels the stripped branches and naked roots into a shredder next to smoking piles.

Something is going on farther north. From here, I can't tell what it is—smoke or simply fog settled into the basin. I move carefully, keeping well within the tree line and close to the ground to get a look at the lower level.

Circling wide around the machines, I find myself farther Offland than I have been for months. Near the edge of the plateau, the lower level of the one-time stream turns into a long alleyway that is no longer trees and water but mud and fire. Arrayed along the length of the basin are large staging grounds, some already denuded and burning. Some have nothing but an access road and a pyramid of pipes.

And they all line up perfectly in an arrow pointed directly at the Gin, at the vulnerable back door onto Homelands.

Choking on a long, low growl, I whip around, headed back for the High Pines, for Home Pond, for the Alpha. Whatever our lawyers are doing, they're looking the wrong way or moving too slowly. I crouch, creeping quick and low along the trees of the plateau.

The route back up to Norþdæl is harder though. Water undercuts the soil, leaving what looks like solid ground but is really just a ledge of soft dirt resting on air. As I scrabble up the slick side, a large ledge gives way, sending me plummeting down, showing uneven flashes of dark-gray and light-gray fur that don't stop until I hit a fallen tree hard enough to push every last bit of air from my lungs.

When did the truck stop?

A door opens with a squeak, and a heavy body jumps to the damp ground. There is a moment of silence, and a shot slaps the granite face right above me.

Another truck goes silent, and a few shards of the rock shower down onto my fur and into my face. Burrowing deeper into the ground, I pull my body in as small and tight and still as I can.

"*Sam!* What're you doing?" The voice yells to be heard over the one remaining truck still grinding in the distance.

"Saw something. Over there."

"He's gonna know you got a gun."

"He's all the way back at the road. No way he can hear, so unless you tell him."

Another shot sounds louder than the first because it's closer. More stone chips erupt behind me.

"Jesus, Sam." This other voice sounds nervous. "There's nothing there."

"Yeah, there is. Just you wait. Saw it move. I'm going to make it move again."

No, you're not. The stone here is too slick for me to run fast. The slope is too steep for me to zigzag the way we have to when we're trying to avoid bullets. I have no choice but—

Something cuts through the air above me, so fast that the humans don't react, don't make a sound until the man's wrist collapses with a sickening crunch between Eyulf's jaws. The gun thuds to the earth, and then the *westend* falls to the ground, screaming.

The human next to him lurches for the gun, but both

Eyulf and I lunge at the same time. He stumbles back, and Eyulf rears above him, bloodstained and furious.

I throw myself between the two, and Eyulf's jaw glances against my shoulder. With my jaws wide, I scrape at his muzzle. A warning that doesn't stop him, because he doesn't believe that I will protect this human until I bite down on his lower jaw and hold it fast.

He's not Pack. He doesn't know what it means to have a territory. A wanderer will make a mess of things, then pick up and go. We can't just pick up and leave. This is Homelands. It was created by hundreds of years and thousands of wolf-hours. If the humans kill me, it's a trophy on their wall. If we kill them, they will come and destroy this final fragile sanctuary.

A heavy door slams behind us. "Willis. Sam," says a new voice, drawing closer. "What exactly are you doing?" With each step he takes, the scents sort themselves out. I let go of Eyulf's jaw and stand beside him. My wolf doesn't know what a Shifter is, and he looks confused as he tries to understand what this thing is that smells like carrion and steel mixed with the wilder fragrance of reeds and water's edge.

He may not know what a Shifter is, but he knows it's not human.

My first real Shifter is as tall as Tiberius, but gaunt and nothing like the giant thing of my nightmares. I know he's full-grown because his black beard is flecked with gray. If he lived someplace with sun, his skin would probably be bronze, but he clearly doesn't and it is khaki instead.

The ancestor we shared with Shifters endowed their descendants with senses and size. But unlike Pack, who have spent the intervening centuries breeding to power, they have come to rely on power they can carry in their pockets. He picks up the gun from the mud.

"Sam thought—" says the human who isn't screaming and must be Willis.

"What did I say about guns?" the Shifter interrupts.

"They're fucking wolves. *Shoot them*."

He turns to me. "I'm presuming you did not attack him?"

I lift my lip over one canine, the wolfish equivalent of a rolled eye.

"Are you crazy, Constantine?" Willis whispers. "*Just shoot them*."

"Willis, take Sam to my car. We'll get him to the hospital as soon as I am finished here."

I have to agree with Willis. *Are you crazy?* What the hell is he doing talking to me? In front of a *westend*? I look at him out of the corner of my eye, but I will not acknowledge him further. Evie already let Elijah Sorensson's human live. We cannot afford another human who knows.

"Mr. Leveraux," he continues, playing idly with the safety of the gun, "has a proposal. So far, your Alpha has refused to discuss it with him. But she doesn't have a choice anymore. We are here now. Tell her that."

He heads back to the car and the two men struggling to get in. I check on the driver of the third truck. Encased in headphones, the cab of his truck, and the noise of his engine, he has noticed nothing. He continues to scoop up branches and put them on the fire.

We don't rush back up the slick, eroded mountainside, because we can't. Part of the way up, the door slams. A little farther, the engine starts. Farther still, a gun fires twice in quick succession.

That's why Constantine spoke to us so openly.

As far as he was concerned, these humans were already dead.

It's only when we are almost at the crest that the third yellow truck stops. The driver jumps down into the mud, pulls out his earbuds, and circles around, wondering when he became alone.

Chapter 23

"There were gunshots," Eyulf says as I clean out the reopened wound with a rag dipped in the last of the Seagram's. "They could have hurt you."

"Still, you shouldn't have followed me. You could have killed them. Turn over? Wolves don't reveal themselves to humans, and they certainly don't kill them unless it is a matter of the life or death."

He turns onto his belly, and I start to pick out more embedded forest litter.

"But it *was* a matter of life or death," he says. "They were shooting at you."

"*The life or death of the Pack*. A single wolf means nothing."

I pluck out several bits of fur.

And a beetle wing.

"It does mean something. *You* mean something. You mean something to *me*."

And small stones.

And a single pine needle.

"I have to tell the Pack."

"Are you listening to me?" He turns quickly, his hands on either side of my face.

"Your leg is—"

"Fine. My leg is fine. I could leave now and be no worse off. It's what I do. A new place. Another page in my book. Except I *would* be worse off because now I know what's here and what I want but don't have."

I stare down at the collection nested in my palm—stone, fur, wing, needle. Tesserae in the mosaic of the Great North. Of Homelands.

What have I done? Wolves are raised with uncompromising loyalty to Pack, to land and to our wild. Even our exiles would never betray our existence, but Eyulf was not raised like we are.

"You can't tell anyone about the Pack." My voice sounds panicked. Not at all like the Alpha command I'd intended. "You can't—"

"I wasn't talking about the Pack, Varya. That's where your mind always goes, but not mine. I was talking about you."

He bends down, looking me in the eye. How could anyone think his eyes were a curse? Blue and green. The promise of heaven and earth.

"I'm talking about you," he says again.

He moves his hand to my hair and sweeps it back, touching my neck gently. He leans close. "You said before that another wolf's mark had to be offered. That it meant they are responsible for each other. That they belong together. I want to belong. But not to the Pack. I want to belong to you."

His thumb moves across my cheek and moves until his jaw almost touches mine, and then he stops. Waiting for me to say no or simply move away. I move closer, partly because I feel woozy and partly because this is what I want. I have only taken the Alpha's mark, the mark that binds me to the entire Pack, but now...now I want this single scent, this single wolf, this single belonging.

Eyulf takes a deep breath and rubs his cheek along mine. "Is this how you do it?"

I feel everything: the coolness of his skin and the sharpness of his cheekbones and the cool eddy as he sucks in my scent and the warm current as he sighs.

Yes. That is how you do it. This—I turn my head so more of my skin touches his—*this is how you do it.*

He nuzzles closer, the damp softness of his lips against the spot where jaw joins neck, and I feel the promise of it all.

Then he whispers in my ear.

———

The weight is heavy on two legs, and the ground is uneven and cold and covered with rigid twigs that puncture and scrape my bare soles.

It's good, I think. The distraction. Reminding me always of the harsh realities of Pack life. Surviving means strength to strength and power to power. It does not accommodate the coming together of two scarred and lonely wolves.

———

"Yours," he said.

"Mine."

———

In one leap, I make it to the top of the stairs leading up to the Great Hall. How long has it been since I was here last? Already there are claw marks on the wood.

The wood of the lock rail is splitting on the storm door. Too many heavy-handed wolves slamming in and out, and Sten, the wolf in charge of carpentry, has too much to do, and anyway, he will be replacing the storm door with screen doors in time for blackfly season.

The foyer is crowded with boots and chew toys, and the hook-lined headboard walls are festooned with clothes waiting until their wearers have skin and need them again.

The heavy main door, like all doors in the Great North, has a levered handle so that wolves can enter and leave at will, whether they are wild or in skin, but some of the wolves are not careful and have left claw marks on this wood too. The base of the little swinging door constructed for the pups is darkened by the near-constant comings and goings of the Pack's youngest.

My hand reaches for the lintel of the thick frame before pushing through to the fragrant hall.

It is quiet. Most of the Pack will be working on the thousand things required to provide for our two forms. But someone is here. I hear the voices. Teresa, the 11th's Alpha, sticks her head out from the door next to Evie's office. She turns away, calling into the library.

"Lorcan. Your shielder is back."

Of all the places in the Great Hall that remind me of last winter's loss, the library is the most haunted. The books burned fast and thoroughly, and unlike the Pack documents, we didn't have a safe with the originals somewhere else. All records are gone, too, leaving only the memories of individual wolves. A chipped brown clipboard hangs on the door with a pencil tied to red-and-white baker's string, so the Pack can write down what books they want and what books they remember having and Gran Jean can replenish the library with the books that shaped the minds of the Great North.

The big room is filled mostly with empty shelves, with a few books scattered to hold the places for absent volumes.

"Shielder," says Victor, leaning against one of the few shelves that actually does have books.

"Deemer." I lower my eyes.

Lorcan cranes his neck around the end of one of the empty stacks. A moment later, he tosses his flannel shirt to me. He gives it to me not because I might be uncomfortable, but because all these years later, the sight of my naked body still makes him uncomfortable.

"I'm looking for the Alpha." I thread my arms through and roll up the sleeves. It annoys me to have Lorcan's smell on my body. I keep the fabric well away from my face, so it won't muddy the Arctic fragrance.

Victor exchanges glances with the wolves I can't see, but I can smell the warm, damp scent well enough. Dominants of some of the younger echelons. The 10th, the 13th. All the youngest echelons are represented here except for the 14th.

"She is with Elijah's human."

"The *westend* is back?"

"Not only is she back," Lorcan says. "She has taken over as the environmental conservation officer for the county. She is living"—he stops as though waiting for the drama of his next statement to build—"in the cabin next to the fire tower."

"*Our* fire tower?" I ask, even though it isn't ours. It is just across the border, but it dominates the bend in the access road.

"And Elijah?"

"He's there now," says Victor. "With the Shifter. *And* the Alpha."

"So you said." He is looking at me carefully. He knows I don't believe the *westend* should have been allowed to live, let alone walk away from here as a human who knows.

He is gauging my reaction to the news of our Alpha's meeting.

"She went *alone*," he adds, emphasizing *alone* to make sure I understand that Evie doesn't mean to kill the woman.

"My shielder understands," Lorcan says, but Victor ignores him and keeps looking at me.

The only thing I care about is the safety and order of the Pack, and I am always careful to give the Deemer the respect that is due his office. But he is not speaking as Deemer. He is not speaking about the law. This is just Victor, a wolf faced with changes he does not like. He is saying something to me, asking me to side with him against our Alpha.

And in my mind, I hear Silver's voice.

"*He is* wrohtgeorn, *Alpha*."

He is strife-eager.

I don't answer either Victor or Lorcan. They share glances, and Victor heads back to the table where he'd been sitting.

I smooth out the spines of books that had been misaligned by his shoulder.

Chapter 24

I HAVEN'T WORN SHOES SINCE I'VE BEEN AT THE PERIM-
eter, but my soles are raw following my frantic run from
Westdæl. Now, the socks and work boots feel stiff and
alien, like they did when I was introduced to them my
first year with the Great North.

The access road is bordered on one side—the Pack's
side—by a thick tangle of woods. With the exception
of the time before the Iron Moon, when we all gather
at Home Pond for the change, it is patrolled by a half-
dozen wolves. On the other side is a steep incline. The
incline is also ours, but Offland starts at the brow of the
hill, where there is an old wooden fire tower built before
the Pack bought this land. It has been deserted for years,
but it looms over the access road at the point where it
turns, burrowing deeper into the wild.

It is the last reminder of the world of humans.

Mostly, the Great North relies on the crowded tangle
of its forests to dissuade casual wanderers, but at the
head of the access road, where the ground is level and
clear, they have installed a tall chain-link fence that
extends deep into the woods. During the Iron Moon,
if someone wants to hunt our land, they'll be dragging
their kill over a mile through nearly impassable terrain
to get back to their illegally parked cars.

Along the side of the hill leading to the fire tower,
a dozen or more wild Pack lurk downwind and out of

sight of the cabin windows. They avoid looking at me as I pass.

"Does the Alpha know you're here?"

Every last one of them backs away sheepishly. They were not in an aggressive posture, simply curious. Still, I doubt Evie meant for such a large contingent of wolves to be listening in on her conversation.

When I open the door to the little cabin, the 9th Echelon's Alpha looks irritated. For some reason, he has a towel around his waist. The human has a sheet wrapped around her like a toga. The cabin smells of sex.

"Oh, for fuck's sake," Elijah barks. "Didn't Leonora teach any of you about knocking?"

He really does talk like a human.

"Alpha," I say, knocking loudly on the door.

Evie looks up from a little table holding a mud-colored canvas case on a table stenciled with the name *H. Villalobos* in big, red letters.

"Is it urgent?" Evie asks.

"I will wait."

"Just give me a minute." Evie turns back to the human. "Tiberius already has a gun. I can't allow another one on Homelands."

"It would never be on Homelands," the *westend* says. "It will be in this cabin, except during the beginning and end of the Iron Moon. During the changes. When you are…vulnerable. Then I would take it to the fire tower."

"You say you haven't used it for five years?" Tiberius looks up from the window where he is examining the long gun. "It's in pretty good shape."

"I just cleaned it," the human says. "Need to zero it though."

"She needs to check the sights," Tiberius says to Evie. "But to do that, she'll have to fire it."

"Not here," Evie says.

I have walked into the middle of a conversation, not that it's hard to figure out. The human is offering to guard us during those times when the whole Pack is deaf, blind, mute, and helpless. When we are a turbid mess of changing bone and skin and fur.

The Alpha knows that guns are the beginning of a slippery slope. Tiberius has one. Now there will be another, maybe not on Homelands, but close enough.

"Alpha," I begin softly because it is not up to me to tell the eavesdropping wolves in the woods why I came down from Westdæl. "It *is* urgent. What I have to tell you."

I hesitate for a moment but then switch to the Old Tongue so the Shifter and the human will not know about the trucks and the fires and the Shifter. Evie stops me.

"*Saga gean,*" she says. "*On westendspræce.*"

Tell it again. In human tongue.

I hesitate.

"How long do you think this will remain a secret from the Pack, Shielder?" she says, her black eyes holding mine firmly. "And I need Tiberius to know."

Dropping my eyes to my Alpha's clavicle, I repeat what I'd told her about the men, the trucks, and the Shifter at our northern border.

"Shifter?" Tiberius asks.

"And humans both. They have burned away the trees to the north and established staging grounds all along the basin that leads to the Gin. It won't be long before they carve away what little remains of the forest north of us."

The *westend* whispers her wolf's name, and he rubs her arm absently.

The Alpha takes a deep breath. Evie's short tenure has been so fraught, but that has made decisiveness all the more important. "How many were there?"

"There may have been others farther north, but across our borders there were three humans and one Shifter. His name was Constantine."

Evie's glance toward Tiberius is met with a single nod, meaning, I presume, that he knows the man.

"You went Offland."

"Yes, Alpha. And I got caught. I will accept any punish—"

"I am not worried about punishment, Shielder. But… this Shifter talked to you in front of the humans?"

"Two of them. They are dead."

Thea flinches; Elijah wraps his arm around her shoulders.

"The Shifter killed them."

Tiberius doesn't look surprised.

"He said that August Leveraux has a proposal for the Alpha that would 'benefit us all.'"

"I have heard August's 'proposal,'" Evie snaps. "Over many weeks and from many numbers. I have ignored it because this *proposal* would make every sacrifice we have ever made meaningless."

She looks through the window toward the access road, her arms crossed in front of her. We wait, but she says nothing more about it, just keeps staring out at the access road, but beyond it past Home Pond, past the

Great Hall, past the woods to the Clearing and the spot where John, her mate, died.

"Alpha." I don't like telling her this now, but Evie knows better than anyone that the Pack cannot afford weakness. "He said one other thing. He said to be sure to tell you 'we are here now.'"

Evie takes a deep breath, steels her jaw, and turns to the little human.

"How many shots will it take you to zero in on your gun?"

The *westend* frowns for a moment. "Ten, Alpha."

"So many?"

"The fire tower stands at the angle of the access road. I'd like to work out both legs."

"Tiberius, you will help her. Come, Shielder. There's something that needs your attention."

As soon as she opens the door, the scent of two-score wolves wafts into the cabin. The human doesn't notice. Tiberius pretends not to, but Elijah stomps out onto the porch, the towel fisted at his hip.

"*Þa gefremminge endaþ!*" he yells angrily at the invisible assembly. "*Agaþ onweg.*"

The show is over. Go away.

The *westend* says his name from inside the cabin. Elijah's expression changes, softens, and he returns to the human he thinks he loves.

Curious wolves start to creep forward again, but Evie, who is already halfway down the hill, calls to them in the firm and stony voice of primacy.

"Your Alpha," she says, "will have you leave the 9th's Alpha and his mate alone."

Evie doesn't look at me. She knows how I feel about

humans, without adding in this unnatural coupling. She must also know that some wolf will tell Victor what she said and he will use it against her.

Immediately, her wolves begin to scratch and scrabble their way down the hill and across the access road. She commands them to find the Alphas and tell them to reassure their echelons, because there will be gunfire at Homelands.

From this angle, I can still see the summit of Westdæl.

Yours.

Mine.

I need to go back.

"I should return to Westdæl, Alpha. Keep an eye—"

"I agree, but not yet. There are things that need to be taken care of here before you return."

Evie sniffs the air as soon as we walk into the Great Hall. Without hesitating, she calls to the little crowd in the library. Victor appears with a volume in his hand, his finger holding his place in—I turn my head to the side so that I can read the title—*The Elements of Crew*.

Why does this irritate me so much?

Because it so blatantly disparages the Alpha's intelligence. Because wolves, real wolves, solve their conflicts openly. In challenges or in front of the Pack. Not like this. Not hiding behind the pretense of some lupine book club.

Evie ignores this thinly disguised deceit and sends the Alphas of the 10th, 11th, and 13th away with the same message. To find their echelons and offer them reassurance when the shooting starts.

She does not send Lorcan. "Come," she says and gestures toward her office.

I touch the lintel.

Chapter 25

"A MOOSE WAS KILLED ON ENDEBERG," THE ALPHA says, leaning against her desk facing us. Lorcan is seated, scratching at a scab on his wrist. Whatever this is about, I don't think he knows, but I can tell by the way he frowns that he is nervous about something.

The moose John reintroduced to our territory several years ago are doing well, but they are not self-sustaining, and Evie has continued the ban on hunting them until they are.

Then we will begin slowly. First chasing. Then rounding up. Then injuring. So that when the time comes, they will not be tamed. They will be afraid of us and run.

"A prime, healthy female."

With that, Lorcan winces. Killing even a dying moose is a transgression because it is a breach of the Alpha's command. But killing a healthy female is so much worse.

We are not like human trophy hunters, always looking for the best and the biggest, for no better reason than to post a picture on Facebook, without caring what the loss of leadership means to the battered herds and packs and prides left behind. This is why we call them *westends*, wasters.

Packs cull herds, and what is left is healthier for our hunting.

In the distance, dominant wolves call to their

echelons, rounding them up so they can be warned and marked and reassured.

"The wolf who did this ate only the heart and liver. The rest, *Alpha*, was left for carrion."

And that…that is the worst of all, a blatant disregard not only for her word, not only for our custom, but for the most basic law that requires we respect death by eating everything we kill.

"Tonia's scent was found on the underside."

Wolves scattered through the territory answer their Alphas' calls. Soon they will be gathering around the Alpha pair, jumping about, curious at first, then needing comfort, the feeling of belonging. That ineffable connection.

Yours.

Mine.

I stare out the window toward Westdæl.

Lorcan wipes at the scrape and smears the beaded blood down his forearm. "I will see to it that she is disciplined, Alpha."

"No, your shielder will. You have an echelon to comfort," Evie says in a tone that makes clear that the conversation is over and he is dismissed. "See that you do it."

Lorcan is torn, as he always is, between concern for the dignity of his position and his loathing for the more unpleasant aspects of leadership. He takes a breath, but then shuts his mouth and lowers his eyes.

"Close the door," Evie says. She listens as he thumps through the Great Hall, listens as he calls members of the 12th who are wild to summon his echelon in the only way that can be heard throughout the territories.

"I am glad to have you watching the border, but the 12th does not do well without you."

I say nothing.

"Tell me, why have you never challenged Lorcan for primacy of the 12th? You would win."

I know she wants me to be Alpha. So did John before her. But being Alpha requires many things. It requires a wolf who can direct and discipline. A wolf who can protect and provide. But as important as any of these, an Alpha must also be able to comfort.

And I know myself. I know that I have no comfort to give.

"It is better as it is." There isn't long before the shooting starts. "Alpha, I should get back to Westdæl. The Shifters—"

"I know what the Shifters want. They won't move against us while there is any hope of getting it."

She says nothing more, and it is not my place to question her when she clearly doesn't want to talk about it.

When the first shot comes, it is distant, but not nearly distant enough. It wakes my mind and sends it running down the hallways of memory at a sprint. *Pitter. Patter. Pitter. Patter.*

Pity.

It's only when the Alpha's hand reaches for mine that I realize my teeth are clenched and I'm growling. I feel the sweat on her palm and see the tension in her shoulders and smell the salt-and-old-leather scent of fear.

I hold her hand tighter.

In front of any other wolf, it might seem like weakness on the part of two of the Great North's strongest members. But we know. Only Evie and I have ever experienced the systematic slaughter of wolves. Only we have lost our packs to the staccato sound of gunfire. It took Shifters a matter of minutes to massacre hers. Longer to flay them and take their skins to market where they sold them for a handful of shillings.

It took the humans a few years to hunt the once-great Pack Vrangelya across our cold and barren island. But the outcome was the same. A collection of rotting, headless bodies, the heads having been turned into the authorities for the ten-dollar bounty.

It takes longer for the sixth shot. Evie turns to me and rubs her right cheek along mine. I wonder if she can smell Eyulf's stony cold that is so clear and comforting to me. She moves her left cheek to mine. I guess not.

"They don't know what it's like," she whispers against my ear. "We know, you and I, how fragile it all is. But..." She stops as another thin crack splits the air. "I would not have them live with that despair."

Was that the eighth?

"It serves no purpose, Shielder, just as it serves no purpose to live in the past. We are more than the sum of our memories."

For a long time, I stay where I am, buried deep in her tight black curls, breathing in her scent, the scent of an Alpha, saturated with the complexity of this land and this Pack.

The storm door bangs shut, and I draw back.

"Leave your boots here," Tiberius says in the distance, "and hang your coat anywhere."

"The *westend* is in the hall?" I whisper.

Tiberius squeezes through even this new, bigger door,

carrying a large smudged piece of paper rolled in his hand. He is followed by the *westend*, and finally Elijah, wild still, nosing her hand like an incontinent puppy.

"The gun?" Evie asks as soon as they enter her office.

"In her cabin," says Tiberius.

"And?"

The Shifter's face is impassive. We all know why now: the mixture of his Pack mother and Shifter father has gifted him with the same sharp canines that his mate has. But while Silver embraces every trace of her wildness, Tiberius keeps his hidden.

Still, by the quirk of the corner of his lip and the calm expression of his eyes, I can tell he's pleased. He pulls out the paper and unrolls a poster of an *æcewulf*, a real wolf. A forever wolf. It is a reddish-brown female standing in the snow, against a scrim of pine trunks. Her body is covered with crosshairs: fifty points for a headshot, thirty for her chest, ten for her belly.

NEW YORK:
LET THE HUNT BEGIN!

There are no bullet holes in any of the crosshairs. There are three scattered around her body and a larger splattered one in the air near her tail.

Then Tiberius turns the poster around. Someone used the blank expanse to draw the rough outline of a small human. Now that large explosion makes sense, because every shot is gathered in the center of the silhouette's head.

Tiberius sticks the tip of his finger through the single hole in the figure's chest. "I was guessing the distance,"

Thea says. "But now I've got the drop. If it's all right with you, Alpha, I'd like to try one more round, so that—"

"Homelands has had enough of guns for now," Evie says before turning to the sable wolf who is rubbing his head into the human's hand draped behind his ear and the back of his jaw. "Elijah, tell the Pack it's over and take Thea back."

He jumps up, twisting in midair like a pup, and when he lands with a floor-shaking thud, he is already at the door. He turns back to his human, whose laugh is deep and throaty.

My hand reaches the lintel.

Chapter 26

ALL ECHELONS HAVE PROBLEMS. THAT'S WHY THEY have Alphas. To take care of those problems before they come to Evie's notice. Things have to be pretty bad for the Alpha not only to notice, but to suggest that a challenge might be in order.

To find out what is going on, I need not the strongest wolf but the weakest.

Arthur is always around but never noticed. He has no skin in any of the games played by Pack. No one cares about the loyalty or advice or support of a *nidling*. As far as the Pack is concerned, he is invisible.

I locate his woody, slightly burned scent and follow it out of the Great Hall, past the Bathhouse, deep into the woods that divide Home Pond from the Clearing and the route further north toward Westdæl.

These are easy woods, domesticated by the comings and goings of humans, their fires and farmlands. The Great North has reused most of the stone that once marked boundaries and houses, but there is still the occasional moss-covered wall. Then I come across the dark-gray wood of Cabin 97, the one John assigned to Tiberius and Silver when they were first mated.

Kicking the toes of my boots on the single step to loosen stray mud, I press my hand to the lintel and open the door.

All of Homelands' cabins are the same, whether

they belong to the Great North's Alpha or to the 14th
Echelon's Theta pair: small with a high-pitched roof and
a sleeping loft. They smell of musty wood and smoke
and the tang of creosote and the musk of wolves. Under
the sleeping loft is a tiny kitchen and bath area. The main
room is dominated by a big, garish sofa upholstered with
orange and green leaves. A pair of large stockinged feet
rests sideways on the arm.

Because pups take a while to learn how to control
their tiny claws, the sound of their scratching against the
floor is one of the first signs to walk carefully. A skinny
tail waves excitedly from under the sofa. Another sticks
out from behind the cold iron stove.

With a flicker, the tail disappears under the sofa, and
its owner emerges held aloft by the long arm belonging
to my *nidling*.

"Arthur."

Arthur's head pops up, followed by his shoulders.
One tiny brindle pup looks at me from behind the
nidling's ear, his needle-sharp claws dug into Arthur's
head until he lifts the pup off.

"Tiberius had to do something with Thea, so I'm
watching the pups while Silver hunts."

Ah. Usually males hunt for their females until they
are completely recovered from the lying-in. But Tiberius
was raised human by his Shifter father. In skin, he is a
lethal hunter of Shifters and humans. Wild, I doubt he
could catch a dead frog.

"It's good that you're back, Alpha," Arthur says.

"I'm not back. I am returning to Westdæl. I need you
to tell me how things are with the 12th."

"Me?" he asks, the smell of his anxiety rising. He

won't lie to me, but he fears Lorcan. "I…I… Perhaps you should ask the Alpha?" He bends his head down until his chin is pinned to his chest. It's what he does when he fears he is being impertinent. One of the pups jumps on his chest facing me.

"If I had wanted to ask the Alpha, I would have asked the Alpha. But I didn't. I am asking you." I have neither the time nor the skill for cajoling the answer out of him.

Arthur cringes, but that pup—that tiny, still stumbling bit of fur—lunges at me. As she does, low, abbreviated growls rumble from her littermates.

Since the little brindle female, barely bigger than my palm, is clearly the dominant, I give her a real snarl, throaty and toothy, the kind of *Weorg* snarl that has made many a grown Pack lower their eyes and submit, but not her. She stands on Arthur's chest, her tiny tail held high and barks.

"*Opswig*, Sigeburg," he says. Quiet, Sigeburg. The little female does not understand the words, but she understands the tone and the hand on her back. But while she quiets, she does not back down.

Arthur sets Sigeburg next to the other nurslings in the corner of the sofa, then stands in front of it, interposing his body between me and the pups. I ask again what he has heard or seen that I should know, adding "for the good of the echelon and the good of the Pack."

Victor, he starts reluctantly, whispers about Tiberius and Evie and Silver and Elijah too. Now that the human has come back, things will get worse.

"Who does he whisper to?"

"Anyone who will listen." Arthur is prevaricating.

"And who listens, Arthur?"

He pinches the bridge of his nose. "I am just a *nidling*, Alpha," he says.

"You are not *just* a *nidling*, Arthur. You are a wolf of the Great North, and your first responsibility is not to Lorcan or to me. Your first responsibility is to the Pack. Just like it is for every one of us."

He takes a deep breath and, with a slight tremble to his voice, tells me. The younger echelons. The 10th, he says. The 11th and the 13th. They all listen to Victor.

"And the 12th and 14th?"

The 14th's Alpha, Arthur says, is loyal to his own wolves and will not hear talk about Tiberius, who Victor despises, and Quicksilver, whom he hates even more because she challenges him all the time. "Not physically," Arthur is quick to add, as though that could ever be an option. "About the law. It makes him angry."

I don't push Arthur about the 12th because his body is collapsing in on itself: head down, shoulders hunched, toes pointed inward, arms wrapped tight around his waist. This defeated posture tells me everything I need to know about my echelon.

Sigeburg watches me unafraid. In this offspring of Silver and Tiberius, of a runt and a Shifter, I see the fierce protectiveness of a real Alpha.

Chapter 27

THE PUPS OF THE GREAT NORTH GROW UP TOGETHER. Once they are no longer nurslings, they move into the children's quarters of the Great Hall. The Grans, the elders, live in the Great Hall, too, because it is warmer there and the pups need constant guidance in their responsibilities and what to do and not to do with those pin-sharp teeth and claws.

Then they graduate together into the Juvenile quarters. They had already been there for a year when I first moved in. They did not trust me, and I don't blame them. I was strange and hard. I spoke the Old Tongue with an accent and English, the language of their every day, not at all.

I came right when all of them were wrestling with the Year of First Shoes. They had spent their early lives running wild in a protected corner that had nothing to do with the real world. They were fantasists, coddled and protected by the full strength of the Great North, the strongest remaining Pack. They could not understand why any of that had to change. Why they had to put on skin. Why they had to put away everything they held most precious.

When I arrived, I was still a child. A child with too much experience. I knew how precarious their existence really was. But I didn't try to tell them. I couldn't. I didn't want the responsibility or the failure.

Then something happened, and the 12th became my responsibility.

The Great Hall is back to normal again. The 6th and the 10th are working on dinner. With the whole Pack here, Evie keeps the food flowing so that the territory isn't picked clean of prey by hungry wolves.

The 12th is scattered among the tables in pairs and small groups. I have never been away from my echelon for any length of time, and it shows. A number of other wolves have injuries, but nearly half the 12th's do. Simon has a broken nose, and Willa has a mark on her cheek the shape of a Monopoly hotel. Those two should never be allowed to play unsupervised.

Evie is discussing something with Tara but spares me a tight-lipped look that needs little interpreting before returning to her Beta.

When I hit the wooden table in front of Tonia, our Gamma, with the heavy handle of a bread knife, the Great North goes silent.

"Gamma." My voice is quiet, but the Pack listens, as I mean for them to. I mean for them all to understand that there are consequences. Some wolves look toward Evie, but with nothing but the slight lowering of her chin toward me, she lets them know that I speak with her approval.

Tonia looks up nervously, her mouth full of spinach dumpling.

"What does *westend* mean?"

Tonia chews and frowns and looks askance at Lorcan.

An Alpha cannot let wolves doubt for a moment who is in charge. I leap on the table, heedless of food and plates, crouching with her face in my hand. A daub of green spit dribbles from the corner of her mouth. She freezes, her eyes lowered, not daring to look anywhere.

"What, Gamma, does *westend* mean?"

"Hoom'n," she chokes out, trying to swallow. She dabs her mouth with the back of her hand. "Human."

"No. What does it *mean*?"

"Waster." Her voice is smaller now. "Destroyer."

"And what are you?"

"Pack," she says, her voice almost inaudible, and as sharp as their hearing is, her packmates have to lean in closer. "Wolf."

"And wolves"—I wipe the spinach spittle from my hand with a napkin—"do not waste. We finish what we start."

"Finish…?" She looks again to Lorcan for help, but he concentrates instead on pushing the bits of tempeh and green pepper in the coconut curry sauce onto his fork with a piece of bread.

"Some days ago, a prime moose was killed by a wolf. By *you* and only the choicest parts were eaten. Now, you will finish what you started."

"*But it was… It's…*" Tonia's face begins to turn the color of yellow birch. Then she grabs her stomach and races for the bathroom.

"When you're done, Gamma, I will take you to Norþdæl."

I grab a hazelnut rye roll and head out. Behind me, Victor calls to Lorcan.

Before all but the oldest of these wolves were born, an enormous tree fell in some enormous storm. Rather than moving it, the Pack lopped off the branches for firewood and then carved deep into the heart of it, creating a bench of sorts. It hadn't been doused with accelerant like the Great Hall, so while embers landed here, they smoldered briefly, then died out, leaving only black spots that join with the green moss and dark blood left by wolves who lean on it for a moment after losing a challenge. Or winning.

Sitting on the back of the log, I eat my rye and hazelnut. When they see me, Pack both in skin and wild avert their eyes and run a little faster. I look toward Westdæl, my fingers feeling the scrapes left by generations of pups and gouges left by adults.

The door to the Great Hall shuts behind Victor.

"Is she ready?"

"Alpha," he says, "while I agree that Tonia Luisasdottir must be punished, I would like to suggest something not quite so—"

"She finishes what she started."

"She would have called the Pack, if she'd been allowed to hunt prey that is *our* right on *our* land."

The law is clear, but he is subtly shifting the blame to Evie. To John. Silver is right. He is *wrohtgeorn*. Strife-eager.

I brush the crumbs away from the corner of my mouth.

"She disobeyed the Alpha, which is bad. She killed a prime female who had not been trained to fear us, which is worse. She wasted that death, which, *Deemer*, is against the law. She. Finishes," I say slowly and deliberately, "What. She. Started."

Then I hold up my hand, gathering the moon between my fingers, pretending to squeeze it and make it smaller.

"Alpha?"

Because when the moon reaches its full size, we will

all lie on the ground utterly helpless, and I am afraid of what will come between the thighs of our mountains. But it's not only that.

Varya Wearg, Varya the Indurate, is afraid, not only of who might come, but of who must leave.

The door slams again, and Victor whips away as another heavy tread *thunks* down the stairs. He hisses something to Lorcan. Something about knowing my "responsibilities."

I know my responsibilities. They have always been terrifyingly, painfully clear to me. Never more so than now when I want those responsibilities less than ever.

Lorcan whispers something back. I can't hear the words, but I can hear the tone. It is nervous but meant to be reassuring.

Then my Alpha takes a seat next to me on the back of the bench and breathes in deeply.

I lower my fingers and release the moon, letting my hands fall to my lap. "I need to get back to the perimeter. Will she be ready soon?"

I see his nod from the corner of my eye. He stares off to Endeberg, the Final Mountain, the easternmost mountain of the High Pines.

"Do you remember our Wild Hunt?" he asks.

"Of course." I bend down to my boots, loosening the laces.

The Wild Hunt. That's what the Great North calls an echelon's first unaccompanied hunt. Traditionally held in February, it's an important test of the juveniles' organization and ability to work together to find and take down larger prey. During the Wild Hunt, none of the adult wolves will give juveniles a place at their kill, making hunger as well as pride a powerful motivator.

"Nils called me into his office after the moon," Lorcan says, watching me pick at a knot in my bootlace. "D'you know what he said?" As it is a rhetorical question, I say nothing. "He said, 'That could have gone better.'"

It could have. That Wild Hunt was wild only in the sense that it was complete pandemonium. Rather than working together, the 12th's wolves competed with one another to be the first to find prey. Or to find the biggest prey. Or to find the most dangerous prey.

All they succeeded in doing was scaring away every warm-blooded thing on Endeberg. It had been reserved, as it always is, for the Wild Hunt, so the juveniles wouldn't have to compete with more seasoned hunters.

An outsider who'd had enough of responsibility, I had settled quite near the bottom of the hierarchy. I caught a hare to feed my own hunger and was no help whatsoever.

The 12th was dispersed far and wide when it came, the repeated bark followed by the long, sharp howl. A coyote was hunting something too big to take down by itself and calling for its pack.

I knew what that meant, as did every juvenile on the Wild Hunt. Having scared off everything on Endeberg, *we* were the only prey left.

Lorcan, as the presumptive Alpha, raced around trying to gather more wolves, reasoning that an adult coyote was an almost impossible match for a juvenile wolf, and more coyotes would be answering the call. When more coyotes responded, Lorcan decided to wait until he had the whole echelon.

And, of course, the adults had left this mountain to the juveniles.

Alone.

I don't remember much, except for the tearing of undergrowth that had been frozen for months and would no longer bend beneath my weight, the slickness of the south face that had once been coated with snow but had melted and refrozen to ice.

I remember the taste of the first coyote as his hind leg shattered in my jaws. Another coyote went down, his eye socket ravaged, and finally, I came to the Alpha coyote, standing a few feet from her prey, a juvenile wolf bleeding from a compound fracture.

Maybe the Alpha was expecting the usual posturing of predator meeting predator, but I wasn't of the Great North. I was Vrangelya, and we had never had much use for posturing.

Suddenly, I was no longer Varya, the withdrawn and sullen interloper with the strange accent that the 12th knew.

I became again the wolf I had always been, and I had the Alpha's throat in my jaws before she had finished breathing in my scent.

The rest of the coyotes dispersed, and as coyote blood froze on my muzzle, I threw back my head and howled my real self.

Varya Wearg. Varya the Bloodthirsty. Varya the Outlaw.

And Tonia, with her broken leg, bent low into the snow beside me until the rest of the 12th arrived. Nils knew the whole Great North was wary of me and wouldn't have forced me on anybody. But it must have been around this time—the time when Nils said "that could've gone better"—that Lorcan asked our Alpha to make me his shielder.

"We make a good pair, you know. We always have. Our young will be fearsome."

I pretend that I don't understand what he's saying and pray that Tonia will come soon. When she doesn't, I struggle to take off the flannel shirt he lent me. Lorcan pulls at the sleeves, careful, as always, not to look at my ravaged breast and torso. If he didn't need to fasten his teeth to my shoulder, he'd probably ask me to keep it on.

I fold the shirt in a neat rectangle, and then the pants, and bend forward, my cheek to the rough back of the bench. In the depths of the forest is a gap where an oak once stood. A birch stand has taken root there. Tall, pale beacons in the dark, wet wood.

Yours.

Mine.

I twist my hips, pulling away from Lorcan's thrusts.

"Shielder?" he asks.

I don't answer, beyond pointing to the tiny pile of my clothes. "You'll take care of those?" I ignore both him and the unwelcome erection that will have to find a truly receptive female, not just one who bends over because it's her fucking duty.

The door to the Great Hall opens, and Lorcan hurriedly finishes buttoning up his jeans. Tonia moves slowly down the stairs.

"You don't think she'll die, do you?" He tucks the clothes under his arm and hooks his fingers through the laces of the boots. "I mean, if she eats that and dies, what was the point of saving her at the Wild Hunt?"

"She won't die."

"How can you know that?"

I shrug. "Because I never did."

Then I sink deep into my hips and wait for the change that will block it all out.

Chapter 28

DESPITE WHAT SHE THINKS AND LORCAN THINKS, I don't want Tonia to die. So I keep watch over her, making sure she isn't eaten by a coyote during the change.

It doesn't take long to find the moose. First, the smell draws me, then the rustle of tiny animals.

Tonia lowers herself, her tail between her legs, her ears pulled down, her head scraping the ground before me, until one eye looks up, begging for understanding.

She is slow, and I am impatient. She tries to pick through the insects, but that just makes the whole process longer, and the insects are hardly the worst part. Snarling, I show my teeth and she eats faster, holding her breath. She isn't starving, so she gags with every swallowed mouthful and vomits a fair amount back up.

It feels like forever before the rotted carcass is gone and Tonia staggers off gagging and vomiting. Still, the Great North will smell the rot on her muzzle and will think twice before wasting another life.

Past the High Pines and across the rough, sloped terrain of the Gin, I go through hardwoods that haven't woken yet, and the canopy is an open lacework for the moon on leaf-flecked snow until I reach the rock pond where I'd first learned what an endling was. I lie down on the rock still warm from the sun.

I feel sullied. My obligatory couplings usually leave me impatient and irritable, but not like this. I push back into my hips, and when the change comes, I slide into

the icy water, feeling the play of the moon's gravity
against my naked spine until my lungs are near burst-
ing. I scrub hard at my teeth, my mouth, my hair, and
hardest of all between my thighs and at the join of my
neck. I break through the black surface and suck long,
deep breaths before diving under again.

When I come up for breath, I hook my arm over the
ledge and pull myself above the surface, water draining
into my eyes.

"Do you love him?"

I push my hair back with my wrist.

"Love who?"

Above me on the overhang of schist that glints in the
moonlight, Eyulf sits naked save for a few last windblown hairs of his undercoat.

"The one who did that." He beats one finger at the
join of his neck and shoulder, mirroring where the lay-
ered marks of Lorcan's teeth will always be, no matter
how hard I scrub.

"No."

Bracing one hand against the rock, he leans forward,
his hand wrapping tight around my wrist, and helps me
clamber out. The cold water puddles around me, and he
moves away.

"It is very hard for us to get pregnant." I twist my
hair tight, squeezing water into a stream from the black
rope. "So strong wolves try to breed stronger wolves.
It's meaningless. A duty; nothing else."

Even as I say it, I feel how weak it all is. I have never
felt anything for Lorcan except vague exasperation, and
yet I let him touch me because it is my responsibility. I
let him inside my body because it is my duty.

His white hair falls in a heavy wave over the tough sinew of his shoulders. "It's not meaningless to me," he says.

I look out of the corner of my eye at Eyulf. *Yours*, he said. *Mine*. And I feel it. I feel that belonging like a thread, thin as a single strand of his white hair, but crazy strong, pulling at me. Insistent.

"I made him stop. I've always let him before, but this time, I made him stop."

Eyulf turns his head now, his cheek resting on his knee, looking at me.

"Why?"

There are a lot of disjointed images that shouldn't be in my mind but are. The delicate yellow of the Arctic poppy, the awkward boy with the gunshot wound, my scars magically transformed on a page into something fiercely beautiful. His frightened eyes in his contorting body, and my hand running like water across his skin. The girl in The Last Place on Earth with her mouth on him.

I can feel something unraveling inside me.

"Because I didn't *want* him. I never have. But it didn't matter before, and suddenly it did. The not wanting,"

He picks up something, a blade of grass, a strand of hair, I don't know. He wraps it around his finger.

"You know what they call me? When they think I can't hear?"

He shakes his head, unwrapping and wrapping the strand on his finger as though it was the most engrossing thing in the world.

"Varya the Indurate." My hand finds the bone that knits up my ribs and covers my heart. "They say I am hard. Empty." I press deeper into my sternum. "But I feel like there are cracks in me. I don't want them, but they're here. Things are leaking out. *I* am leaking out."

The wind kicks up, and my skin is buffeted with damp hair and the stone-and-electric smell of cold, and my mind is filled with the whipping of pale hair and the dark slashes above those haunted, beautiful eyes.

He reaches for me, moving his hand to my face, his long fingers caressing my cheek all the way to the crook of my neck in slow, liquid shocks. Shivers run the entire length of my Arctic body, and he asks if I'm cold.

"Never," I say. "I am never cold."

"No," he says, moving closer, his arm touching my arm, his knee leaning against mine. "I don't think you could ever be."

His tongue darts out, making his lips glimmer in the moonlight.

I've never known what expression Lorcan wore during our obligatory matings. The only thing I'm very sure of is it has never been this. The black of Eyulf's eyes, deep and wide, and in the thin circles of blue and green.

I touch my own lips. They've always been cool, even against my fingers. He takes my hand away and, holding my fingers tight in his hand, leans over and doesn't quite touch his lips to mine. His mouth is open just enough to draw the damp of mingled breath.

What does cold taste like?

My tongue flickers into his mouth. I take from him the taste of rock and air and ice, without all that extraneous life. The earth stripped bare. It's not enough, though, and his lips move closer, ticklish and electric, sending tremors through my neck and chest, sparking the mangled nerves of my clawing, and igniting my body's core.

When I ease against him, he slides his other hand around my lower back, pressing hard so that when his mouth surges against mine, I feel the involuntary spasm of the thick ridge pressed against my hips. I push back, the bone of my hip against a muscle that might as well be bone.

His mouth clashes against mine. Neither of us have experience, not of this, and our teeth clash. I bite his tongue and taste blood. His groan vibrates against my lips as he turns his head so he can slide deeper, painting my mouth with the taste of copper. I suck at it, warm and beating and alive.

His hand touches my ruined breast, not tentatively but encompassing the hard ridge and the soft furrows in between, and where the nerves don't join up properly, it feels like lightning.

I freeze.

Eyulf's forehead drops to mine. "Varya?" he asks.

My eyes fall to the long, pale fingers stretched across the darker skin of my breast.

"He can't look at me. Lorcan. After all these years, he looks away until my back is to him. So he won't see."

One hand slides around my waist. "I don't know what his problem is, but I see you, Varya." His eyes focus on my chest. "I feel you. Varya." His hand traces every naked inch of the path carved by Illarion's claws all those years ago.

"I want you," he exhales. "Varya."

Then…then he bends down, pushing his hair to the side, and takes my torn nipple into his mouth. My hand slides against the back of his head. At first, I mean to pull him away, but as he explores with the top of his tongue and the even softer, silkier swirl of the underside, I push him closer instead.

This has nothing to do with the quick and dutiful fucks that fulfill my responsibility to the Pack. Unfamiliar heat tears through my veins, making my body warm and liquid. Fitted to his. One damaged, awkwardly healed wolf to another.

He shifts and closes the distance between us, thigh against thigh, hip to hip, hand to shoulder, to waist. He smells musky and green, more like the bright spice of coriander than Lorcan's crude rutting buck.

My mind, which has always been divided between then and now, is suddenly completely present.

I growl deep in my chest and feel the answering rumble in his. His hands glide down my back to cup under my ass and pull me in and up. The ridge of his cock pressing between my legs. I drag him down to the rock, which softens and warms under the heat of my thawing chill. Someone else might need a softer spot, the dry, thick, fragrant floor beneath the firs, but not us.

He touches my hair and runs his hand down my naked body. It feels like water. I touch him, too, try to pull him closer. I need him inside, I need him to fill me, really fill me. Not like wolves whose filling has always left me feeling emptier than before. I need him to leave a part of himself inside me.

Supporting himself on strong arms, he shifts his leg between my thighs and spreads me open.

His hair falls down on either side, and I am grateful to be shielded when he comes to me, when he enters me, when I knife my hips, forcing him further in, and then he does, driving deep and hard through that break in my shield, and touches the ache that is at the very center of myself.

I stay awake long into the night, listening to all the riotous sounds of Homelands.

I turn away, so as not to wake him and whisper my own chorus.

Listen to me. Look at me. Love me. Make life with me.

I have always been on guard when I sleep, waking fully alert at the slightest noise or smell or shadow that doesn't belong. Never waking up like this: slowly, uncertain about where I am and what I've done and whose cold skin and hot blood is entwined with my body. I stare at the pale arm crooked across my torso, the hand stroking the scars that have defined me for so long.

Everything I am belongs to the Pack, except for this. This one thing belongs to me.

"It's called a *Clifrung*. A clawing."

His finger follows a single line. "You don't have to tell me," he says.

"I know I don't. I've never told anyone, not really, because I didn't care if they understood. But you are…"

What is he, Varya? He's not your mate, your bedfellow. He's not even part of your pack.

No, but he is the holder of my secret self, and I lay my cheek on his cool skin. "I had a shielder once," I whisper. "His name was Mitya."

"What is a shielder?"

"Just what it sounds like. I'm a shielder now. To Lorcan, but pups have shielders, too, mostly to help hunt and protect us during the change. Mine was a white wolf. Like you. The only other one I've ever known."

His chin settles against the top of my head.

"But Mitya was more than that, more than a shielder. This was before the Great North. On that island in the Arctic that no one cares much about anymore. The humans had set a bounty of one hundred rubles for every wolf head. They said it was one hundred dollars, but it wasn't. More like ten, but ten dollars was enough. I don't know when it started, but I'd never known a time when we weren't hunted, and it made my pack very...hard."

There's something prickly in a depression in the rock under my back.

"Except for Mitya. He was gentle and unspoiled, the *only* gentle and unspoiled thing on that island, and I did everything I could to protect that in him."

"Did you love *him*?" Eyulf asks, his fingers moving up and softly picking away something in my hair.

"Mitya had hope and kindness in him, and because I needed that so badly, I needed him. I'd never needed anything more. Is that love? I don't know. Maybe it is."

He smooths my hair back down.

"I was the strongest of the young wolves, and Illarion, our Alpha, tried to give me a more powerful shielder, but I refused. What he never understood, *they* never understood, was how much strength it took to be gentle in a place like that. Anyone could be hard and bitter, and I knew that without Mitya, that's exactly what would happen to me."

Eyulf doesn't say anything. I'm glad. I'm not sure I'd be able to continue if he did.

"The juveniles were the worst. They were desperate and angry, and they took it out on Mitya. Tried to. But I was desperate and angry, too, and when I got angry, something happened. Everything dropped away, and I was beyond pain, fear, obedience. A wolf who knows no pain, no fear, and no obedience is a terrible thing. So they became afraid of me."

I move slightly, dislodging that thing that's been digging into my back. A sweet-gum pod.

"It must have been almost exactly this time in our last year as pups, when the adults went hunting and Mitya howled. I don't know why. He knew better than that. We all knew better than that. We knew it would frighten off prey and attract hunters. I'd never heard a wolf howl in Vrangelya. Ever.

"We all ran, hiding like scared rabbits wherever we could. And you know what happened? Absolutely nothing. No planes, no guns, no hunters. And because no one got hurt, I thought there would be no consequences. I was proud of him even. He'd been a real wolf and howled.

"But there were always consequences in Vrangelya, and the next morning when I woke up, Mitya and Illarion were both gone.

"There was so much threatening us... I hadn't understood how easily the Pack would sacrifice individuals to protect the whole. I understand better now, but I didn't then. Anyway, the Beta said Mitya would not be coming back. That the Pack could not afford to coddle him any longer, and besides, summer was coming and would bring more hunters, and we didn't need a white wolf standing out like a beacon against the dark gray of our island."

Rubbing my cheek against Eyulf's chest, I twine a strand of his white hair around my finger.

"*I* did, though. I needed that beacon against the dark. Then Illarion came back, and I don't remember much after that. Just the blood drying on the underside of his muzzle and the world dropping away.

"I don't think he took me seriously at first—he'd never watched us fight—then he did and fought for real. I wasn't even a juvenile, yet I almost killed our Alpha.

"I had to be punished. They held me down while Illarion clawed me. After, no one was allowed to care for me so that the wound would leave scars and I would be marked forever as *Wearg*. Bloodthirsty. Outlaw. A savage, doomed to a short life outside the Pack. What they didn't know was it was already too late. It was the beginning of the end."

"But you survived?"

"I don't mean the end of *me*. That wouldn't have mattered, and that's not what happened. It was the beginning of the end of Pack Vrangelya. Because of me, the Pack lost faith in Illarion, but there was no one stronger to take his place. Because of me, when death was outside, there was no order inside. Because of me, when the summer ended, there were no more wolves."

I suck at my teeth with a soft *tchck*.

"The irony, if you can call it that, was that I survived because I was less of a target alone than I would have been as part of the Pack. That and because the hunters were humans. They didn't eat what they killed, and I learned not to be picky."

I look down at my hands. "They wasted so much death."

Eyulf touches my skin, softly stroking it. His hand runs like water down my jaw and my neck to the spot between my breasts that feels not like it is cracked but broken wide open. He holds his palm tight against my heart, as though he understands that something has to be done to stanch the bleeding.

Chapter 29

THERE ARE MANY KENNINGS FOR WOLVES IN THE OLD Tongue. Some come from Pack, who needed ways to talk about us that kept our secrets from humans. Some come from humans, who feared conjuring wolves by saying the name outright. Which left us with, among others:

The bitch of wounds (my own personal favorite)
Mountain's enemy
Night prowler
War lynx
The hound of the roaring sea of the dead
Evening rider
Fenrir's spawn
The dog of blood
Sharp-eyed death dealers of the forest
The untamed dog of Sif
Gray heath-walker
Guardian of the marches
and
Wealdgast
Forest spirit.

If I am the Bitch of Wounds, Eyulf is the Forest Spirit. Even when he is doing something as completely human as drawing, he imbues everything with the *Wealdgast*. He gives a beech bud's coppery scale weight and significance. He gives the mighty Norþdæl lightness and fragility.

In his hand, nothing in Homelands is expendable. And nothing is invulnerable.

He feels the subtlest pulse of the land. The thickness of the air and the curvature of sound and the shift of clayey soil. When I ask him about it, he shrugs and says only that it's intuition.

Maybe, but I believe this "intuition" is really the distillation of years of experience as a lone wolf and in hiding. It has become so deeply ingrained that he is no longer aware of where it comes from.

What distracts him from the tiny beginnings of trillium that he had been nosing? Why do his ears start twisting and turning until he takes a step south and turns to look at me so I know to follow? It's only after we've been running for a while that I finally hear the unusual quiet of the animals of Homelands.

That's when we see him. A human warmly dressed in dark clothes with a backpack and a big grease-stained canvas tool bag slung over his shoulder with a long drill bit sticking out the back. Black scopes, attached to a convoluted array of straps crisscrossing his skull, stick up from his forehead.

The man has come back with his traps, and he knows he's trespassing. If he didn't, he'd've spared the expense of night-vision goggles and just used a flashlight.

He looks around to the front and the side but never to the back. That's where I run, taking his scent onto my face. My shoulders shake with the painful desire to rip open his skin, to crush his windpipe, to tear out his entrails and feed on his liver. But instead, I do what wolves always do.

Lawyer up.

Josi's gone hunting with her echelon. However, I track Elijah to the human's cabin. "I'm busy, dammit!" he yells as soon as I open the door. Pulling the sweat- and seed-soaked blankets off with my teeth, I shove my *westend*-scented muzzle into his nose.

"What is it?" the human asks.

"Hunter," Elijah says, kissing her hard before he pulls on his pants. He rearranges his stiff cock. "Oh no you don't, Thea. I'll be right back."

The human doesn't respond, simply continues to get dressed, and Elijah Sorensson, one of the most powerful fighters of the Great North, purses his mouth, silent as this little female throws on two additional layers. The only time she looks at him is before slipping on her hol- ster. When he shakes his head, she puts it away again. Dark-green coat with a badge on the front and arm. She doesn't comb out her hair, just ties it under a cap that has a badge on it as well.

Bright-yellow vest that says *Police*.

In case anyone has any doubts.

I head out the door, my claws clicking on the wooden porch and steps, then trot into the wind blow- ing in from the mountains. There are a lot of trees and branches downed by winter storms. The Pack will col- lect these later for firewood, but for now, they are too wet and combine with the endless mud to make the already difficult terrain much harder to traverse. When one pair of boots falls behind, I ignore it. I do not wait for humans.

At the edge of the woods, invisible to the hunter but close enough to see, Thea Villalobos catches up with me, breathing hard, her hair rimmed with sweat that glistens in the low, long afternoon light. My ears circle and my nose flares as I try to search out Elijah.

"He's not used to this kind of mud on two legs," she says. "I'll take it from here." Then without waiting for Elijah, she squares her shoulders, hooks her thumb through her belt loop, and hikes out across the soggy ground, heading directly for a man who certainly has a gun.

As much as I disapprove of Elijah's choice, she has a right to be here. Not like the man who trapped the coyote and left her to suffer in the hopes of catching something bigger.

Keeping low, I parallel her in the lengthening near-night shadows of the forest.

"Hello, sir," she calls loudly. "My name is Thea Villalobos. I'm the environmental conservation officer for this area. May I see your license?"

I dodge from the forest to the remains of a water-logged spruce, to a Labrador tea, still holding on to its scruffy folded leaves. I settle in to watch. Or kill.

The man wipes a gloved finger under his nose. "You got some ID on you?"

Thea doesn't argue, just takes a little wallet from her jacket and opens it for him.

He looks from the picture to the woman herself. "Thea Villalobos. What kind of name is that?"

"The name of the ECO for this area," she says coldly. "Your license."

He fishes out his wallet and hands her a piece of paper. Thea looks at it and takes a picture with her phone.

"Mr. Anderson," she says, handing the license back to him. "What are you trapping for?"

"Beaver."

"Season's just about over."

"Just about means it's not."

"Hmm-hmm. What size trap are you using?"

"Usual."

"Looks like a sixteen. Four seems about right for beaver."

"You do it your way, I do it my way."

"I'm afraid that's not the way it works. Because there is no right way to trap on posted land."

"Is it posted?" he says, staring right into her eyes. "I didn't see any signs."

"I think you did. I think you did last time too. Because last time, you set your duffel next to the post holding that sign that you didn't see, and because you took the wheels off the duffel, it makes a very distinctive imprint in the snow. Like this."

She holds up her phone again, showing it to him. His mouth thins. "So now, Mr. Anderson, maybe you can tell me what you keep looking for on private land with night-vision goggles and a bear trap."

His face is red, the color of a man who has spent his whole life hunting for slights and finding them.

"There is something going on up here. These people, they buy up all the land they can. And they don't do anything with it, right? They don't take care of it, don't clear any paths. They don't put in drainage, don't cut down trees. Don't plant a fucking flower. Nothing. You know why I think? Because they don't want people up here. Because they're hiding something."

"And what do you think they're hiding?"

"Let me show you something." His hand slides to his

lapel. My legs coil, ready to spring, until he takes out a phone. I don't trust this man.

"Look at that."

Thea strips her glove and looks. She swipes at it with her bare fingers. "I'm not sure what I'm supposed to be seeing."

"Right there!" says Anderson, jabbing his finger into the air above the screen. "That print is nearly twice the size of my hand. *That is the print of a fucking monster*. Now do you see?"

"You know what I see, Mr. Anderson? I see two things: a fine example of the kind of distortion that happens to coyote tracks with snowmelt. And a great deal of blood and fur and suffering caused by a pattern of trespass on *private land*."

"And here's what I see: a fucking public servant *policing* private land." He stands too close, trying to intimidate Thea, but aside from a slight shift to plant her feet more firmly, she does nothing.

I can't help it. It's not loud, but my low, warning snarl is enough to send him reaching for his gun and pointing it a few feet from my direction. My legs tighten until they spasm. If he shoots, he will miss. I will not, but it will be a mess for the Pack.

Thea moves, putting herself between Anderson and the Labrador tea.

"Put your gun away, Mr. Anderson."

"You heard that. Don't tell me you didn't."

"Put your gun away *now*, Anderson." With that slight change in tone and the loss of the *Mr.*, Thea Villalobos makes something clear. She isn't afraid or even angry. But she is in control. Anderson just doesn't know it yet.

Then comes the sound of someone who is really not in control. Elijah clears the forest looking like he's tripped over every branch and into every mud slick in Homelands. The roar that comes from the 9th's Alpha as he tears toward Thea in his squelching boots is not human.

Anderson pulls down his night-vision goggles and turns toward the raging thing bearing down on him, his gun drawn.

"Don't," Thea says, her hand abruptly shoved into the air in my direction.

As soon as she shines her high-intensity flashlight into Anderson's goggles, he stumbles back, blinded. Then she whips around and does the same to her furious mate, who trips and falls.

"Now, we're all going to calm down. Mr. Anderson, your gun please."

I slink back behind the Labrador tea.

"Elijah?" Even she must be able to smell the peculiar bitter burn of rage rolling from his skin.

"I know him," the man says, slipping the gun back into its holster and brushing the back of his pants. "I know you. You're the goddamn lawyer."

"I represent the interests of the Great North LLC," Elijah finally manages through gritted teeth. Thea keeps her body firmly planted between him and Anderson.

"That was my land over there," Anderson says, waving in the general direction of Home Pond.

"The junkyard. Yes, I know," says Elijah.

"Salvage! *It was a salvage yard*. It was a legitimate business, but you people were always complaining about some violation or another. Thought you could force me into selling it to you. Well, the joke's on you, because the man I sold it to? You know why I sold it to that Canadian? Because he promised me that he would never let you have it. John Torrance would have paid me double, but nothing was worth as much to me as August Leveraux's promise that he would be a thorn in your side for-fucking-ever."

Thea coughs and hands the man back his phone. He wipes the screen against his jeans and shoves it back in his pocket.

"I'm letting you off with a warning, Mr. Anderson, but I've got your license and I'm going to strongly advise you—"

"Fuck off." He slings the canvas duffel over one shoulder. "There is something going on here, and I'm not the only one interested in finding out what it is."

Elijah takes a step forward, neck bent down, teeth bared. He can't help it. This man is threatening his wild, and his wild responds.

"Stop," Thea whispers, pushing her back against Elijah's chest, pitting her frail humanity against the mountainous body of the 9th's Alpha. "Breathe, Elijah," she says, and finally he does. I leave the shelter of the Labrador tea and join them watching Anderson work his way to the other side of Beaver Pond.

"He has a picture."

"What sort of picture?"

"Here." She hands him her phone. "I took a copy when he was ranting."

Elijah looks it over carefully, tilting it so that I can see too. Then he does exactly what she did, widening his fingers to look more closely.

"We don't have a white wolf. Never have that I know of."

"White?"

"Right there. The hunk of fur." He hands the phone back to her. "There are no packs anywhere near here, so this wolf must have wandered a long way looking for sanctuary. Shielder," he says to me, "we should look for the body." He takes one last glimpse at the bloody mess in the snow.

"Pity," he says.

Chapter 30

I SPRINT ACROSS THE ICY MUD AND DRIED WEEDS, FOLLOWING the smell of cold up the south slope of Westdæl. I hit the tree line and find the body, *my* body, the body that lost so much blood but didn't die because I wouldn't let him. I am surrounded by white fur, by the frantic rubbing of jaw against muzzle and soft-jawed wolf kisses. He can tell that there's something wrong and, with his chin, pushes me down. He lies down facing me, his front leg across my shoulder. We are so close that even in the blind vortex of my change, I feel every shudder of his.

"There was a picture," I whisper when I finally can. "So much blood. You lost so much blood."

"Shh," he shushes, his voice still garbled like a wolf at the end of his change.

"*I wasn't supposed to be here.*" I blink frantically, trying to forget the image of blood-pitted snow. Trying to forget how arbitrary death is. How if I hadn't gotten exasperated with the crowds around Home Pond, I would never have come here. If the helicopter hadn't arrived, I wouldn't have sought cover. If I hadn't been raised cold, I would never have known he was there.

Who knows how many years it would have taken before some adventuresome juvenile found what was left of his body?

I hold out my hands, cupped tight around this precious

and fragile thing that I can't explain but I have to take care of. That I have to protect.

But even without explaining, he seems to know. He covers my hands with his own and sighs.

"You can't always protect, Varya. Things happen in the world that are beyond even your control. Sometimes all you can do"—he gently pries apart my hands and kisses each palm—"is love."

Dropping my head to his shoulder, I stare at one hand, half expecting to see the trace of his lips like a brand on my palm. Nothing's there, but I need that burn, that combination of fire and ice, and press my hand to his chest, feeling for every jolt and spark and ripple under that marble skin. My mouth fits to the entry wound beneath his shoulder, while my hands touch his cabled arms. I move down his ribs with their crisscrossed musculature until, falling to my knees, I follow his hard, flat stomach down the long, hard lines of his thighs.

There are so many things that should have killed him that being shot almost seems like the least of them. The desertion of his pack, the years of wandering, the decades of not knowing what he was, but none of it did, and in the hard, yearning insistence of his cock and the smell like the bright musk of coriander, I know he is stubbornly alive.

I mark him, my cheek and jaw taking on his scent and leaving mine, and when I look up, his eyes have darkened from ice blue to storm, from summer leaves to winter needles.

He stands still, but I can tell by the slight tremor that it's taking effort. "If I change," he chokes out. "If I fall…"

"If you fall," I whisper, my breath eddying across the already weeping crown, "then I will catch you."

I let my tongue run over his head. It tastes like salt and wild mushroom. I raise my hand to his pale nipple and flick it with my finger. Almost immediately, it tightens into a sharp point and his hips jerk forward, brushing against my cheek.

"Careful."

He steadies himself, his hand on my shoulder.

In all my dutiful couplings, I've never done this—never licked or nibbled or dragged my teeth across or felt the contrast between the unyielding core and the silky skin that has enough play to pull down.

And I've certainly never covered a cock with my mouth, feeling the throb of my wolf's living pulse echoing the speeding of his heart.

A deep growl resonates through the chambers of my mouth and he groans, his scent sharpening, his arms and legs trembling.

I push down and pull back, without letting up. And when my arm is tired of playing among the planes of his chest, I weigh the heaviness between his legs in my palm. Squeezing carefully, rubbing my thumb against the little seam and—

"Let me in, Varya. Take me inside you."

I am not Homelands. I am not a territory that needs to be protected from every invader. He must feel it when he cups his hand between my legs.

The colder the land, the more passionate the thaw.

"Yours," he says, driving into me.

"*Mine.*"

"Yours," I repeat.

"*Mine.*"

Humans measure their time by the sun. Always so blus-teringly, predictably full. We measure our time by the moon, changing minute by minute, a painful reminder of transience and passing. With each night, the moon unfurls and my chest tightens.

With each day, winter dies a little more. Eyulf doesn't understand why I don't want to watch the cold roll back from the land. Why I don't want the goddamn white flowers of the serviceberry or bright-yellow coltsfoot or the tiny pink hazelnut or the trout lily or the tightly curled fiddleheads or the sprays of horsetails sprinkled with the first dew.

Why I don't want to hear the sparrows and winter wrens and flycatchers and pewees and mergansers call out the same song across the Great North's territory.

> *Listen to me.*
> *Look at me.*
> *Love me.*
> *Make life with me.*

The song he loves the most is wolf song. If it comes when I have words, I tell him what it means.

> *Human has entered Homelands.*
> *Human has left Homelands.*
> *Wolf injured.*
> *Fresh kill.*

And most often:

I am.
We are.

Then, too early, it comes. Rising high, it falls, and then after it surges halfway back up the register, Evie lets her call float down, disappearing as her breath gives out.

Come home.

Not yet. Please, not yet.

The sun is high in the sky, and Evie starts again.

"We're being called home," I whisper into his hair.

"Now?" I don't see his face, but I feel his body stiffen. "It's too early."

It is early. Earlier than usual, but that's not the way packs work. The way packs work is that the Alpha calls and you come. I see him staring at the scars at my neck.

"He won't touch me," I say, looking into his eyes. Eyulf covers the join of my shoulder with his hand. A callus scrapes against the muddled, faded teeth marks that Lorcan has left in my skin over the years.

It irritates me, the idea that I am marked by Lorcan. "I want you to do something for me."

"Hmm."

Pulling my hair to the side, I stretch out my neck. "I want you to—"

"Forget it." He smooths my hair back down, covering my shoulder. "I'm not biting you, if that's what you're thinking. I'm not making another mark on your skin."

"And I refuse to have my past be the thing that marks me." I hold his hand to the subtle ridges at my neck. "Wolves are physical. Our stories are written on our skin. And *you* are the story I want written on my body."

He feels every ridge and indentation left by

Lorcan's teeth, his lips tight. He shakes his head. He doesn't want to hurt me, but he doesn't like the idea of having me marked by Lorcan any more than I do. Finally, he nods.

I begin to turn over onto my hands and knees, but he stops me. "I have to turn over."

"No," he says, holding me tighter. "If I'm going to do this, I will not have your back to me. I want to make it clear that I see you. All of you. You say your story is written on your body. Well, I want every piece of that story. Every hard and painful thing that has brought us here. And there's one other thing"—he shakes his hair back and bends his head to the side—"you mark me in the same way."

He strokes my cheek. "It goes both ways, Varya, or it doesn't happen at all."

There is a fire that burns inside Arctic wolves. Banked, it keeps our bodies from freezing in the long nights of ice and snow. We are careful with it, though, because if it rages out of control, there is always a chance it will turn those around us to ash.

We balance on that knife's edge between control and release. He—we—are flushed and slicked with sweat. His pale hair falls down onto his face in rivulets. His hips push until the root of him is tight against me. He is so thick inside me that I know there will never be space left for anyone else. Voiceless, I growl at him to tend the cramping need that balances between pleasure and pain. Only then does he press my head to the muscled cord above his collarbone and his own mouth over the hard, scarred join at my neck. As soon as I strike, his teeth tear into the skin at my shoulder. I am not gentle because I

know the force needed to bite through the small, accu-
mulated marks of my past.

He breaks me open, just as Evie calls again.

Chapter 31

IT HAS FALLEN TO THE 12TH AND THE 5TH TO SET UP THE Great Hall to accommodate the Pack's full numbers when no one is hunting. To drag out every table and every bench. I haven't seen Evie yet, and if anyone else knows else why we've been called home early, they're not saying.

"Lift it. Don't drag it along the floor."

"It's very heavy," says the 5th Echelon's Beta mate.

"Put it down then. I'll find someone stronger."

I don't say it loudly, but several more subordinate wolves in his echelon watch him with interest. He picks it up without another word and lifts it high with one hand.

Pointless posturing.

By tradition, it falls to the Year of First Shoes to set the main table, putting out hot pads and piles of mismatched plates and hillocks of cutlery. Because they are not yet comfortable with opposable thumbs, there is an almost constant noise of things dropping.

Tara signals to me from the corner. "Evie would like to talk to you," she says as soon as I am out of earshot of the other wolves.

I scan Tara's face, looking for some explanation. For her to correct herself, but she just nods so that I know it was no simple oversight or sloppiness on her part. *Evie*, Tara had said, not "the Alpha." *Would like*, she said, not "would." And she didn't address me as Shielder.

No, Evie is asking something of Varya.

Touching the lintel, I knock on the door to the Alpha's office. Evie answers, her finger to her lips. The answering machine beeps and she bends over, leaving some message about the Great North LLC and a board retreat to cover for the fact that with the Iron Moon coming, she will have no hands to pick up the receiver and no words to speak into it.

She hits a button and turns back to me.

"I'm taking precautions this moon. Rather than gathering in front of the Great Hall, I will be dispersing the echelons throughout the High Pines. I have also consented to have Tiberius guard the access road. Along with Elijah's human."

If she hadn't asked me here as wolf to wolf, I would have said nothing, only acquiesced, but she didn't. I am here as Varya talking to Evie. "Is that wise?" I ask. "Ælfrida warned the Pack that those who guard us in our weakness will always end up exploiting it."

"She was thinking of the mercenaries who killed Pack Wessex. Tiberius and Thea may be outsiders, but they love their mates. Love *us*. I believe even Ælfrida would say it was different."

The water drips from the rooftop in slow, steady drops down the window that looks out on Westdæl.

Sometimes all you can do is love.

"Thea Villalobos will be joining us for the last meal before the Iron Moon," Evie says.

I suck in a breath too quickly and choke on it.

"The human didn't ask to join us," she says. "Elijah did. The 9th's Alpha would break from the Pack before letting her go. He is not asking that she be part of the

Great North, just that we become used to her, know her
scent and know that she will not betray us.

"I hoped you would guard over her when she is here."

"*Me?* Why *me*? Wouldn't an Offlander be better
suited? Alpha, there must be someone else. *Anyone* else."

Or just someone who hasn't already promised to kill
her, though I don't say that part.

"Why not Elijah?"

"Elijah," Evie says, exhaling slowly, "will kill anyone
who looks at her sideways. I have no doubt he could
guard her, but this is as much about protecting the Great
North as it is about protecting Thea. The Pack respects
you absolutely. They know you have no love of humans.
That is what makes you my best option. I also know if
you say you will do this, she will be safe."

A plate falls in the hallway beyond the door.

"I'm not commanding you, Varya. I wouldn't do that.
I am only asking."

Adult voices bellow, answered by panicky juveniles
making excuses.

"The Pack is already nervous with so many outsiders."

"*Two* outsiders," she says. "There are only two." She
listens until the tinkle of broken plates being swept into
a dustpan by a broom is finished. "I remember a story
from my childhood," she continues. "My Deemer told
us about a wolf who had a wonderful home. The earth
was soft under his feet, and the trees and sky shone
bright above him. Then one day, a wolf's head pops
from among the trees. 'What are you doing in the trees?'
he asked. 'What are you doing in the trap?' the tree wolf
answered. Something like that. It was a long time ago.
But the point was perspective.

"I think about that sometimes. I believe the outsiders understand what is precious about the Great North in a way that wolves who are born here never can. Tiberius loves this"—she waves her hand vaguely in the direction of the Clearing and the little cabin he shares with Silver and their four pups—"as much as any wolf. More. So does Elijah, who was away from it for so long. So do I, who came here frightened and alone.

"And so does Thea. I trust her. She doesn't want to be part of the Pack. She clearly has no interest in belonging to any hierarchy. All Elijah wants is that the Pack accept her enough to let her live."

On my way out, I rub the lintel.

This evening meal is already off to a bad start, with wolves snarling at one another. The subordinates are tired of being bossed around. The dominants are tired of being responsible. Evie watches with a careful eye to make sure that the Alphas keep their echelons in check, putting out the thousand small fires.

It doesn't help that Marco got stabbed yesterday. It was a flesh wound, but now seaxes must be sheathed during meals. Wolves feel the absence of their carefully honed daggers and jabbing at food with dull knives just makes them surlier.

The front door opens, and the hall falls silent. Some Pack stand frozen, their plates at the ready in front of the table clotted with bowls and casseroles and platters; others hover with one leg half swung across the bench; still others close their mouths, cutting off the rough babble of the Old Tongue or the oilier language of humans.

I head immediately to the door, the one that stands

between the foyer and the main hall. Elijah suggests Thea put her boots on the windowsill, because the pups, he says, *will* mark anything with an unfamiliar scent. He puts her coat on a hook and then covers it with his own; he doesn't say it, but I know it's so no wolf's outerwear smells like human.

He is making reassuring noises, but because *westends* don't hear well, the whisper meant only for the female is loud enough for the wolf standing at the door.

As soon as he sees me, he holds Thea against him, his chest out and shoulders forward, an instinctive attempt to look stronger.

I lick my teeth before turning to the human with lips curled up in greeting. "Welcome, Elijah and *westend*."

"Oh, for fuck's sake, Shielder," Elijah says, looking away with a shudder. "Do *not* try to smile."

I let my mouth fall back, glad to be relieved of that particular burden.

The Pack remains silent as the three of us head to the serving table. The *westend*'s jaw is clenched, but that is the only sign she gives of discomfort. Her back is straight, her head held high, and she does not smell of fear. Elijah seems more on edge. His eyes move back and forth, his top lip curling upward in the near-snarl that dares any wolf to challenge his mate's right to pack hospitality.

I follow them to the serving table. Trying to maintain her distance, Evie only nods before continuing her conversation with Tara. The Pack listens as Elijah explains the various dishes. She is, it turns out, a vegetarian, which would explain why she stinks of steel but not carrion, that other defining human smell.

Victor stands suddenly, dropping his napkin to the

plate in front of him. He glares at Evie, who spares him a disdainful glance but no more. Clearly, their relationship has deteriorated further. Then he heads for the tables to the east side, the tables occupied by the younger echelons, catching his toe on a bench sticking awkwardly into the space between tables. He stumbles, his face red, but then tugs at the cuffs of his shirt, waiting.

The 10th, the 11th, the 13th. Lorcan. One after another, the younger Alphas look briefly toward Evie, then to Victor.

Victor is forcing them to choose their loyalties, but Evie says nothing. They are not children who must be made to eat dinner.

I watch as too many of these younger wolves stand and follow Victor lightheartedly. They don't understand what they're doing, and their mood is more like juveniles making mischief than like wolves embarking on the dangerous business of pulling a pack apart. A few in the 12th are more hesitant, looking toward me, but I am not here as the 12th's Alpha Shielder. I am here as Varya, who told Evie that I would make sure nothing happened to a human.

There is one member of the 12th who doesn't go. Nobody notices that Arthur is left behind, standing in the corner, waiting and watching.

The human looks stricken. Elijah whispers to her, rubbing her back through her long, black hair.

When the last of the 12th files out after Lorcan and Victor, Eudemos, Alpha of the 14th, stands and my heart sinks. Alone among the younger echelons' Alphas, he had refused to follow Victor's lead, defending Silver and Tiberius. He is gruff, a little sloppy, not the most brilliant strategist. I'd come to admire his courage and understanding of what it means to be an Alpha.

There are strong wolves in the older echelons, but the Great North needs leadership in the younger echelons, too, if the Pack is going to survive.

Eudemos picks up his plate, the saltcellar, and a water jug, stuffs the last roll in the breadbasket into his pocket, and with a nod to the 14th, moves to the table next to the 9th. Gathering their plates and food, his echelon follows, closing the gap left by Lorcan and the others. Now when Elijah and Thea sit with the 9th, they will not face table after empty table left by angry wolves.

Tiberius stands, a plate in one hand and a pup balanced on each of his huge shoulders, while Silver calls to Arthur to join them.

When they are finally all rearranged and reseated, Silver pats the seat next to her for Arthur, who swoops in carrying two more pups. One wriggles desperately until he reaches the floor and then skitters off between the big legs and big feet that will be his playground for years to come.

I've always come late to the serving table, waiting until the 12th is hunched over their plates, before taking whatever is left. With so many wolves gone, though, the table is still laden with a confusing array of choices. Dumping the remains of whatever is in the mahogany stoneware crock, I turn back to find a place to sit.

Elijah motions for his Gamma to move over, making a spot for me next to the human. A pup whimpers under the table, little black paws on the human's knee. She leans down, her head to the side, and emerges holding her tiny namesake, Theo Tiberiusson, cupped in her hands. He stretches his head up for her marking, and even though she is human and can't truly understand what it means to mark and be marked in return, she rubs her cheek against his muzzle on both sides. He licks his nose and crawls up against her neck until he is perched on her shoulder, under her hair.

Many of the wolves who stayed did so because they felt constrained by Evie's example or the example of their echelon's dominants. Doesn't mean that they are reconsidering a millennia-old hatred of the hunted for the hunter. Too many of them look to me. They all know something about the end of Pack Vrangelya and my abiding fury at the *westends* who killed them, but those humans would never have allowed a pup to nuzzle into their necks, completely hidden except for the scrawny black tail beating against the curtain of her black hair.

They would never have confronted one of their own to protect us. I know enough about those other humans to recognize that there is a difference.

Pins prick my own leg. A brindle pup digs her tiny claws into my jeans and clambers up the slope of my shin. I try to shake her off, but she rides my leg until I pick her up. She clings to my lap like Velcro, this little bit of fur, and won't let go. Ignoring her, I go back to my food. Then she lifts herself up on her hind legs, her paws on the table, looking first at my eggs and mush-rooms, then, in case I'm too dense to understand what she wants, she turns her head to me.

In Vrangelya, pups knew better than to beg for scraps. Those who were strong and fast stole. Those who weren't starved.

The little brindle's tail wags hard, banging against my ribs.

I look down at her fuzzy pleading face, her tiny pink tongue, her sharp teeth and hopeful eyes. I wasn't lying when I told Eyulf that the reason I loved Mitya was that I loved hope. I love it still. I would not want the Great North to be like Vrangelya. And to spite Vrangelya and Illarion and all those bitter adults, I hold pieces of egg between my fingers and feed them to the tiny pup with the needle-sharp teeth. She eats so eagerly, biting me twice, but the fuller she gets, the sloppier she gets. Until almost all of it ends up in my lap. Only then do I stop her.

"Hæfst þu genoh, grædig wulfling."

You've had enough, greedy wolfling.

Greedy wolflings never know when they've had enough, so she mewls a complaint, but when I push the plate away, she gives up and crawls into the crook of my arm, turning and fussing until she is on her back.

I stare down at her little belly, so exposed and vulnerable.

"Sigeburg likes her tummy rubbed."

The human has to learn to speak more softly. Her voice carries too far. I will remember to tell Elijah.

Sigeburg's little legs stiffen, then bend, relaxing as I stroke her rounded belly with my thumb.

Thea suddenly puts her hand on Elijah's much bigger one, holding tight to his pewter mug. "Whatever it was, don't."

Theo peeks curiously from under the curtain of the human's hair.

"You promised. No matter what. That was the deal."

I hadn't been paying attention to the conversation of the 8th's Beta pair. They'd been talking in the Old Tongue about planting, though I suppose I should have been suspicious about why they needed to use the Old Tongue, which is not particularly suited to modern farming. Then Kieran, the Beta mate, lowers his voice further.

"*Ne biþ ðǽr nǽnig mǽþ umwǽstmbǽre lond becswincan.*"

It is too soft for either Arne, the 8th's Alpha, to hear or for Evie. It was meant for Elijah.

It is not fit to plow barren land.

Elijah's face turns white, then red, and when he lets go of the mug, the crushed pewter topples over, water spilling across the table.

By law, an open insult can be met with a challenge across echelon lines. No one would dispute that, but this was not an open insult. It was a carefully couched taunt aimed at Thea, who because she is human, will never bear Elijah's young. She rubs the head of the tiny pup on her shoulder. I cannot discipline wolves who are not of my echelon, but here's the thing: while *mǽþ* means rightness or fitness, it also means honor. And whether he meant to or not, Kieran has left me an opening. Wolves fight to protect their own. They fight to maintain discipline. They fight for position in the hierarchy.

And for centuries, they have fought for honor.

Not so much anymore. Not here, in the gentled Great North. But in Vrangelya, that bellicose pack, we certainly did.

I don't bother to turn around. "*Ne biþ ðǽr na mǽþ on lǽðendum þara mǽgenleasena.*"

Nor is there honor in speaking ill of the powerless.

With a seax, the crusty loaf in front of me would be easy to cut. But because some wolf cut some other wolf, my seax must stay sheathed, so instead, I stab the butter knife into it over and over again until the last cut, when I thrust the dull blade through bread, through wooden trencher, and into the table. I leave the knife shuddering next to the perforated hunk of rye.

"But, Kieran Thoriansson, there is honor in fighting me."

With the use of his Pack name and the word *honor*, Kieran began to exude the peculiar scent of salt and old leather that is the unmistakable scent of fear. I do not look at him, because I do not intend to acknowledge his submission. It has been so long since anyone has consented to fight me. My tongue toys with my dismally flat teeth. My fingers flex and remember the feel of hide giving way under claws. The elation that is both mind-numbing and clarifying and peculiar to fighting wild.

"Shielder, I meant no—"

"Kieran Thoriansson, by the ancient rites and laws of our ancestors and under the watchful eye of our Pack and our Alpha, I, Varya Timursdottir, challenge you to *mæþ holmgang*, to prove the steadfastness of your purpose and the strength of your marrow. With fang and claw, I will attend upon you the last day of the Iron Moon."

Technically, this does nothing to our positions, as we are not in the same echelons. But a wolf who loses the *mæþ holmgang*, the honor challenge, loses respect, and the wolf who loses respect loses everything.

At least that's how it was in Vrangelya.

The stench of salt and old leather picks up his damn plate and turns toward the kitchen.

"Take this," I say, pointing to my own plate. And he does.

Chapter 32

EVIE CALLS FOR THEA AND TIBERIUS TO READY THEM-selves at the access road. She sends Tara to find Victor and the others, but I ask to go in her place, because I want to hear the excuses of the wolves who would tear this Pack apart over a human they have not taken the time to know. Before the moon takes my words, I would have them with the Deemer.

"Alpha! Wait." Quicksilver lopes down the stairs, flying toward me. "Sigeburg?"

I don't know how I could have forgotten the brindle pup snuggled in the crook of my arm, asleep. Her tail and one little leg swinging loose against my wrist.

Silver scoops her up, leaving my arm oddly cold, though I am an Arctic wolf, and spring is coming.

Sigeburg.

"Quicksilver." As the Alpha did with me, I address her by name, not by rank, because I am asking her as one wolf to another. "You named your pup after the previous Deemer?"

"A sign of my great respect."

"You did not name either of your males after Victor?"

She rubs the jaw of the little pup in her arms, who turns and begins to gnaw on the finger with her tiny white teeth. Quicksilver doesn't say anything, but she is a wolf and doesn't insult me by equivocating either.

"I am asking because there is a fault line in the

Pack. Except for your own echelon, all the younger wolves follow Victor unquestioningly. I am trying to understand."

Her eyes catch mine, her nose twitching. Even in skin, she is more wolf than most.

"Victor," she says, weighing each word, "has always taught the law as infallible. What is on paper is absolute and must be followed exactly as written. For him, it is a simple matter of cause and effect. But Gran Sigeburg was always subtler, teaching the law in context."

"Because of my leg"—Sigeburg looks up at me, still chewing on the runt's finger—"I couldn't always run with the echelon, so I'd be left with Gran Sigeburg, and she told me not the law, since I had to learn that from Victor, but our history and our stories, the things she knew gave flesh to the bones of our law. She also knew that we could not understand the intent of the lawgivers unless we understood the minds that created the law. She said the stories were the keys that gave you entrance to those minds.

"Not so hard," she says to Sigeburg, tapping her nose with her finger. "And you, Alpha? Who Victor has always held up as the most *æfast*. What about you?"

"I am law-strong because I believe the law serves the interests of the Pack." I raise my head, sniffing at the breeze from the east. "But I have never believed that the Pack serves the interests of the law."

In these hours before the Iron Moon, it's dangerous to be wild. Nobody wants to take the chance that moonrise will come before they've had a chance to change completely into skin and will find themselves stuck as a forever wolf. Our wild may be sacred, but it is also dangerous.

Even in skin, though, it's easy to follow the thick muddle of four echelons of wolves. At least until it is not. The muddle disappears into Bear Creek and does not come out the other side, which means they walked up or down the river before coming out and confirms my suspicion that they are up to no damn good.

Running back and forth, I finally track them downstream through the tangled woods to a little house with a steeply sloped roof, topped by a cupola, and an attached shelter that had been emptied of logs years ago.

I am no skulking sneak thief and don't bother to disguise my footsteps or keep downwind. The voices inside slow, then stop.

The sap-house entry is made of two doors of weathered wood wide enough to accommodate a sled. One warped long ago and has been unusable for years. It just needs to be kicked hard enough, and it swings opens with a splintering crash.

The warm scent of a hundred wolves mixes with moldering wood, smoke, and burned sugar and rust. And salt and old leather.

"The Iron Moon is coming." Wolves clear a path, pressing against the walls of the little space to get away from me. "You all have responsibilities. The Alpha is dividing the Pack. The elders, the 2nd, 3rd, and 14th have already left for the High Pines. The 12th will follow your Alpha to the Great Hall. I will meet you there. The rest of you better find out where you're supposed to be."

One wolf begins to ask why.

"If you had been with your Pack, you would know," I growl, and no one says anything else.

Watching the wolves file out, I lower my eyes for none of them. Not the Alphas, not my Alpha, and definitely not Victor.

"You will wait here with me, Deemer."

"I...?"

"*Will wait*," I snap.

He shifts from foot to foot. He is always given a place at the kill and no longer has to hunt. If he did, he wouldn't expend that kind of unnecessary and noisy energy.

"I know," he says when the last of the wolves have disappeared into the forests heading toward Home Pond. "I know that you stayed with the *westend* because your Alpha asked it of you. I know—"

"You know *nothing*. I stayed not because the Alpha asked me, but because Evie did. I stayed because it is my duty to protect the Pack. I stayed because I wanted to find out for myself whether Thea Villalobos was so dangerous that she was worth tearing the Pack apart."

"She is a *westend*," he spits out. "They are all despoilers of land and wasters of life. Have you forgotten what they did to Vrangelya?"

"Do *not* dare to lecture me about Vrangelya. *I* was there. I saw each and every death. But if the humans built the trap, it was the wolves who stayed in it, fighting among themselves instead of finding a way out."

I am close enough that my belly grazes the button on his white shirt. "I know the price of lawlessness, but I also know the price of whispered dissent. If you speak your mind like a wolf, I will always listen. But"—I lean in, my nose touching his, my fingers a claw just below his rib cage—"if you shuffle *wrohtgeorn* through the Pack, know that I will eat your liver and pay whatever price the law demands."

Victor looks at my hand sinking into the softness under his sternum and touching the offending organ. His skin suddenly grays.

"Your Alpha is waiting for you, *Deemer*."

He turns on his heel and catches his toe on a loose floorboard that smells of lavender and turpentine. Then he races after the rest of the Pack.

It is not something that I am proud of, but I know my reputation. I know what they say about me.

That I have eaten my own kind.

They are, of course, right.

Chapter 33

THE PACK HAS ALWAYS GATHERED TOGETHER, WAITING for the waning evening light of this last day to give way to the inexorable pull of the moon's iron law. We'd sit together on the snow or ice or mud or rough grass of the land between the stairs of the Great Hall and the edge of Home Pond.

But that was when the thing we had to fear most was a coyote or bobcat coming upon us helpless in mid-change and eating us. There was strength in numbers then and in a well-marked territory.

Having all of us naked and immobilized in the same spot when the Shifters came would be, as the humans put it in a particularly inept phrase, "like shooting fish in a barrel."

Evie has emptied the barrel. The echelons are scattered throughout the High Pines, so that even if the Shifters with their superior senses can find some, they will not find us all before the change is over and the rest can either escape or fight.

The Grans, 2nd, 3rd, and 14th have taken the pups as deep into the wild as our lands allow. Far from roads or what passes as paths into the harsh, trackless, wolf-welcoming dark of the forests.

The 9th and the 12th and the 7th—Evie's own echelon—gather in small groups hidden among the trees near but not on the access road.

The other echelons—the ones that aren't as strong or that she simply doesn't trust to stand watch over our entrances or our pups—are scattered throughout the interior of Homelands.

I help distribute the 12th along the near edge of the access road. Lorcan will take up position closer to the human road. I remind him to take the rubber band from his hair.

The 9th is on the far side. The 7th at the top of the road, so that if anyone should be able to get past us, there is one more barrier to cross before getting to the gate across the road that marks the true beginning of Homelands.

By tradition, the Alpha closes the door of the Great Hall, marking the official beginning of the Iron Moon. This time, Evie double-checks the new heavy chain locking that gate.

"*Ēadig wáþ*." She says the traditional blessing, hoping—praying, really—that her wolves have three good days of wandering and hunting.

"And be yourself not hunted" comes the subdued answer.

Then she returns to the bend in the road, overshadowed on the Offland side by the spindly fire tower where Thea lies armed and waiting. On the inside of the curve, Victor, Tara, and I all sit, naked, our clothes in neat piles in the Great Hall. We sit, because once the Iron Moon begins her pull on pelvis and phalanges, there is no standing upright, and it is not worth the potential for injury. I have a place with good sight lines; Evie sits nearby. We both strain our senses for any sound that doesn't belong.

Tiberius stands in the middle of the road, his hands buried in the deep front pocket of his dark jacket. He is already a shadow, and as the sun sets, he will dissolve into black, leaving nothing but the two luminous green eyes of this deadly bulwark between the human world and the wild he loves.

The hope is that the Shifter and the human, the two who can keep their fingers even after sunset, can delay any invaders into the Great North long enough for those of us who must be wild to finish our change. Then the three echelons arrayed along the length of the access road will kill as many as we can, giving the other echelons time to run.

I keep pressing through my hair at the tooth marks at my neck. *Alys us. Alys hine.* Save us. Save him. I pray—as I did when I was a pup and believed that it might actually help—that if the Shifters come, they cannot smell cold. That if they come, he knows not to wait for me, because if they've made it as far as Westdæl, I am already dead.

Then it starts. The change of the Iron Moon is not like the changes I trigger myself. It doesn't start with one part of my body and move from there. Instead, it starts with the increasingly urgent rush of my blood, the moon pulling at it like the currents. Now, I lie down in a tiny, clear space, my arms and legs crooked in front of me, so that as soon as the change is over, nothing will be awkwardly positioned and I'll be able to move fast.

Dark swirls surrounded by white start to float across my eyes. My eyes and nose start to feel clotted and heavy, and soon all I see is a snowstorm of pale floaters and all I hear is the dull roar of the inside of my skull and all I smell is my own bone and blood as my face rearranges itself.

My pelvis and legs and chest narrow; muscles ripple as they shorten and lengthen. Finally, I am awash in the warmth of my powerful heart and thickening coat and I am almost done and I pray to the moon to let me not be shot before I have killed at least one Shifter.

I stumble to my feet, searching with my still-compromised senses for any distant gunfire or smell of cordite.

It's silent. Not silent, but forest quiet, the sound of peace. Only the fast, metallic creak of a barn owl makes me jump.

Evie and other larger wolves are still changing, so I lope toward Tiberius.

"Nothing," he says, staring into the moonlit dark of the road that leads Offland.

It won't be long before even the largest wolves will be changed and Evie will decide whether to call the all clear.

A little whimper of relief steams from my nose, but just as it does, I know it was too soon. Tiberius stiffens, so he has heard it too. From far away, where our rough access road meets the smooth human pavement, comes the grind of rubber turning onto dirt and rock. Tiberius and I look at each other. I back into the forest, to Evie. Maybe Victor heard the sound of wheels on rock because he, too, is circling around our Alpha's changing body.

Evie tries to get to her paws with muscles that won't obey yet. I stand at her side while she shakes out her enormous body. She lurches against me but doesn't fall.

The cars move slowly closer. Elijah is the only wolf large enough to still be changing, but Tara is across the road and is more than capable of leading the 9th.

Now Evie lifts paw after silent paw, her shoulders rolling under her black fur like waves as she creeps through rough, dead stalks that come summer will be primrose and fireweed and Queen Anne's lace and yarrow, clinging to the sunlit border of this road.

Wolves on either side silently follow her lead, all finding spots deep enough to remain hidden, but with nothing blocking an attack.

Evie's shoulders and legs are bent tight, her lips drawn back over her teeth, her ears cocked, listening.

Rocks crunch under the wheels of the two huge black SUVs until their engines sigh to a stop. Inside the tinted windows of the lead car, a click sounds, followed by the slick *whoosh* of a seat belt. I can smell nothing through the overwhelming assault of plastic and paint and solvents until the door opens and a foot reaches for the ground.

Tiberius shifts his right hand just slightly inside his pocket.

The driver jumps down, and now we can smell him. Carrion, steel, the sweet oleaginous smell of alcohol. And somewhere underneath, the scent of ferns on damp wood.

His hair is the color of Lorcan's, but his skin is ruddy, crisscrossed with tiny blood vessels.

"Tiberius," the Shifter says. The wind changes, and a wolf on the other side who'd moved too close to the road steps back into the brush, licking her nose, trying to get rid of the smell.

"Lucian," Tiberius says. "What are you doing here?" He doesn't say it as if he's actually curious. There's no rise at the end. Instead, it's a statement that this man has no right to be on our land.

Lucian hooks his thumb in his belt loop, trapping the

fabric of his coat behind him, showing us all his holster, if not his gun. The passenger door opens with a thud and another thump as one more Shifter jumps to the ground. He starts forward, but Lucian lifts his hand. He stops, but I still recognize the gaunt Shifter with the flecks of gray in his beard and the khaki skin and the smell of reeds on water's edge.

"Constantine," Tiberius says without taking his eyes from Lucian. He must know him by smell. Constantine nods in response. Lucian takes a step forward.

"That's close enough." Tiberius lifts his palm, the one that is bent and deformed by the dog spike his father used to fasten him to a wooden post.

"Give us some credit," Lucian says, pulling a glove from his pocket. "If we had come to kill you, we would not have waited this long."

"I give you credit for nothing. What do you want?"

Lucian smooths the glove over his left hand, pulling it tight over each finger before wiggling them.

"Your father has been trying for weeks to talk with the Alpha of the Great North. She has been ignoring him."

"He killed five of her wolves, including her mate. She doesn't owe him an audience."

Lucian closes his eyes and throws back his head, breathing in deeply, his mouth just slightly ajar, then turns toward the tangle of trees and underbrush where Evie is crouched and ready.

"Evie Kitwana," he says, scanning the brush. "I know you're listening."

Evie doesn't move.

"Your idyll is at an end. The Great North has been able to protect this land for so long because, to be frank, nobody else much wanted it. August has made sure that very powerful people have been alerted to its worth. Its resources. Its very attractive position between those who produce energy and those who consume it. The humans who come now are backed by the will of nations, and when they tear through your territory, there won't be anything you can do about it. Sadly, there is nowhere left for you to go."

Lucian holds on to the lapel of his jacket. "Having set this in motion, August is the only one who knows how to stop it."

A breeze rolls down from the north, ruffling Evie's coat.

"This isn't about money," Tiberius says.

"Nothing as crass as that."

Lucian's hand moves toward the inside of his jacket, and Tiberius stiffens.

"May I? I only have the gun in the holster. This is just a photograph."

Tiberius doesn't respond and doesn't relax.

The man pulls out a small rectangle and shows it first to Tiberius, then stiff-armed, he turns so that wolves on either side of the access road can see a picture taken overhead with a long-range lens. A picture of John, Sigeburg, Solveig, and Theo—Tiberius and Silver's young—tussling over an antler.

By the time he has turned full circle, Tiberius's gun is pointed steadily at the center of Lucian's forehead.

"It's not a threat, Tiberius. It's simply a picture taken for a proud grandfather."

Tiberius's only response is the almost silent snick made by the gun's safety.

"August wants this back." He slips the photograph in his breast pocket and pats it. "None of us believes it is a coincidence that the only successful Shifter births of the past half century were with Pack."

"This was not a Shifter birth. *I* was not a Shifter birth. I was forced to be a Shifter when my father chained me to a fence every moon for—"

"You were *trained*. We were all the same. Once. But we fought against the worst, most bestial part of our natures. August believes he can train your—"

"*No.*"

"Can you put that down?" Lucian nods toward the gun, still pointed at his head. "I wouldn't want you to get nervous and make a mistake."

"I don't get nervous," Tiberius says. "And I don't make mistakes. Not with guns."

Lucian turns once again toward Evie. "Alpha? What August is proposing is that we join. We will protect you and protect your land for this generation. You must see that there is no room for the wild anymore. We are offering to free your children from this endless cycle of vulnerability. All we ask in return is that you join us and save *us* from the slow extinction of our breed.

"It is a fair deal, Alpha. A future for a future."

I follow the huge black wolf with dark eyes as she steps out of the shadows. Elijah and Tara emerge from the other side as well.

Lucian undoes the snap of his holster.

A crack splits the air followed by an explosion of mud that covers Lucian's lower legs.

"I would take my hand away from the gun, if I were you."

Muddy water creeps into the depression in front of Lucian's toe as he turns his head, trying to locate the scent of the sniper watching from the heights.

"The Great North already has its defenders," Tiberius says.

"Ms. Kitwana," he says. "Mr. Leveraux will call you Tuesday so that you can talk. He would truly prefer an arrangement that was mutually agreeable."

"*Prefer*," Tiberius spits out. "But if the Pack says no?"

"This is life or death, Tiberius. You know your father; what do you think?"

Lucian signals to Constantine to get back into the SUV. The passenger door closes with a dull thud.

"Tuesday," Lucian repeats to Evie. "Late morning. Mr. Leveraux does not like to wake up early."

Then there is another dull thud, and the big, black, blind cars start to back up. Evie follows them, her muscles twitching with every step. I wonder if she is feeling what I am, the futility of our claws and our fangs and our strength of heart against metal and fire.

And I follow Evie all the way from the rough stone to the smooth crushed pavement Offland. Once they are really and truly gone, Tara howls the all clear. Few of the Pack know what has happened. Some saw the lights of the SUVs bobbing along the rough access road. More heard the single gunshot. There is a lot to say, but no words to say it with, so the Pack will do what they always do: wander and hunt.

Evie sits erect and silent among the trees girding the road, and I sit next to her. Aside from a slight turn of her head, she does not acknowledge me as we wait there deep into the night.

Chapter 34

WHEN I FINALLY GET TO THEM, THE WOLVES OF THE 12TH ARE anxious. They don't like change. In skin, they were willing to follow Lorcan and Victor in a show of petty defiance. Now that they are wild, they stand with their tails drawn in, their ears circling, waiting for any other sound. A few run toward me, sniffing my face, hoping that something on my muzzle brings comfort or at the very least news.

I have neither, but what they do find is the scent of a failing buck near the waters at the easternmost border of Homelands. I run around quickly, spreading the scent. They are hungry and nervous, and I spend too much time growling and nipping at their flanks, until the 12th finally concentrates enough to be able to hunt.

I move them along quickly, snapping at stragglers, because once I have done what I must do, I will leave them to Lorcan and George, our Beta mate.

The 12th has no trouble hunting down the old buck, but I have no heart for it. The sound of tearing hide and the impatient growls mix with the smell of blood and the damp heat of fresh kill, but I'm not hungry. I stare blankly as the consciousness of a lifetime fades in big, round black eyes that reflect the silhouette of the moon over Westdæl.

Evie is running everywhere, checking on her Pack, reassuring those made nervous by the sounds of cars and

guns if they were close enough to hear, or by the change
in routine if they weren't. Victor has been too. I know
because when he lopes in to take his place at our kill, I
smell the scents of many wolves on his muzzle. I watch
as the 12th backs away, letting him eat his fill.

When he is finished, his long tongue swirls around his
blood-spattered mouth before striding over to Lorcan.
He props one paw on Lorcan's head and marks him
before turning to me. I can feel the 12th watch. They are
nervous. They want cohesion and consensus.

They want to know that their dominants are agreed.
But I don't agree. Victor is not like Evie, who has been
helping with hunts, reassuring, disciplining, and marking. Victor is like the human politicians Leonora once
described. The ones who kiss babies and pat backs and
hug warmly in order to gain power.

Victor turns to mark me, and I lunge. It is a feint;
there is no actual menace in it, just a line he knows better
than to try to cross.

Licking his muzzle, he kicks the dirt with his hind
paw, a subtle slight, before moving on to the other members of the echelon. One after another, wolves I have
grown up with but have never truly known line up to
take his mark.

With no more than a bend of my head to acknowledge my Alpha, I leap up, twisting in the air, and run.
Jumping over moss-covered logs and lichen-covered
rocks, I stumble into the soft new mud, the thin layer of
ice giving with a delicate break.

Biting the ice lodged between my pads, I glance
back up to the 12th. Victor stands impatiently in front
of Arthur, waiting for him to offer his muzzle. Just as

I am about to return to my paw, something entirely unexpected happens: Arthur—*Arthur*—carefully and deliberately turns around, presenting the Deemer with haunches and tail. He has no rank in the hierarchy, so it is an empty gesture.

At least I thought it was an empty gesture, until others of my echelon move away. Not all, by any means. Most—either from loyalty to Lorcan or to Victor or by habit—still receive his mark. But those who were uncertain have been given courage by a *nidling* who is braver than they are.

They are complicated, these wolves. They are frightened and stouthearted, stiff and flexible, infuriating and wondrous, and I would do anything and everything to protect them and this wild place that is their only home.

When I stand on the promontory overlooking this corner of the land that has been carved and painted and protected by the Pack, I understand better the *Bredung*, the braiding. I have never seen one, as they are silent, private affairs joining two wolves not only to each other, but to the land and the Pack by bonds that end only in death.

My breath comes slowly and mixes with the thawing earth and all the life that clings to it.

And the smell of cold as Eyulf pushes his damp nose against mine and holds me with his green and blue eyes.

I leap on his shoulder and jaw his ear, and he rubs my muzzle with his until I stumble backward over a thick, moss-covered branch and fall on my back, legs stretched toward him, and he bounds up, pretending to pounce down, his paws landing near my belly. Then I twist around, my forelegs stretched in front of me, and snap at his tail when it flashes through the air in front of me. He licks my chin, and we jaw spar a little before falling down and over and biting gently and nipping a little harder, followed by chasing and stopping and posturing and skittering and slipping through the damp and leaf-rot of the undergrowth.

There is no word in the language of men for the courtship games of wolves: run-and-jump doesn't begin to cover it, because in the Old Tongue, *behleapan* is to leap upon, but also to settle on. To be devoted to. It is the metaphysical made very physical.

We both stop, ears turning and noses quivering, attuned to the presence of other wolves. Seeing me, they back away, but when I look over my shoulder, Eyulf has disappeared.

I snap irritably at the wolves, whose only crime was to run as wolves together. I'm irritable because Eyulf has slunk away and our game of run-and-jump is over. I'm irritable because it must feel so good to run thinking of nothing else, just cold air and the scent of prey. The soft give of the forest floor, as the wolves mingle their scents into the land. With an almost imperceptible angling of the head and tail, they change directions, and shoulder to shoulder, they run. They even run across the Clearing where anyone could see them.

I follow Eyulf's scent to the top of the Gin and down the loose stone through the thin strand of trees and over the gash left by the trucks.

Something races past me, bright and fast and silent like a knife through the air, and runs up the unstable rock and then slides down it until he stands in front of me, his forelegs extended in front of him, his hind legs coiled, his tail up, not wagging but shivering at the top.

Play.

Puffing out a breath, I turn my head to the side. *Come back.*

Come home.

But he backs away, leading me deeper Offland, into this place that isn't his home and isn't mine either.

A low, steady howl drifts across the bowl of our mountains, joined by another higher howl that weaves back and forth across his. It's nothing: no wolf is calling a warning or asking for help or announcing a kill. It's just mates being playful.

His tail shakes again, and this time, his hind legs do too. *Play?*

Stretching beyond him is the ravaged wound down this hollow that once housed a river but now holds intersecting lines of tire tracks, the herringbone patterns filled with water that glimmers in the moonlight.

Yes. Play.

I jounce gracelessly down the rounded rocks and land splat in front of him. He jumps and twirls in midair, then takes off through the ruined ground, his feet a blur leaving a spray of muddy water.

I can see every liquid movement as his powerful back undulates under white fur. He doesn't have to look behind him to know that I am chasing but not full out. That's the difference between prey and play.

Then he veers left and churns around, drawing almost parallel to me before running on ahead. Something startles to his left. Instantly, I am alert to my responsibilities; I stop fooling around and swing wide to stop any possible escape into the woods.

In the end, we have a rabbit. Not a big rabbit. Spring

is still too new and the rabbits are thin, but I know to be grateful for every mouthful of hot blood and fresh flesh and narrow bone.

It's inevitable on such a small kill that noses touch and muzzles rub.

Mine.

Yours.

Ours.

The endless rains gather in the canopy overhead and fall in heavy, irregular drops onto my face. Mud coats the pale fur of my chest as I vault over an ancient trunk. He races past me. I don't know this land at all and shouldn't be running flat out. It's only when it's too late that I realize there's a rill or a stream that I can't see, and I slow. If I'd kept going at top speed, I might have cleared the gully, like Eyulf did, a jagged bolt of lightning sailing across in the moonlight.

But I doubted and slowed and missed the far edge. My claws scrabble on the eroded edge, scraping, trying not to get up, just to slow my tumble to the bottom. The earth falls away in a thick slurry under my churning claws, until my hind leg catches in a thick root and the dirt under my front legs melts away. I fall backward, my head…hurts. It hurts, and pain shoots across the back of my head and around the front of my muzzle and into my sinus. I have to get up. I have…responsibilities. I must stand guard. A soft tongue laps against my scalp.

He pats my shoulder, pushing me back down. He nuzzles my ear and then gently touches his nose to mine and gives out a soft questioning whine deep in his throat. It's what we do when we are worried and without words.

Are you okay? it means.

Please be okay.

Then he sits next to me, alert, his nose twitching, his ears circling, the lucidum of his eyes glowing as he watches the dark. After a lifetime of shielding, I allow myself to be shielded.

When I wake up again, he is just the same, except one paw is propped on mine so that when I move, he curls down around me, nuzzling into my fur.

Wild, it's easier to touch him and show how I feel than to say those words that seem so remote from our true selves. When he gives me a big open-jawed kiss, I stretch my head back, looking upside down at the periwinkle blue of the morning sky.

Eyulf nuzzles me some more, making whining sounds, because he doesn't understand what it means when a wolf exposes her throat. I stretch out longer, even more vulnerable, until by some ancient instinct, he moves that open-jawed kiss down and sets the points of his teeth so gently on either side of my neck. He is so careful that those teeth, powerful enough to break through bone, barely touch the tips of the longest guard hairs.

For wolves, fucking is far from the most intimate thing we do. But this…this is what wolves do when they have no words. It means I give what is most vulnerable about myself and know you will not hurt me.

It means I trust you.

It means I love you.

Chapter 35

THE LAST DAY, AS I STRAGGLE BACK TO HOME POND, Tara calls to Kieran, who already looks thinner and weaker and more threadbare, though it has only been three days since I challenged him.

The final day of the Iron Moon is the traditional time for challenges. It gives the restive Pack something to do when they are too full to hunt. It starts with the lower ranks, like the fight between the 10th's Theta and its Iota for *cunnan-riht* to the Iota's bedfellow, which was a whole lot of spit and snarling and not a single injury. Very few wolves even from the 10th bothered to show up.

A few fights involved strength and strategy, and since there was the promise of blood, the audience share was inevitably higher. We're not so different from humans that way.

Because I am an Alpha and Kieran a Beta, our challenge was always going to be near the end. Since a *mæþ holmgang*, an honor fight, is rare, it comes at the very end, so I nestle into a hollow beneath the roots of a nearby tree. A thing I never imagined happening happened, and I didn't want to lose a single precious minute of my time with Eyulf to something as meaningless as sleep, but now I fluff my tail over my nose and breathe in deeply, napping until Tara wakes me, announcing that it is my turn.

A lot of wolves have gathered to watch, arrayed

around the paddock and near the big log bench. Some even have gathered on the steps to get a higher view. Pups try to clamber up on adults, not quite understanding what all the fuss is about. Lorcan and Arne, the 8th's Alpha, stand at the sides of the paddock, Evie and Victor on either end to make sure no one is hurt. That Kieran isn't hurt. Not badly. Or fatally, to be precise. Nobody is much worried about me.

With a yawn, I shake the dirt and dry bark from my fur. Then I give in to a good stretch, letting the muscles ripple from my shoulders all the way to the tip of my tail.

Evie puts her damp nose against mine and snorts, blinking her golden eyes once. *Avoid the face. At least try to avoid the face*, she tells me. Kieran will be going back to his job at Global Foundries, and it would be better if he did it without fang or claw marks shredding his cheeks.

Unfortunately, wolves in the middle of a fight don't always remember.

And I don't remember anything after Tara threw back her head. A short howl that started high, then got lower before rising again. When I jumped over the paddock, my mind was already empty: no pain, no sadness, no honor, no Alpha, no loss, no Pack. All that's left inside is the ember of old fury stoked to a purifying burn.

Kieran is in unfortunate shape, but there is a reason we don't have challenges at the beginning of the Iron Moon. Soon Tristan will change, and he will hopefully be able to knit Kieran back together. I forgot that thing about his face.

Lorcan opens his mouth hesitantly. He is my shielder and will do what needs to be done, but I can already tell he's praying that I don't need him to debride my wounds. I don't. I really don't want his tongue anywhere near me.

The real pain comes after, when the Iron Moon is over. Every tear in my hide rips open again—and further to accommodate the changing flesh underneath. I stand under the gentle drizzle of the ice-cold shower in the Bathhouse, watching the bright-red blood slip down my legs and onto the tiled floor before mixing with other wolves' soap and briars and pine needles and dirt and swirling down the drain.

They look away as I head down the stairs to the basement to dry storage. Big metal shelves are fitted with large plastic bins labeled with sizes (most XL and above). My power is not in my size, so I rummage through one of the few bins labeled simply *Large*, quickly pulling out sweatpants and the pale-gray Henley, because Evie is about to announce the beginning of the Iron Moon Table.

The Pack gathers at the Great Hall. Some washed, but many are just shifted. Combing fingers through their hair to get rid of burrs and seed pods, they wait in line to scrub blood and mud from their hands at the big trough sink in the kitchen before taking plates of scones and eggs and bread. Some gnaw on the stone-dry Baltic rye bread that is served after every moon to help scrub our teeth clean.

"In our laws are we protected," Evie says.

Taking the stairs three at a time, I get to the hall in time to answer with all the other wolves.

"And in lawlessness are we destroyed."

Evie leans against the head table, looking out over the expectant eyes of her Pack. "By now, I'm sure even those of you who were in the High Pines know that we had visitors.

"Shifters came as soon as we had changed to present a proposal from August Leveraux. I have heard it before, but since it was made to me directly, I ignored it. Now he has made it to the Pack, and I can't. I will tell you the basics, and we will see if anyone is willing to be the for-speaker.

"The bottom line is that we join with the Shifters. Through us, the Shifters hope to be able to have children. In return, he promises us his protection."

There is a long silence, while every wolf waits to see if their Alpha will clarify. Finally, Eudemos stands, scratching at his beard. When Evie nods, he says only one word.

"Children?"

And that's the question. *We* don't have children. We have pups. They may change back and forth in utero, but once they have come into the world and felt the connection with it that is their birthright, they stay wild for as long as they can.

"He believes he can train them." Evie stares at her coffee mug, her long, dark fingers turning it slowly against her palm. "Train all our young to resist the change, make the Iron Moon irrelevant. Make them children."

"Like he did with Tiberius?" Silver mutters.

Evie does not mention the threat implied in the Shifter's last words. "He would truly prefer." She is trying to keep to the facts, keep her voice neutral, because it is the Pack's decision and only one thing can stop it from going to the Thing.

"Are there any for-speakers?"

Almost as a whole, the wolves of the Great North drop their heads, only daring to sneak a side glance to see who might consider being a *fore-spreca*, an advocate. If no wolf feels strongly enough to speak for it publicly, then it is not worth the Pack's time and consideration and will not go to a vote.

Several wolves slide hands under muscled thighs, just to be sure. Evie stops looking at her coffee, and I can see that she is relieved the Pack doesn't want this any more than she did.

"Alpha, I know it is not customary for the Deemer to be *fore-spreca*." Victor fingers the ironed collar of his shirt. "But custom and law are not the same, and the law allows it."

Evie grimaces and then nods to Marco. I didn't know that Victor is allowed to be for-speaker; the Alpha is not. She is considered to have too much influence, too much sway. That was why Evie was trying so hard to keep her words, her voice, and even her face cool.

But once Victor has said he will do it, she has no choice but to start the Thing. Marco lifts the massive wooden box bound with metal straps. It is new, a careful duplicate of the ancient one that went up in flames this winter. The fire set by the same Shifters who now offer their protection.

Then Marco opens the lid, retrieving two heavy bags filled with stones collected from Homelands rivers from inside. He hands one, filled with dark stones, to Henry, then follows behind carrying another filled with pale stones. Those who agree with the for-speaker, with Victor, will put the light stone in the Thing. Those who don't will cast the dark stone. The lid has a hole as round as the moon and big enough for the largest fist, so that a wolf who does not want the color of their stone known can hide it easily enough. This is how the Pack makes decisions.

Next Evie asks for a *wiper-spreca*. An against-speaker.

There doesn't have to be one, but I can tell by the Alpha's expression that she fears that without one, the Deemer will carry—

"Oh, by the Moon!" Victor barks toward the table where the 14th is seated.

Quicksilver Nilsdottir is holding the hilt of her seax with one hand, while trying to extract her leg from the crowded bench.

"I will be the *wiper-spreca*, Alpha," she says, and Victor looks away with disgust.

Tiberius sits upright, his shoulders expanded, so that his mate, who is still recovering from her lying-in, can lean against his big arm without looking weak.

She doesn't. The Pack cannot coddle weakness, and no one is more aware of this than the runt, the least significant wolf in the Great North.

Still, there's a saying that is common in one form or another among all Packs: a wolf who discounts the power of the smallest has never had to sleep with blackfly.

Mosquitoes, they said in Vrangelya.

"Alpha, I need Adrian to get something for me."

Evie signals for Adrian, the oldest and fastest of the juveniles. Not yet an adult, he can't vote. Silver whispers to him, slipping her hand up and under, indicating some invisible place, then checks to make sure he understands. He whispers something. Tiberius breathes deeply, his lips tightening over teeth that are just as sharp and inhuman as Silver's.

Victor stretches his neck, looking through the window as he strains to catch a glimpse of where Adrian is going.

"Deemer?" Evie says.

He shakes a crease free from his pant leg.

Chapter 36

I AM CURIOUS WHY VICTOR, OF ALL WOLVES, WANTS TO SPEAK on behalf of the Shifter proposal. Victor, who has been so dead set against all strangers and now is speaking on behalf of joining with a whole swarm of them.

First, he walks slowly and silently before the arrayed tables. It is theater, but the Great North watches him hungrily.

"Only a few weeks ago, you said that while it was my duty to preserve the Old Ways, it was your duty to preserve the Pack. At least I think that's what I recall."

Evie doesn't say anything. She knows and he knows that was exactly what she said.

Now the Deemer turns to the Pack. "When the Shifter first announced that he had a proposal from August Leveraux, I immediately thought no. Whatever he was thinking, the answer had to be no. There is nothing the Shifter has that can be of any use to our Pack. But during the three days that followed, I could not speak and had time to think. My mind wandered back to something else our Alpha had said." He stops in front of the 11th. "Do you remember what it was, Sylvie?"

The 11th's Beta bedfellow shakes her head.

"I do. She said, 'We do not fear questions.' So I started to ask myself questions. Starting with the most basic one: Should I listen? If it is for the good of the Pack, the answer must be yes."

Evie smears some fig spread on a slice of rye, then adds some cheese. Irony is usually avoided by wolves, who count it among the various forms of human misrepresentation. Leonora teaches it using a mnemonic. JAFFEWIP—Jokes. Advertising. Falsehood. Flirtation. Exaggeration. White lies. Irony. Politics.

The Deemer turns to the 10th. "What is the fundamental purpose of our law?"

The echelon's members look at one another, not sure what the Deemer wants.

"To keep order?" one says.

"Partly, but that is only a part that serves the larger purpose." No one says anything. "It's not a trick question. The Alpha just said. She says it at the start of every Iron Moon Table."

Sarah, the Epsilon, scratches her cheek, lifting three fingers in a diffident raising of the hand. "To protect?"

"Exactly. To protect. Everything about our law is constructed to protect the Pack. And protection is precisely what we are being offered. We have managed to survive so far, but each year brings new threats. More hunters, more threats to the land itself. The world is changing and what... Julian? Was that his name? Tiberius, you know."

"Lucian," Tiberius says, his obsidian eyes unyielding. He understands, as I do, that Victor is trying to tie him to the other Shifters. "His name is Lucian."

"Lucian. So what Lucian said is true. There is no longer room for the wild, and if there is no room for the wild, there is no room for wolves. And if there is no room for wolves, there is no room for us." Victor waves his hand, dismissing the sudden rumble in the room. "We have to be practical. We have Shifters at our front door, humans at our back.

"Now"—he picks up one of the pups and rubs his cheek against it—"supposing we no longer had to live in fear of the gun or the trap? To live in fear is to be enslaved. What we are being offered, then, is nothing less than freedom. If August Leveraux can do what he promises, then this pup"—he holds up Nils Johnsson, making every muscle in Evie's body quiver with fury—"will no longer know fear. He will be able to do anything, go anywhere, not worrying that the hour is coming when he will turn into a nuisance species that can be killed with impunity."

I try to read the faces of wolves to see who is swayed and who is not. Too many are: younger echelons because of an ingrained habit of deference, and even a few of the older Offlanders who have become accustomed to life among the *westends* and find the monthly return to Homelands an unwelcome complication.

I've only wanted to see the Pack safe, to know that whatever else, the thing that happened to Vrangelya will never happen to the Great North. But I wanted to see the *Pack* safe. The idea that we can only be saved from humans by *becoming* humans tears at my soul.

When the Deemer sets Nils down, the pup runs awkwardly over to Evie, who is both his mother and his Alpha. Her nose is flared, and the scent rolling off her skin is like charred resin.

"Ælfrida thought that we could use the laws of humans to protect us, but law is not enough to control humans. We need power. And that is something the Shifters have. Now, before…"

Adrian comes in out of breath. He must have run

far, I suspect to Silver and Tiberius's cabin deep in the woods. He hands Silver a small canvas bag. A shoe bag perhaps. Silver seems to weigh the contents in her hand.

"May I continue?" Victor asks tightly.

Silver's lips curl back from her sharp canines, and she growls at the Deemer. I have little tolerance for humans, but Silver simply doesn't understand them. She never did manage to pass Introduction to Human Behaviors and has no tolerance for those little humanisms like facetiousness.

Victor shakes his head. "Where was I?"

"Shifters have power," Tara says in a low, cold rumble.

"Yes, Shifters have power. Before, I might not have trusted them, but now I realize that while they can give us freedom, we can give them something they need as desperately: a future."

Silver stands, setting the bag on the table next to her plate, her hand on the hilt of her seax.

"What do you want?"

"I just want to be clear," Silver says, "that when you say 'we,' you don't mean yourself. The future that we are promising is in our females' bodies."

"There are many things they want—"

"No, there aren't. There is only one thing. Tiberius was the last Shifter birth. They want us to help them breed. Whether we like it or not." Silver makes way for Henry so he can continue distributing the light and dark river stones to the 14th's table. "I believe at the end, Lucian said that August would 'prefer' that this be a mutually acceptable agreement. To me, that does not sound like I have the right to say no."

"You already have a mate who, conveniently enough, is a Shifter."

"And you are trying to change the subject, so let me rephrase: to me, that does not sound like a female has the right to say no."

Whatever is in the bag clinks slightly in her hand.

"What is the word, Deemer, for when a human mounts a human who is not receptive?"

In the silence, a purse snaps open and shut. Every head turns to Leonora, the only wolf who carries a purse on Homelands. She's a tall female, made even taller by the spiky heels she wears so that wolves will understand the peculiar ways in which humans hobble their own.

Her pup-chewed clutch is under one arm, but in her other hand she holds the hilt of her seax.

"Rape, Quicksilver," she says, daring the Deemer to deny her expertise in the world of humans. "The word you are looking for is 'rape.'"

"Thank you, Leonora," Silver says, turning back to Victor. "So what you propose is to buy our security with the bodies of our females. That is not who we are.

"You said, Deemer, that you did not speak immediately because for three days you had no words. *That* is who we are. You said we would not be tied to the land, but that, too, is who we are. You said we would not be forced to gather every month. And that is who we are.

"Maybe," she says, "what you say is true. Maybe the Great North would be safe. But we would no longer be the Great North. Because the land, the Pack, and our own wild is *all* of who we are.

"Yes, the Iron Moon is a dangerous time, but it is a sacred time and, like all things worth having, involves risk. Without it, we will be like Shifters. We will live on the fringes of the human world, separate and alone. The question is not do we want to be *safe*. The question is do we want to be *us*."

Chapter 37

QUICKSILVER STOPS AND PATS THE BENCH NEXT TO HER mate. "Adrian? You should eat something. Corn bread? Apple sauce?" She starts piling the plate with food.

"What—" Victor starts to say, but one look at Evie's face stops him.

Like all juveniles, Adrian's hunger is more imperative than his table manners. As soon as Silver puts the loaded plate in front of him, he bends over and starts shoveling food into his mouth as quickly as hand or spoon will put it there. He notices nothing else. He doesn't notice when she upends the little canvas bag. He doesn't notice when she shakes the silver thing out. He growls slightly when she wraps it around his neck. Only when she snaps it tight does he sit up and look around. He tries to bend over, but even from where I'm standing, I can see the skin at his neck yield to the metal spikes of the prong collar. If he sits utterly still and straight, the spikes don't dig farther in, just touch the surface of his skin.

He starts to scratch frantically at the thing, so frantically that Silver can't get it off until Tiberius holds Adrian's hands in one enormous fist. Silver unlocks and holds the prong collar behind her. Then she sniffs the juvenile's neck, checking for blood.

Evie taps the table. "Adrian, come," she says in a gentle voice. The juvenile runs to his Alpha. She holds him still and marks him slowly, letting him stay close, his face next to hers, until his breathing finally calms. She whispers something to him, and within moments, his clothes are on the floor and he is too, twisting at his waist to trigger his change.

"This"—Silver holds up a chrome chain with spikes around the inner face—"is how August Leveraux trained his son. This was what he used to drag him back to Homelands in the winter." She places it around her neck and stiffens. "I've tried it before. So that I could know what the wolf I love lived through every moon. You should try it," she says, taking it from around her neck and holding it toward Victor. "See what it feels like."

Victor refuses to look at the spiked thing and keeps his eyes focused on Silver. "This is nothing but theater."

"I am a wolf, and wolves do not have use for theater." Silver's voice drops to a menace. "Theater is fake. This is real. This is what they did to Tiberius for four years, and he was only half Pack."

"There are humans just to the north of us." Victor's voice rises up the register, sounding shrill in my ears. "What do you propose we do about them? Arm ourselves? Oh, wait, we can't. Or at least not always, because *we must be wolves*."

"Yes, we are wolves, but at least we are *wolves*. What August Leveraux is proposing, what *you* are proposing, will kill our wild. And then what are we?"

"*Alive*. We are alive, *Theta mate*." Victor draws out her place in the hierarchy to emphasize her weakness and lack of rank.

"I'll tell you what we are. We are wolves broken to the will of others. And wolves broken to the will of others are dogs."

There is a momentary silence as the d-word hangs in the air, and then all hell breaks loose. It was a cheap shot, maybe, one guaranteed to rile up the Pack.

Too many wolves get to their feet, which usually means the fighting is about to start. Evie bangs the pommel of her seax against the table and shouts for the Alphas to control their echelons.

After a second thump, the noise fades. After a third, it all but disappears. "Marco?" Evie says. "The Thing."

One noise continues, a tremulous sound in the corner, where Henry and Victor stand with Arthur, who is arguing in a desperate voice.

Silver bumps into me as I stride toward my *nidling*.

"It's not right!" Arthur whispers when I get close enough to hear.

"Arthur?"

"I am taking care of this." Victor starts to angle his back to me. He stops only when he slams into the hard corner of my elbow. Holding his arm, he looks first to me, then to Evie, to see if she saw. Saw that someone hit her Deemer.

"I will not see your back, Victor."

The runt twists her mouth to the side and scratches at her nose.

"I have no stones, Alpha." Arthur shows me his empty hands. "I need stones to be able to—"

"The *nidling* has no say in this," Victor snaps.

"Since when?" asks Silver.

"The Thing is only for adult members of the Pack.

A Pack is hierarchy, and he has no position within it. A *nidling* is not a place; it is the lack of a place. It—"

"I was there," Silver interrupts, "this fall when the Pack was deciding whether to allow Tiberius in. Allow me back. You didn't object then."

It's true. But something has changed. It's not the law; it's Arthur. He stands straighter now, his hands fisted by his sides. He has developed a backbone, and during the Iron Moon, he turned it on Victor.

I don't know how long Evie has been standing behind me.

"I'm not sure I've ever seen you smile before, Shielder."

"No, Alpha."

"It's an odd time for it."

"Yes, Alpha."

"I disagree with you, Deemer, but I can't afford to have this decision side-tracked by Arthur's status. I need to know where the Pack stands before August Leveraux calls."

Arthur's jaw tightens, his lips curl back slightly, and I can smell the anger on him as he glares at Victor. Then he turns on his heels and strides toward the kitchen where the pups and juveniles are already gathered, waiting until the voting is over.

I can't help but feel as he strides away that the Deemer has misjudged seriously.

Marco bends his legs and hefts the heavy box, beginning the slow procession through the ranks of wolves. The first stones dropped ring hollow on the wood base, though soon enough the sound changes to a muted click. A few—they are all supporting Victor—try to display their vote, but that is not the way things are done, and Tara, who is following the proceedings wild, bites the shins of the first two who do. It is only temporarily debilitating but quite painful, and everyone else chooses to be discreet.

Some wolves I know will vote with Silver: Elijah, Tara, Evie, Eudemos, Tristan.

Leonora.

But the weaker wolves, those who are afraid, clearly have chosen safety. Especially the males. After all, they won't have to deal with either the pronged collar or the lying-in. The consequences belong to someone else. The benefits belong to them.

Some of these look toward Victor, their hands still in the Thing, as though they are hoping for approval. Oddly, I can't tell about Lorcan. He looks at no one and nothing but his fisted hands until the moment the Thing is in front of him, and then he just stares out the window.

But the strongest wolves all wear the same grim expression of fierce determination in the face of almost certain doom.

This is who we are. We are wolves, and wolves fight to the death.

"Alpha?"

"Hmm?"

"Your stone?" The rest of the Pack looks to where I stand as always. In the back. Where the sight lines are good. "The Pack has voted. You are the last."

I look at the two stones in my hand. The white one for Victor and the proposal that we can break free of this cycle of weakness and we will have safety.

The black one for Silver, for the proposal that our wild is sacred and makes us what we are.

As soon as I drop my stone, Marco returns to the head table, which has been completely cleared. Victor and Silver, the for-speaker and against-speaker, stand on either side. By tradition, they are naked. I suppose at some point a wolf must have tried to drop something into a pocket or secrete something into a sleeve, so this was the simplest expedient for excluding foul play. It hardly matters. Every Alpha gathers around the table, watching as each stone is extracted. At first, it seems that Victor has carried the decision, but as the counting continues, his expression rises and falls with the piles of stones.

At the very end, he seems to have lost by one stone. He demands a recount, which is done, but every wolf knows, because every wolf has been watching carefully.

We will stay as we are. Strong and vulnerable and together and wild.

When Henry comes around with the empty bag to collect the unused stones, most wolves push their hands in so that no one will see the stone they didn't cast and know the one they did.

I don't care who sees the pale stone that would have won the thing for Victor. If I'm not strong enough to face my Pack, I am certainly not strong enough to face what is to come.

Chapter 38

"YOU? YOU VOTED AGAINST THE DEEMER?" LORCAN says as Henry pulls the cloth bag tight. "I was sure you would vote for peace."

"I didn't vote for 'peace' because Silver is right. The sacrifices needed for that peace would be borne by our pups and by the suffering of our females. Sacrifice is the duty of an Alpha, and no real Alpha could possibly support something that requires more sacrifice from others than from themselves."

"You don't trust Victor," he says, "because you weren't born here. You don't know him like I do. The Deemer only wants what is best for the Pack. That's all he has at heart. That's all he's ever—"

"You've seen it?"

"Seen what?"

"His heart. You've seen Victor's heart."

"Shielder," he says in a vaguely irritated tone. "You know that's not what I meant."

"Then you don't know. Any more than you know my heart. I know I wasn't born here, but I would pit my love for this place and this Pack against anyone's."

"I know," Lorcan says, the little angry fire already dying in his eyes. He pushes his hair back into the sprout at the back of his head and wraps the rubber band around it. "You've been gone. The 12th was already nervous and combative before all this. Now things are just going to get worse. They need you back here, and they need to see us united." He scratches his forehead. "I think we should just go ahead and do it."

"What?" *Please no, please no, please—*

"It'll calm the 12th," he says, sighing again, "if we are mated."

My blood beats against my ears, camouflaging all other noise. I can't hear what is said to Arthur; I just see him cringe. I don't hear Tiberius's angry voice, just see him catch the falling Silver and turn on Poul, his canines out and glistening. I can't hear Evie, just see her holding two wolves apart. I can't hear Victor, just see him furtively whisper to Esme.

It's all so familiar. A different time, a different place, but the outcome will be the same.

The ground loses its solidity and undulates beneath my feet. I float from one member of my echelon to the other, pointing to the table where we had been sitting. I don't say anything, but maybe there is enough in my eyes to encourage them to obey. At first one by one, then in a stampeding herd.

I circle the table. "There will be no whispering. If you have the courage of your convictions, you will speak to all of us. If you don't, you will say nothing."

Lorcan sits back down, looking smugly at other Alphas who are having trouble keeping the peace. Between Evie's discipline and Lorcan's smugness, the other Alphas get their echelons settled. We eat in silence.

"I left some things in Westdæl," I tell Lorcan at the end. "When I get back…then we can tell the Alpha and the 12th. Find a date. After blackfly season."

"When you get back then." He looks distracted for a moment, then he says it. "Varya," he says.

Every nerve in my body, every muscle, every sinew, every beat of my heart screams out *NO!*

I am not yours.

You are not mine.

But nobody hears the deafening "NO" except me.

―⁓⁓―

I'd barely entered Westdæl when Eyulf skitters out of the dark and jumps up, his front paw across my shoulders, his teeth across my muzzle.

I shake him off, continuing slowly up until I find a spot wide enough to accommodate my change.

Eyulf is larger than I am, so it takes longer for him to change. Still, his fur is almost gone when I am done. I grab at the molting hairs from his undercoat before the breeze sends them dancing away like the seeds of a dandelion.

"Varya?" His voice is throaty and worried as he pulls himself up. "Look at me?"

Instead, I look out over Homelands. A few thin ribbons of melting snow still streaking the upper peaks, the glazed-green slopes, the dark forests, the water dropping or trickling or rushing everywhere. Stone and thorns and flowers and trees and mountains and valleys.

"You have to leave." My throat is tight, and my mouth is dry. Remnants of the change, I suppose.

"What?"

"You have to leave." I don't want this to go on any longer than it has to. "I am going to be mated to Lorcan."

"*Mated?*"

"Like being married, but—"

"*You don't love him.*" He grabs my arm, forcing me to face him. "Look at me, Varya, and tell me that you do."

I am more tired than I have ever been. Even when I'd spent months on the run, eating badly, sleeping barely at all, I was never this tired. Too tired to even pull my arm away.

"It's not about him."

The trees below the High Pines are just touched with the brightest green. Up above, the remaining veins of snow are melting into the trickle and rush of water. I know birds are padding their nests with the stray tufts of our heavy undercoat. A creak followed by a crack followed by the sound of branches slapping against water signals that the beavers are changing the world one tree at a time.

"Do you see it?"

"See *what*?"

"The land. Everything. This is the last refuge of the last truly great wolf pack. There is no other place for them. You said I couldn't always protect, that some things are out of my control. Maybe, but not this. This I can do. I will do." I squeeze my fist tight, surprised to find that there is something in it. "You and I were playing a game. Pretending. But this was never really yours. *I* was never really yours. You were never mine."

"And what about me? What do I do?"

They call me Varya the Indurate when they think I'm not listening, but supposing I really was Varya the Hard? What would Varya the Unfeeling say?

"You will start over," I say coldly, pulling my arm away from him. "It's what you do. A new place. Another page in your book."

There's a sudden intake of breath and a long pause. Then the sound of things breaking underfoot. Someone walking away who doesn't care if he makes noise. I regret the last bit. It was beneath me. Beneath him. Nothing but a pointless attempt to end a conversation that I no longer had the courage to continue.

I look at the felted mass of white fur in my hand.

———∿∿∿———

How did I get here? I had been at the heights of Westdæl, and now I appear to have been standing among the trees behind the Laundry for some hours. The sun is already low against the tamaracks. What happened to the time? A wolf in front of me looks down at his feet, not sure what to do.

"You're with the 13th, aren't you?"

He nods, the bare toes of one foot crossing over the other.

"The 13th is helping Tristan clean and restock the med station."

"Yes, Alpha," he says and turns on his heel without looking at me once.

With the changing seasons, two of my roommates will be moving out, joining a handful of other misfit wolves in the Boathouse while Lorcan moves his small box of possessions in. With me. I don't remember agreeing to it, and now Lorcan is pawing through my clothes, none of which I would care about, except that somehow they smell of that other warmer, receptive me that I will never see again.

"You smell different." Lorcan lifts my underwear to his nose and breathes in deeply. "Warmer somehow." He smiles. "Mating agrees with you, Varya. Which side do you want?" he asks.

"Doesn't matter."

He hammers a nail into the wall and hooks a dingy gooseneck lamp to it. When he turns it on, the light pierces my eyes.

I head back down the ladder and crawl outside, running through the woods until I find the corpse of a black walnut recently torn from its roots.

A half hour later, my ax is moving as if on its own. One branch after another falls off until the crown is gone, and I put on a drag harness and pull the trunk step by struggling step to the woodshed.

I need to work. To make sure that this Pack, at least, will survive. So that all the sacrifices of all the wolves will mean something.

That's how each day passes. A blur of work. The 12th is one of the echelons building another fence, one to replace the chain link we currently have. Made of slats of galvanized steel, when it is done, it will extend far deeper into the forests on either side of the road.

There are three echelons working on it so it will be done by the Iron Moon. I am setting the pace for the wolves whose job it is to sink steel posts into the still-frozen ground, but it makes me nervous to have one fence partly down before the other is finished.

At the end of each day, other wolves drag themselves off to sleep or the Bathhouse or the Great Hall. I drag more windblown trees from the forest to restock our winter-depleted firewood.

My shoulders are raw, there is a knot the size of a quince below my shoulder blade, and my hands bleed, but I can't stop. I feel like I will never stop again.

Chapter 39

"ALPHA."

"Alpha."

"Alpha!"

I arc the maul down against a half log that splits with a crack and falls to the ground before settling another full log on the chopping block. I swing the maul high and wait for Silver to speak.

"The Alpha asked to see you."

I slam the maul down again. Two halves fall to the ground.

"Should I tell her you're coming?" Silver asks, threading her way through the undulating piles of wood back to the path that leads to the Great Hall.

I set one of the halves back on the—

"Do you know the story of the wolf who chopped so many—"

"*I'm not in the mood for stories.*"

Leaving the wood for when I get back, I wipe the edge of the maul before hanging it in the woodshed. Then I lope after Silver. I check my pocket, feeling for the little compressed pellet of white fur, which is getting smaller. Despite all my care, it's getting smaller.

"Wait, Theta. There is one story… The Bone Wolf. Tell me the story of the Bone Wolf."

"Which one?"

"What do you mean?"

"There are two. There's the one everyone knows, the one that says the Bone Wolf watches over heaven and earth, waiting to announce the end. When men will be as wolves to men."

"And the other?" I ask numbly.

"Gran Sigeburg preferred that one. The entire story is the same, except for one word: the Bone Wolf watches over heaven and earth, waiting to announce the *beginning*.

"When men will be as wolves to men."

Something whimpers. Silver looks at me sideways but says nothing.

I run toward the Great Hall.

At the top of the stairs is a huge black wolf covered with nurslings, four of his own, two belonging to the Alpha. For a wolf who had never been a wolf until last fall, Tiberius is very tolerant with the pups, playing Chase the Tail, Chew the Ear, Bop the Nose, and other nursling games. He occasionally opens his mouth, gently nibbling a muzzle, or bats away sharp claws too near his eyes, but mostly he waits patiently.

"As soon as Arthur comes"—Silver strips off her clothes and lies down next to her mate—"we can go hunting."

Tiberius suddenly jumps up and the pups go tumbling. He paces back and forth, snapping and snarling and batting the pups away from Silver's changing and very vulnerable body until a cry of "Wulflings!" comes from the direction of Home Pond.

All six of the pups rush to the top of the stairs, *orrrooo-orrroooing* for Arthur, who looks...different. He walks rather than shuffles. He doesn't wrap his arms around his waist. His neck isn't curved down. He is straightened and unbent like a sheet someone found crumpled in the bottom of the closet and shook out.

"Alpha," he says with a nod and the momentary lowering of his eyes. As is right.

"Arthur." I lower my head briefly but not my eyes. A sign of respect but not deference. He says nothing else until I am almost at Evie's office. Then the pups *orrrooo-orrrooo* again, and Arthur *orrrooo-orrrooos* with them.

Evie's head is bent over her desk when I wrap my fingers around the lintel of her office. She waves me closer and turns to a blueprint with a number of small suites arranged in an L around a play area and a grooming station.

Along the bottom, Sten, the monosyllabic head of carpentry, has written *The Great North's Fucking Kennel*.

"This isn't—?"

"Yes, it is," Evie chokes out. She stops for a moment, her hand smoothing the paper. She takes a deep breath. "For when the Department of Agriculture and Markets comes to inspect."

"We are going to cage our own?"

"Pups and juveniles," she says, her voice dry with fury. "It's the only way we can keep the helicopters away from Homelands. I don't know when they'll come, but Josi says we should be ready as soon as possible, so I'm putting the 12th on this. Get help from the 14th if you need it."

Evie rolls up the blueprint and considers me carefully. "But before you do anything else, Shielder, eat something."

"I'm not hungry."

Evie slips a rubber band from her wrist. "I didn't ask

if you were. Get something from the kitchen, or hunt if you'd rather." The rubber band slides down the paper tube with a hollow scratching. "Your Alpha," she says, leaning against me. Can she smell that I've marked myself over and over with the dingy ball of fur that carries the sharp, ionized scent of clean stone and the earth before a storm?

"Your Alpha would have you eat, Shielder."

I head to the kitchen from the back. It's busy as it is all the time now. The scents of garlic and turmeric mix with yeast and cinnamon. The sounds of knives chopping against wood, whisks clattering against glass, water splashing in the big trough sink. All the wolves talking at one time, until the 8th's Gamma sees me and they fall silent. I cast my eyes around, but I don't feel like walnut rolls or lentils with cauliflower. If I have to eat, I'm going to eat something that bleeds.

I've only just finished changing when Victor sounds the call to law from the front porch of the Great Hall.

"*Nu is seo mæl for us leornian þine laga and sida.*"

The Deemer has the door open, shooing the pups and juveniles inside, even though it is warm enough outside.

"Nils. Nyala. You too," he says and picks up Evie's nurslings. "Time to come to the law."

I cock my head at him. *That's odd. Why would he want Evie's pups?*

We don't come to law until after the First Kill. Nils and Nyala won't understand enough for another couple of years. Victor doesn't look at me, just brings the pups inside with the rest.

Silver has just finished feeding her pups and jumps down the stairs to her waiting mate. She writhes on the ground in front of him and flicks his muzzle with her legs, then Tiberius jumps up and sets his jaw on his mate's shoulders.

Sigeburg scrambles on top of me, getting a better view as the two of them run away. I shake her off, but the pup is tenacious, digging her claws into my hide.

She starts to slide down, just as a wave of short warning barks come from the direction of the access road. Heavy footsteps run across the hall before the barks are even finished. Tara jumps down the stairs, followed by Evie, her phone to her ear. I get up to follow, but the Alpha yells for me to stay.

"Guard them," she says, heading down the path past the woodshed toward the gate. It's probably a hunter or a teenager, but there is too much going on to leave anything to chance. Whoever is on gate duty will hold them until Evie and Tara arrive to take care of it.

Elijah runs past, pulling on a sweatshirt. For whatever reason, they need the lawyers. Standing at the edge of the porch, my ears circle, listening. Because I'm listening, I hear the rapid *thump* and *thunk* of a car on uneven ground. A car that is coming fast and not up the access road. I growl for Arthur and the pups to stay behind me.

My *nidling* looks at me worriedly. I snarl along my flanks for the wriggling foursome to be still. As young as they are, they stop immediately, making themselves small and silent.

I roll my shoulders forward and feel the power of my jaws.

Chapter 40

AN ENORMOUS SPORTSMOBILE VAN CUTS ACROSS THE grass and drives right up to the front of the Great Hall.

A door opens, bearing a shield that proclaims it belongs to the New York State Department of Agriculture and Markets, Division of Animal Industry.

At first, all I can see is a foot encased in supportive black shoes and sagging gray socks.

The man rounds the front of the car, eyeing first me, then the pups. He puts his hand on his hip.

"I'm from Agriculture and Markets. Division of Animal Industry," he says to Arthur, who folds back up, his arms around his waist. My *nidling* looks to me for guidance.

I do not trust this man. His hair is thinning, his body thickening, and he smells like anger and disappointed expectations. Like one of those high school bullies we read about in human books. Only this one got older without ever growing up.

"We have to wait for the Alpha?" Arthur says worriedly, still looking at me.

I chuff at him, irritated. He knows better than to talk to a *westend* like that.

The man with the gray socks snorts. "Your *boss* is busy explaining to my colleagues why none of the Great North Kennel's dogs have had their rabies shots. By law, we have to take them in."

He opens the back door of his van, and when he turns around, he has a large crate and a long, thin gun that is green and makes a *whupp* sound. Something pinches my flank. Another *whupp* sound, and Arthur growls and falls.

When I leap at him, my leg responds awkwardly and sends me flying down the steps, my head in the dirt, my ribs cracked against the stair. As I try to raise myself, the man shoots me again, then runs up the stairs and puts the pups into the cage. Theo cries out, and I drag myself toward him. I can't jump, and everything swims loosely in front of my eyes. I dream that I flounder toward the man and grab his calf above his stinking sock. My jaws feel like cotton.

I dream that the man screeches and kicks at me with his other foot. The little hairs of his leg itch the roof of my mouth. The crate crashes against my ribs, and the pups mewl and bark, their claws scraping for a hold on the slick plastic. Then everything is made of water. Something goes tight around my neck and pulls me unrelentingly into the back of the van. I'm swimming at night through the cold water. Even for an Arctic wolf, it's impossibly cold and my sinuses occlude. I can't breathe. I don't know which way to swim. Where is the surface? My body bumps across ground and metal, and a car door slams. I'm paddling as fast as I can. Trying to save them.

Trying to save them all.

But then the dark, cool water covers me and I fail.

—◆◆◆—

It's airless in the back of the van. It smells like many frightened animals, but most of all, it smells like the fear of baby wolves. The pups mewl softly. It takes a lot of effort to roll over to face the crate and Sigeburg's little muzzle pressed against the grating as she reaches toward me with her paw. A bright-blue tarp scrunches to the side, and the corrugated metal floor is hard and cold against my belly. I push myself against it. Road, legs, mind—nothing is stable, and I careen from one side to the next, until I hit the door and let myself fall.

There's no handle here, just a gap in the door panel. I start scraping at it, tearing at it until my claws bleed. Snarling, I lash out with my jaws, and something around my neck pulls at me. Only when I tumble back and a metal cable slaps against the floor do I realize I have been collared and tethered to a winch attached to the front cab.

It's long enough to reach to the door but no farther. I pull and scratch and lash and bang and bleed and fail. Every time becoming more furious, with snarling and snapping that has no effect on the door.

"Guard them," Evie said.

I had only one job, and now they are caged in the back of a van.

You can't always protect, Varya. Things happen in the world that are beyond even your control.

I stare at the tangle of fur and blinking eyes, retreating as far as possible into the back of the crate. Away from me.

Sometimes all you can do is love.

Dragging myself over to the cage, I press my face to the grating and wait.

It doesn't take long for Sigeburg to come forward again. Maybe she remembers that I once rubbed her tummy. I strain my muzzle toward her, awkwardly marking her cheek through the metal wires. John comes next, then Theo, and finally Solveig. Each looking for comfort from the only bit of home they can find.

Pulling against the collar, I curl my body around the metal and plastic that cages them, trying to make a fortress against the world. Whatever comfort they are taking from me, I am taking more from them, from the smell of their fur and the feel of their warm breath and sharp claws as they knead against the scars on my belly that they haven't yet learned to fear.

The dark water sucks me under once more, only to spit me out again when the van slows and turns sharply before coming to a stop. The door in the front opens. Two other doors from another vehicle slam shut. There are voices. I clamber to my feet, grateful that my back legs have some feeling again. The pups whimper, but when I snap, they obey immediately, moving quietly to the back of the crate.

"I need to count it," says the voice of the man with the draggy socks.

"Be my guest," says a familiar voice. "Any problems?"

"Yes, as a matter of fact. I pumped her with twice what it would take to kill a bull mastiff and look... See what she did to my ankle? Now I'm going to have to report—"

Deep treads move against asphalt, and a voice comes closer. "I wouldn't do that if I were you."

"Well, it's not like I can pretend it didn't happen. I gotta get it checked out. They don't have their shots, remember? The insurance won't cover it if I don't report it."

The door opens, and cold air that stinks of oil and

rotting food shocks the draggy workings of my brain into remembering that voice and the scent of ferns on damp wood. Lucius? Lucian? I throw my faltering body toward the man at the door, my jaws just missing him when the collar cuts off my breathing. I hang over the edge of the van, my legs beating frantically to get some purchase on the concrete ground.

"Oh my fucking…" I struggle against the big hand grabbing my hind legs. "You were supposed to get the silver runt. Does this look like a silver runt? Lift her up before she suffocates."

The big hands of a second Shifter push me roughly into the back of the van. The floaters in front of my eyes start to fade. As soon as I am back in the van, I scrape at the collar. When I cough, it hurts my throat.

"I was told to get a gray dog with puppies in front of the big house. And that was what I did. If you don't want this one, I bet I can sell it for—"

A phone dings. Lucian turns away. "I've got to take this."

He takes the call, his back to us, his hand cupped around the speaker. When the voice on the other end grows louder, he moves farther away.

"You still here?" he says to the human when he's done.

"Well, I'm thinking that I may have to make special arrangements about my leg. Get it looked at privately. If I'm not supposed to go through channels and whatnot."

"You're asking for more money? You fucked up, and now you're asking for *more* money?"

"For your sake. For my leg. Otherwise, I gotta go through channels."

I can see the second Shifter raise his eyebrows. "I

was under the impression that you understood who you were working for," Lucian says with a low growl.

"You trying to threaten me? I am a representative of the government of the U S of Fucking A. Period. You tell your boss to grab a two-four and some poutine and watch some hockey, eh?" He snorts at his joke. "Fucking Canuck."

"*You* are a glorified dogcatcher. The last person to try extortion was the daughter of a circuit judge, and she ended up *without a fucking face*."

A soft click makes the air thick with the smell of salt and old leather. The Shifter's gun is flush against the dogcatcher's temple. "As soon as we move them, you'd better get out. You don't want to be here when he calls back and remembers…well, remembers you at all."

When the *westend*'s legs finally move again, they are disjointed like those of a marionette with tangled strings.

The second Shifter pulls at the crate, so I bite him.

He whips out his gun, training it between my eyes.

"You can't shoot her *here*, you idiot." Lucian takes the other Shifter's face in two hands and roughly turns his head. "What do you see?"

"A Dumpster?"

"What else?"

"A car?"

"Think bigger."

There's a moment of silence.

"A Loblaws?"

"Exactly. You don't shoot a fucking monster in the back of a Loblaws. You shoot a fucking monster in the fucking forest. We'll do it on the way back. Allagash or something."

Then he shoots me with that long, thin green gun.

Three times.

In the back of a Loblaws.

The cold and black flow over my consciousness, and in my dream, I hear a sound somewhere between keening and wolf song.

Chapter 41

I HAVE NO IDEA HOW LONG I WAS UNDER. THE DRUGS were stronger this time, and when they open the doors to the back of the van, nothing works. I am as helpless as I am during the change, except that I can hear.

"You take the puppies."

Pups, my brain yells as the crate bumps against my back.

"And make sure you wash them before you take them to see their grandfather."

Someone finds that funny and laughs.

"And that?"

"I don't know. First, he tells me to kill her. Then he tells me to hold off. I didn't ask him what he wanted her for. If she's pretty enough, I'll take her. Make some puppies of my own."

More hilarity. I need to remember something. What is it? What did I need to remember? I thought of it before I went under this last time.

Oh, that's right. *Kill them all.*

"Send Constantine out. We'll need help to move her."

My sluggish mind wanders. I know that name. Constantine. Gray-flecked beard. Khaki skin. Would be bronze if he lived anywhere but Canada.

A door closes. Boots on stone.

"Just take a leg."

Four Shifters. Each of them takes a leg. My head

drops back, toneless, against the collar pressing into my throat and hackles.

It reminds me of all those pictures of wolves being carried hanging from branches by the heroic hunters in human books.

Dead, if they were lucky.

"Where to?"

"Safe room."

It is an awkward trip. One of them keeps stepping on my tail. When they reach stairs, my drooping head bumps along the steps while they strain to keep me elevated.

"Fuck. This," one says and drops me once they reach the bottom. The rest let go, and a door closes with a dull thud. Outside, metal scrapes against metal.

My eyes move around my sockets, trying to see where I am. Solid walls, two cabinets, a toilet, a sink, and a single bed. No windows: the only ventilation comes from a tiny grate in the ceiling.

There is nothing here that speaks to me. No light, no trees, no animals. Even the air smells like nothing. It's…disorienting, and my stomach already feels like it is filled with beetles.

My immobilized back legs don't respond. Twisting my shoulders and forelegs throws my balance off enough. I fall forward, my jaw into the cement. Shaking my head doesn't make anything clearer. The pressure of the collar on my neck makes me gag. I need fingers fast, but it's hard to coordinate my muscles. I keep trying, pushing into my hips over and over, hoping that some combination of spasming and intent will trigger my change.

That, I suddenly realize, was not. A. Good. Idea.

I wake up, my naked body splayed out on the icy floor.

The drugs that were strong in my wild body are a lead weight on the more sluggish metabolism in skin. For some reason, I remember the feeling of Eyulf's hand like liquid on my changing skin. I always remember the feeling of Eyulf's hand on my skin. I'm good at remembering things I've lost.

Crawling to the door, I turn the knob. It is a safe room; isn't that what they said? There are three locks on the inside: two sliding bolts at the top and bottom and a lock in the door handle. None, obviously, are locked, but when I turn the knob and push, it shifts slightly and then jams. A bar lock maybe.

The walls are made of concrete, the door of steel, the spare furnishings of particleboard.

This is not where I want to die. I want to see the ferns unfurl in the shock of bright green. I want to see the red squirrels emerge with their litters. I want to hear the wood frogs.

I want to run with my echelon, feeling the warmth at my shoulder, the sound of their breath, the smell of damp fur. I want to hear my Alpha calling me home.

I want to stand at the promontory where I stood before looking out over the chaotic fertility of the Great North's territory. Of *my* territory. I want to smell the sudden scent of petrichor and stone and cold and look into the green and blue eyes, the promise of heaven and earth.

I want to tell him I love him.

I want to tell them all that I love them.

It's too late for that. But if I have to die here, I will do it killing the men who are threatening *my* Pack. I have loved, and I have failed those I loved. I will not do that again.

The floor pitches under me, and when I reach up to the walls, they lean away from me. Both hands barely skimming the concrete, I keep walking. Round and round. Heart pumping, poison filtering, thoughts clearing.

There are footsteps upstairs, more than one set. Listening to the movements and distinctive patterns, to the combination of weight and stride and rhythm, I decide that there are five. I cannot kill five armed Shifters alone. I just have to wait and focus. I need to focus on August. On killing August.

The first cabinet is nothing but a flimsy container for food and water. I drain two bottles quickly. When much of it comes up into the sink, my head feels a little clearer.

The other cabinet has shelves of clothes: a few packages of men's boxers and tanks. The rest on hangers. I pull a tank over my shoulders and look through the hangers. Even without knowing his scent, I know because his name is everywhere.

"Styled exclusively for August Leveraux."

"Customized exclusively for August Leveraux."

"Tailored exclusively for August Leveraux."

Leaving aside the question of what emergency would require locking yourself in a safe room with a bespoke walking jacket, the word that stands out is *exclusively*. This safe room was outfitted *exclusively* for August Leveraux. His food. His clothes. His toiletry kit. His single bed. As if Evie or John or Nils or even Lorcan would ever imagine locking themselves away when disaster came for their wolves.

I help myself to a pair of canvas pants. "Breeks designed exclusively for August Leveraux," they say.

The last piece of furniture is the narrow bed. Its metal

legs are screwed into plates in the floor, but under the blankets and mattress are metal slats soldered into the narrow frame.

Wrapping my hands in one of August Leveraux exclusive shirts, I plant my feet firmly on either side of the frame, squat down, grab hold, and slowly straighten my legs. The slat curves, then lifts, and then one end comes up, pitching me backward onto the floor and into the chair, which skitters across the room with a crash.

All motion upstairs stops, and when it starts again, someone is running down the hall. I grab the bar in my bare hands and push both feet against the far edge of the frame until I loosen the other end. Shoving the slat under the mattress, I sit on top of it.

A door opens at the top of the steps, and a particularly lugubrious tread starts down the stairs.

Outside, metal ratchets open, and the door cracks just wide enough for a gun. Not one of those long, thin green ones, but a thick silver one. The gunman takes in the room and the chair and me sitting on the edge of the bed, my hands clasped in front of me, dripping blood on the floor.

He calls up the stairs. "She's just waking up. Looks like she banged into the chair."

Someone says something I can't hear.

"I know what I'm supposed to do; I'm just saying it'll take a while." Constantine closes the door. Locks it top and bottom and pulls the chair in front of it, his gun aimed steadily at me.

"What happened to your hands?"

The exclusive shirt on the floor says *A. L.* on the cuff. I wipe the blood on it. "Where are our pups?"

"With their grandfather. Don't growl at me. He's not going to hurt them. They *are* his grandchildren. August wants you to make them change."

Bouncing once on the bed, I feel for the bar through the mattress.

Pups don't change. They can see better, hear better, move better wild. That's why some—my hand slides into the pocket of these pants, reflexively feeling for the grubby little ball of white fur, the talisman I have been clinging to these past weeks—some don't change until they're juveniles.

"Can you?"

I smooth the empty pocket back down.

"Yes."

"He's going to kill you if you can't."

I open and close my hand on the drying, sticky blood. "I'm a wolf. We spend our lives running from bullets. It's just a matter of time."

Constantine has the grace to look stricken.

He pulls the chair closer. "Do I need this?" He lifts the gun slightly in the air.

"Absolutely. If I see any way of doing it, I will kill every one of you."

Chapter 42

"I AM NOT THE ENEMY HERE. I AM..." HE LOOKS AT THE locked door behind him. "I don't have a lot of time, but...August thinks you can save us from extinction. I think he's just going to drag you down with us." He starts talking fast and quiet. "We used to be like you. We didn't have to change, but we did. Not often: just enough to make it impossible to live as human. Then August starts saying we didn't have to live like this. He said all it took was a little discipline, and we could have everything they had: money and power. Freedom. It was easy. All we had to do was give up the change."

I hear the scraping of his fingers along his cropped beard, his eyes distant. "Now, so few of us have ever done it, but I did. Once. Didn't understand what I was doing. It was terrifying: I changed and everything else did, too. I *heard* the dark, *felt* voices, *tasted* the air... I lost the edges of my self."

The smell of reeds at water's edge grows stronger, but then the weight of the gun shifts in his hand and he jerks awake, the scent fading quickly. "I'm not explaining it well."

"Do Shifters use the Old Tongue?"

Frowning, he shakes his head.

"When we are wild, we say we are *manigfeald*: manifold, complex. We are ourselves, but more. We are part of the land and the Pack. Everything. We say that when we're in skin, we are *anfeald*, alone and singular. We think of it like seeing the world through the wrong end of a telescope. It's dangerous, because then everything that isn't you becomes insignificant. Expendable."

Constantine startles, then reaches into his pocket for his buzzing phone. "Almost," he says. "She still has to get dressed." He listens for a second. "I know he doesn't, but she might."

He slips the phone back.

"It was never easy for us to have children, but I think giving up the change killed something inside. August…" He shakes his head and sighs. "August doesn't want to hear it. He's obsessed. He doesn't want to know that all that work and everything he's built may be responsible for destroying us. But what if it happens to you too? What if you stop changing and then there is no future for any of us?"

The phone buzzes again.

"Dammit," he says and flicks it again. "I know. She's ready."

"Listen, there's something else. August wants to cull the Pack, get rid of anyone strong enough to lead it. Somebody got a picture of blood and white fur and this enormous paw print in the snow. I don't know the details. All I know is that August has arranged for a predator hunters association to host a 'Dire Wolf Hunt' during the full moon. On your land. The only stipulation August made was to leave the smaller ones, the younger ones. For future hunts."

"And Victor?"

"Victor?"

"He's the one who told you where to find the pups."

"Only August knows his name, but he's supposed to hide until the change is over. Then he—"

The door to the stairs opens. Constantine looks pointedly beneath the bed before slipping outside.

I grab the metal bar. All the stomach beetles and wobbling floors and leaning walls, all the weakness and sadness of these past weeks disappears in the face of the end of the Great North. Half an hour ago, I had thought only to take as many Shifters with me as I could before dying; now, I want to survive and warn my pack. I pull off the pants.

"What are you doing out here?"

I shred a tank top into long strips.

"She's using the bathroom."

I tie the bar against the outer part of my thigh, so that it sticks up to my waist.

"Don't hear anything."

I pour some water into the toilet, pull up the pants and flush.

Someone knocks on the door. "Hurry up in there."

"Washing my hands," I snap, scrubbing thoroughly to get rid of the smell of metal. Then I open the door.

"Let me see your hand." It's Lucian, the blond Shifter who delivered August's ultimatum. "Why is it bleeding?" he asks when I hold it out to him.

"I tried to open the doors of the van," which is true and easy to say. Lucian narrows his eyes. He signals toward me with his own gun.

"Check her out."

Constantine gestures for me to lift my arms and pats down first my left, then my right, then my back, then my front. His expression flickers as he touches my torso, but he does nothing when he feels the hard metal bar continuing down the outside of my thigh.

"Clean," he says without looking up. He uses the muzzle of his gun to push me toward the stair.

"And what's wrong with her leg?" Lucian asks.

"I took five darts the size of hummingbirds in my ass. That's what's wrong with my leg."

I don't look at either Shifter.

It's easier to walk once I clear the stairs into a long hall of smooth wooden panels that blend almost seamlessly into smooth wooden doors with indented metal fixtures. The kind of thing that no wolf could ever open.

At the end of the hall is a living room with a high cathedral ceiling and plate-glass windows that extend from floor to ceiling. The scrupulously clean glass looks out over a low, perpetually leaden sky that meets the sage-gray scrub and the vast expanse of water beyond.

It's like entering a dream of my childhood. The beach of pebbles, rough waves, tough sedges extending to the ocean. It is a hard landscape, the mating of glacier and rock and sea, infused with the damp salt and sand and cold smell so reminiscent of Vrangelya.

The room itself is not as big as the Great Hall, but that is crowded with tables for hundreds of wolves, sofas and shelves and baskets of wood and kindling. This is a vast white-carpeted emptiness surrounding a U-shaped pale-gray sofa. A young man sits on the sofa, a mug pressed to his cheek as he stares into a fireplace with a "fire" that is smooth and regular and silent and odorless.

"Magnus!" Lucian yells.

The young man startles.

Without warning, Constantine lashes out as fast as a copperhead's strike. All I hear is the snap of skin against bone. All I see is Lucian cradling his cheek.

"You fucking lunatic. I swear to god if you broke my face, I will kill you in your sleep."

"Told you not to talk to Magnus." Constantine wipes the back of his knuckles against his shirt.

This is a very badly run pack.

Lucian rams the gun into my back. Happily, it is aimed at my lung, instead of my spine as it was before.

I clench my thigh, feeling the metal bar dig hard into my leg.

"*Door*," Lucian snaps.

After a moment of looking around for a coaster, Magnus puts his coffee cup next to the fireplace and runs to the door. When he opens it, his jacket swings back, showing his own holster. Three Shifters with three guns.

We step out under a bare metal trellis onto an expanse of small, smooth pebbles neatly arranged in tiny furrows. They are gold-toned and not native to this place, which means that August Leveraux, who lives in a place of nothing but rocks, imported even more. A razor-wire-topped cement wall circles everything, leading all the way down to the ocean and in, until it finally disappears under the waves.

The gun in my back directs me along a flat stone path leading toward the back. A Shifter is busily raking away the tracks left by a car in the pebbles. He has short-cropped red hair.

"Antony," Lucian says, and the Shifter sets his rake against a gate of overlapping steel plates, taking up a gun instead. Even inside this fortress, they are all armed.

Halfway along this windowless length facing the gate, I hear them. A soft whimper of tiny swallowed barks. The sound of pups who are alone and terrified. Without thinking, I rush forward, until Lucian wraps his hand in my hair, jamming the gun tighter against my back.

Then I see them. Our pups attached by chains to the metal trellis, each tiny neck circled with a prong collar, miniature versions of the one Silver used to torture Adrian. The chains are so short that they can't lie down. Even worse, the chains are too short for the pups to touch each other.

I lurch forward, dropping to the ground in front of Sigeburg. Lucian loses his balance and his grip on my hair just long enough for me to touch Sigeburg's little face. Each of the other pups makes an achingly quiet bark, begging to be reassured. Nothing like the loud demands they make at Homelands where that reassurance is their birthright.

Lucian grabs my hair again, but I snarl deep in my chest as I shuffle along the line, marking the other frightened pups.

Then I hear a wheeze and a bump and a monotone vibration.

"You really are just dogs, aren't you?"

Chapter 43

I HAD HEARD FIVE SETS OF FOOTSTEPS, BUT THERE aren't five Shifters: there are six. It's hard to imagine that the thin man in the wheelchair, with his withered, dark-russet skin wrapped in layer after layer of thick clothing against the weather, is Tiberius's father.

Except for the shape of his eyes, which must have once been beautiful. Maybe when he seduced poor Mala, who was so alone and so vulnerable. But I know this is August Leveraux, because the "exclusively designed" clothes smell like him. That, and because Tiberius shot him through the throat and failed to kill him.

The Shifter eyes me coldly, then lifts his chin, and Lucian jerks me up to one knee. I tighten my thigh muscle holding the metal bar.

"Romulus," August gasps and another Shifter standing behind him wheels him closer. He is—or was— larger than I originally thought and wears the appraising expression of a man who is used to power.

He takes several deep breaths and holds out his hand.

Bad hunters see prey, then give chase immediately. Good hunters observe prey before giving chase. Learn which are sick, which are old. Which are aggressive, which are hesitant. Lucian would shoot me without a second thought, but he is sloppy and angry. Constantine is more dangerous but also conflicted. He watches Magnus with a worried eye.

Romulus shakes out a clean, sharply ironed handkerchief from a pile of them on a low table and hands it to August. August holds it over his neck with two hands, then coughs several times, dabbing at his throat before handing the handkerchief back.

"I need grandchildren," he says once he catches his breath. "Don't want pets."

I look slowly and deliberately at the five men waiting on him.

"Then why do you have so many of them?"

For some reason, that makes him laugh, then cough, and Magnus grimaces while making ready with another clean handkerchief.

"Who are you? Not my son's mate. Not the runt that idiot human was sent to pick up. We retrieved the money, by the way, so I suppose we should thank you for that."

"I would do nothing for you."

"I didn't mean you specifically. You were indisposed. I meant your Pack. The *Great* North." He says *Great* with elaborate sarcasm, because he doesn't understand that they are not Great and Vast or Great and Powerful, but *Deore*, Great and Precious.

"They ripped open his car. Him too. That goes without saying." He drags his clawed hand across his abdomen, tracing almost exactly the path of my clawing. "Didn't eat him though. Just left his bits and pieces littering up the woods. Very confused"—he gasps for air—"about that particular law."

Who killed the dogcatcher? The Great North would never have done something like that Offland. It's too dangerous. And they certainly wouldn't have left the body where anyone could find it.

"Poor old Daniel. He ended up being eaten by rats. Did you know that? Rats. Such an undignified end." Clearing his throat, he turns toward the Shifter with the cropped red hair. "Antony, you wouldn't let me be eaten by rats, would you?"

"Never, August. Never."

A cruel smile plays across August's lips. "But you are planning to outlive me, is that it?"

Antony quickly becomes flustered. "No, I didn't mean that. I meant that if somehow I did, I wouldn't... I..."

Unlike our Alphas, who control by a combination of discipline, example, and sacrifice, August controls by force and whim and keeping his followers unbalanced and unsure.

"What is your name, bitch?" August says.

I can't stand the sound of my name on Lorcan's lips. I'm certainly not going to give it to August.

The gun shoves hard against my temple.

"Answer him. What's your name, bitch?"

"You're not offending me by calling me 'bitch.' I am a female wolf. 'Bitch' is just what I am. Call me 'girl,' though, and I will eat your tongue."

The gun is now under the slope of my skull. "What is your fucking name?"

"I am the Alpha Shielder of the 12th Echelon of the Great North Pack."

"Ah, a bitch with a title."

"Wolves don't have titles, Shifter. We have responsibilities."

I tighten my leg again to feel the metal bar against my skin, reminding me that when the time comes, I have more than soft, stubby fingers and flat little teeth.

"You're not from the Great North originally, are you? If I had to guess by your accent, I'd say…Russia? There were two Packs at the end, weren't there? Sakha and… What was the other one? Randall's?"

Once upon a time, they had both been great packs, with many wolves and vast territories, but now they are nothing, just one more thing tossed in the rubbish bin of inexactly remembered trivia. "Wrangel Island. The Pack was Vrangelya."

"Well, gone now. Like Sakha. Like Nunavut. Like Osdalen. All gone. What makes you think the Great North will survive?"

The heat that has been prickling at the back of my neck spreads down over my chest. If I were wild, my hackles would be raised and they would know I was about to strike, but August doesn't notice. Even now, he's a man in love with his own voice. "Chimpanzees and humans once shared a common ancestor. But one chose to stay in the trees, and the other chose to evolve. It is the same with us." He is interrupted by another series of short coughs. "We share that common ancestor, but at some point our paths branched. We suppressed our more bestial instincts; you indulged them, worshipped them. Move out of the way," he snaps at Romulus. "I can't see."

The Shifter scampers out of August's sight line.

"There was only one difficulty. Our ability to reproduce has slowed, but I had barely joined to Mala when she became pregnant. My son hardly touched the little runt when she conceived. We are dying out because we can't reproduce. You are dying out because you are hunted. I was proposing a way forward for both of us."

"It might help if you had females."

"My wife is not the one kneeling on the ground with a gun to her head. We keep our women safe," he says. "You've lost how many? Three females? Four? Because you put them at the front lines. We have lost none. *Our* women are our most precious commodity."

"Commodity? Does a commodity have a choice? Or is it like the 'choice' you gave the Great North, which was none at all."

He slaps his hand against the padded arm of his chair. The weak, muffled sound of a once-strong arm infuriates him more.

"*I will not be made the villain here*," he snaps.

Isn't that what every villain tells themselves? No matter how overwhelming the evidence—our home invaded, our wolves dead, a gun shoved into my head, his own grandchildren being strangled by prong collars—but no, he's not the villain.

His coughing gets worse, and the other Shifters look nervously at one another. Romulus readies more clean handkerchiefs.

"There is no room for wolves in this world," he says. "And it is time for you, for them"—he points to the four pups who cringe behind me—"to accept it." He expels a long wheezing breath. "Don't doubt my will. Tiberius may have been born like you, but I made him a man. It took years, but I made him human."

I look at him, not with a casual glance but with an Alpha stare. August narrows his eyes but doesn't look away. "I saw your son. Right before your dogcatcher took me. He was with his pups. Letting them play with his tail, grooming them. Then he left to go hunting with his mate. For rabbits, I think. Or maybe voles. Whatever you think of your will, it took the least of our wolves a few weeks to undo everything.

"He is," I say and *mean* it, "a glorious wolf."

August begins to cough again, and now it won't stop. He hacks and hacks, unable to catch a breath. The noise worries the already anxious pups behind me. But it terrifies the Shifters. I can feel it in the hesitation of Lucian's gun.

"*Mynaþ, guðlingas,*" I whisper, "*þæt ge beoþ.*"

Remember, little warriors, what you are.

I feel for the metal bar at my waistband.

Chapter 44

AND FREEZE.

Constantine has pulled Magnus back against the wall of the house. Romulus is searching for another handkerchief, the muzzle of Lucian's gun vibrates slightly, and somewhere in my hunter's mind sorting through all of it comes something that they would never understand. Something carried on a wind that smells of sand and decaying seaweed. Clean stone and petrichor, the mineral, electric scent of a storm.

The cold is coming.

The cold is here.

I tighten my grip on the metal rod and bend forward, just as that cold slices like a knife through the air. Lucian stares at the hot intestines in his hands and starts to scream.

Romulus hesitates. Then fumbles around, looking for the thing he hadn't seen or smelled that just tore through Lucian's guts. As his hand starts toward his jacket, the metal bar breaks his skull.

Eyulf tears off Antony's hand holding the gun, and the Shifter stumbles to his knees, tracking big, lurching circles in blood on the stone.

Leveraux opens his mouth, gurgling and coughing for help. Magnus takes one uncertain step forward, but Constantine whispers something and pulls him back.

A good kill is a kill that happens quickly. And that

is what I give August Leveraux. I won't say that I don't feel some satisfaction at the crunch and snap of the metal bar when it slams through the gap in the wool and through the gap in August Leveraux's throat. It slides quickly through soft tissue and bits of bone until it meets the resistance of the back of his wheelchair. The fear and surprise in his eyes start to fade as I hold on to the chair with one hand and twist. Unlike his son, who tried but failed to kill him, I will not leave him alive to haunt us.

The chair rolls back a few feet and bumps to a stop against the trellis's metal supports.

I wrench the metal bar out and lurch toward Constantine, whose gun is trained on my snarling, blood-spattered white wolf.

"I don't want to shoot him, but he has to stand down. I told you, I am not your enemy. If you want to get out of here, you'll need a car. So I'm going to put the gun away"—he slides the gun slowly back in its holster— "and Magnus will get it."

As soon as Constantine's holster snaps closed, I throw myself at Eyulf, rubbing my face into his fur, taking his markings over and over again. He drops his muzzle to my shoulder and makes a strangled sound deep in his chest while I hide my face in his fur.

Solveig lets out a squeaky, questioning *ooowooow*. Eyulf growls over my shoulder at Constantine, who is heading toward the pups.

"I just want to take the collars off," he says. "You need to push here." He shoves his pinkie into a slightly larger link, and with a quiet snick, it loosens enough to slide over Sigeburg's head.

Leaning into her shoulders, the pup growls angrily

at the collar. Then she holds up her tail and her head and, with that lurching martinet trot of the littlest pups, marches over to where her grandfather sits crumpled in his chair, his arm dangling loosely over the armrest, blood funneling from his throat.

She sniffs the dark puddle, then squats down, marking it. Finally, she turns and scrapes dismissively at the cold stone with her hind paws. One by one, her littermates do the same until the spreading sea of bright-red Shifter blood is marbled with gold wolf piss.

A mechanized whirr and the scrape of metal against stone and the pleas of the wounded and dying Shifters. Still, my wolf leaps forward, shoulders high, head down, a growl of anticipation rumbling through his chest. I hold the metal bar at my shoulder, ready. Behind us, my pack of four fearsome pups lines up.

"Just the car. There should be water and clothes for him." He points to Eyulf with his chin. Magnus hops out, a phone and prepaid card in his extended hand. I am struck suddenly by the overwhelming feeling that he doesn't belong here.

"There's still time, Alpha Shielder of the 12th Echelon of the Great North. Not a lot, but maybe it's enough."

As soon as the last of the pups is in the back, Eyulf jumps in after them. I throw the stack of neatly folded handkerchiefs in and pull the door closed. Then I start the engine, my foot itching to hit the gas and take my wolves home.

Just as the gate begins to close, I roll down the window and look toward the gaunt Shifter in the rearview mirror.

"Varya," I call to Constantine. "My name is Varya Timursdottir."

Chapter 45

Do Offlanders ever get used to driving?

Do they get used to hurtling through space, insulated from sounds and smells by glass and metal and speed? Do they ever get used to the way everything zips past unnoticed and unnoticeable? I never will.

Unsure what Canadians would think of a wolf on the A-20, Eyulf stays in the back with the pups, shifting while we are still on the relatively deserted back roads surrounding August Leveraux's compound.

The pups crawl back and forth over his roiling body, sniffing every corner of him and marking him as their own. They do it to all of us, their sharp claws slipping and sliding across our skin. Now they do it to him. I keep peering into the rearview mirror, desperate for everything I thought I'd lost. The hollow voice, the sharp face, the pale hair, the lithe body of my wanderer.

How are you here? Why?

Finally, I catch his eyes in the mirror: one the faded blue of old ice at day's end, one the bright, variegated green of the forest depths. I can tell from the dull light in them that they aren't working yet, but I see him. I see him as he was and will be, and suddenly I don't see the road clearly anymore. The landscape in front of me runs like an ink painting in the rain, and I have so much in this car that I need to care for, that I am responsible for. *That I love.* I pull over to the shoulder, my fists tight on the steering wheel, listening to the sound of cotton sliding over skin.

Eyulf clambers over the front seat in a cloud of loose white fur and the smell of cold.

I stare straight ahead so the pups won't see. Wolves should never see their dominants' distress. But then Eyulf pulls my face toward him. I feel his thumbs running over my cheeks and then his lips.

"I have to get home. There are hunters heading to Homelands. They—" And my voice breaks.

"Stop, Varya, just one minute. Let me...for one minute." He pops my seat belt. "I need to hold you. I know you won't do it for yourself, but do it for me."

I do need it. I need this minute of clinging to him. My frantic hands slide under his shirt to remember the coolness of his skin. My body presses against his, remembering the stretch and sinew. The tiny bead of his nipple. My eyes run over every pale inch and sharp angle of his face, reassuring myself that he is really here. That I haven't lost him. I wipe away the flakes of dried blood. He holds my head so tight that I feel his fingers against my skull. He takes me so close, cold lips to cold lips, hair tangled together, hearts racing at the same frantic, consuming pace.

Yours.

Mine.

Ours.

Sigeburg pulls herself against my hip and looks anxiously from Eyulf to me. I kiss him one more time and tuck Sigeburg into the back.

Then I wipe my face on my hem, wrap my hands around the steering wheel, check the rearview mirror, and do my best to smile at the worried pups. Make sure Eyulf has his seat belt on. Then I look into the side mirror and pull back out.

"You really are a terrible liar, Varya. I could read your decision on your face the moment you came back from the Pack. I could see that you were afraid that what had happened before might happen again. I knew even as I was arguing against it that you would sacrifice anything—yourself, me—to stop it. But if there's one thing I know, it's that the future is a void that is filled by the present. And since you are all of my present, it wasn't possible that you wouldn't be my future too. You did what you thought you had to and left. I did what I knew I had to and stayed."

I don't have the strength to answer. I barely have the strength to lift my hand to my cheek. To bring the fur on my hand that came off when I rubbed his back. With one hand on the steering wheel, I hold it to my nose and breathe in for a long time, rubbing it against my cheek and behind my jaw.

"I had some of your fur. I kept it in my pocket. It's... It's in my cabin." I cough, trying to disguise how hard it's become to talk. "I couldn't go through that again. It wasn't a choice between you and Lorcan. I couldn't even look at him when I got back."

"I know. I saw you. Take eleven north," he says. "Next exit."

Eyulf sighs softly, his eyes half opened. He is exhausted, and any questions about how he found me will have to wait. As soon as we're on the A-20, his eyes close, his breath comes slower.

Flicking on the turn signal, I look in the rearview

mirror, catching sight of the pups. They may have been born to Silver and Tiberius, but they are mine now. Ours.

"By the way…I left a body," Eyulf mumbles sleepily. "Behind the Loblaws."

Chapter 46

I TRY TO HIT THE SWEET SPOT BETWEEN STICKING TO the speed limit like a drug runner and flouting it completely like someone with so much money that they'll pay anything local law enforcement asks just to get back on the road.

Especially now that I have the dogcatcher's body in the back.

Most of it anyway. It was not a good kill, but we rushed to gather what we could find so humans wouldn't use this death as an excuse to hunt anything with pointed teeth.

"Sigeburg! Put that down!"

I did my best to wrap the scraps neatly in the blue tarp from the back of the dogcatcher's truck, but the pups keep scratching it open.

In the rearview mirror, Sigeburg drops the man's finger and sticks out her tongue.

"I told you it was nasty."

The pups finally fall back asleep, but whenever I look back, Sigeburg opens one eye and jumps up, ready to fight.

"*Slæpe, min herewosa weard*," I whisper. *Sleep, my fierce guard.*

She may be too young for words, but she understands by my voice, by the brief downward drift of my eyelids that there is no threat. Circling around her littermates, she settles in and, with a sigh, closes her eyes.

I've told Eyulf about the hunt, and three times I've

tried Homelands. Three times, I've gotten Evie's message about a gas leak requiring the evacuation of the Great North's offices until Thursday. I left a message, but I doubt she'll check it. Once they are this far into preparations for the Iron Moon, they rarely do. By now, their focus has shifted completely from the world of men.

Still, I told her I had escaped, that August was dead, that I had the pups, that she needed to disperse the Pack for the change.

I also told her not to let Victor out of her sight.

With each mile I come closer to Homelands, my left hand clutches the steering wheel tighter. It's white-knuckled now, and the metal underneath the rubber is bent.

August died. But he was a predator, doing what predators do.

Victor is something else. I knew he had betrayed us the moment I regained consciousness in the back of the dogcatcher's van. I knew what had happened. I don't believe in coincidence. I don't believe it was coincidence that Victor commanded Nils and Nyala to heed the call to law, even though they were too young.

"*I was told to get a gray dog with puppies in front of the big house.*"

But I do believe in fate. Maybe it was fate that decided to substitute me—Varya Wearg, Varya the Bloodthirsty, Varya the Outlaw—for Silver the Runt. Who knows.

Not long ago, I thought that fear was cold and that only the heat of anger could burn through it. Now I know that the heat of love works just as well. I love Homelands and these pups and the whole imperfect

motley of the Great North Pack. They aren't spoiled.
They don't ask that life be easy.

All they ask is for a chance to keep fighting.

I love my wolf too. His tangled pale-blond hair. His
mouth slightly open. His leg has been twitching under
my hand the whole way. As if he's been running so long,
his muscles don't know when to stop.

I pull over on the shoulder.

"Eyulf?" He startles, groggy-eyed, straining at the
seat belt. "We're home."

This is human land, but beyond it is the slope leading
up to Homelands, and beyond that is the little cave that
looks like a dark eye in the rocky face of Westdæl.

"As soon as I can, I'll come find you. But if I can't…"

"That is such a shitty smile." He unbuckles the seat
belt and turns to me, his hand slipping behind my head,
holding me tight against his cool lips. I open my mouth,
just to suck in the last taste of cold, and my breath
hitches in my chest.

--- ∿ ---

The pups already know they're home. They knew as
soon as Eyulf opened the door to the damp early spring
air that brought with it the scents of pine and birch and
water running across moss and unfurling cinnamon
ferns and, even though we were not yet at Homelands,
the warming smell of Pack. They immediately started
barking excitedly. I leave the window open so I can
follow the chain of wolf calls as one by one the Pack
announces our return.

At the rusted sign saying Private Drive, I pull too
hard on the steering wheel, almost heading into the deep

gutter on the side of the access road. With a loud thump, I regain the rough road. Through the woods that close in on either side, I catch glimpses of fur from wolves clinging to their wild for the last few minutes before we must change so that the Iron Moon won't force the matter.

A series of sharp, excited howls announce the coming of the Alpha.

The new fence is up, and the gate is locked as it always is now, but as I skid out of the last curve toward home, Evie runs over downed wood and through sodden branches. The pups begin scratching at the door, and Sigeburg jumps up front and onto my lap, looking through the open window, her skinny tail wagging furiously.

She throws back her head and *orrrooos*.

Evie vaults across the last few feet and takes Sigeburg from me, desperately checking her and marking. Then she opens the back door of the car for all the wolves who have no thumbs but are no less desperate to see our pups. One after another they leap in. Enormous and strong and gentle, they lick and cuddle and kiss the pups in a giant writhing ball of fur that keeps getting bigger until Silver comes, slower on two legs but just as fierce. She throws herself into the middle of the wolves, wrapping herself around her pups, smelling them, rubbing her face desperately over the foreign scents, all the while making small whimpering sounds deep in her chest.

"Henry, call Tiberius," Evie yells. "Tell him we have them and to get home as soon as he can."

I have barely managed to unwrap my hand from the steering wheel when I feel Evie's cheek against mine and lean against her, breathing in all the complex scents of Homelands and of its inhabitants, all concentrated in the wondrous fragrance of her hair and skin, and for a moment, I relax into the primordial comfort of my Alpha.

"Where is Victor?" I whisper against her cheek.

"Victor?" She starts back confused. "I'm sure he's coming. Why?"

The tight, elegant curl of fiddleheads gathers around the Pack's feet. The yellow, green, and peach shoots of the red maple leaves frame their heads. The thaw taking root. Pack who are in skin emerge from the woods. Branches that would have broken around the careless big bodies during the winter now bend. In the distance, through a slight gap, I catch sight of the wolf I once called Deemer.

"Victor Karolsson," I scream as I leap down. "I do not call you Deemer."

"Shielder," Evie says in a voice between warning and curiosity.

The embers inside haven't been embers since they erupted into flames days ago. "I do *not* acknowledge the protections of our law." My shoulders curve forward. "I do *not* acknowledge your right to a challenge during the Iron Moon." And when I walk toward him, I feel my hips moving with that familiar predatory roll.

"I do not acknowledge your right to live."

"*Shielder!*" Evie snaps. This time, she takes hold of my arm, holding tighter when my lips draw back in a snarl over my flat teeth.

"Where, *Victor*, is the skull of the rabbit that Nils brought to the Alpha? Where is the skull of the squirrel that Nyala brought her?"

"They're still nurslings," Evie says. "They haven't made their first kills."

"Which means they are too young to be called to the law, but you, *Victor*, insisted that they come with you, leaving Silver and her pups alone. On the porch of the big house. That's what the human was told. That he should get 'the gray dog and the puppies on the porch of the big house.'"

Evie snarls but holds me tighter, her own fury growing as her grip hardens on my arms.

In my head, my voice echoes louder. "You know that humans are coming this moon to kill us. Kill our strongest. You were told to hide, so that when it was over and the Pack was small and afraid and leaderless, you could hand it over to August Leveraux."

"Victor?" Now Evie's voice slices through the air like ice.

"*We were offered a chance at safety. You,*" he yells at Evie, "*wanted to throw that away.*"

"We *decided*," she snaps, "in the way Pack have made important decisions for centuries. In accordance with the law that *you* are sworn to safeguard."

"*By one stone*. I refuse to lose this Pack by *one stone*. August Leveraux—"

"Is dead. I put a piece of metal through his neck, and I made sure that the light of his eyes died. When the Iron Moon is over, no Shifter will be coming to install you as Alpha. All you have done is sell the Great North as trophies to the *westends*."

I lunge for him, but Evie's arms are like iron around me. "*Shielder*," she commands in that firm Alpha voice. "Your Alpha would not have you kill him. If you do, I have no choice but to kill you. Don't make me do that. If August Leveraux is dead, Victor cannot betray us further.

We must have at least the appearance of law, now more than ever. After the moon, we will cast our stones, and the Thing will decide if he has broken faith with the Pack. If he has, then there will be a *Slitung* and we will fight, you and I, over who gets to make the first tear."

Victor's smile is a half smile. A knowing smile. He believes that all he has to do is survive the Iron Moon in whatever hiding place he has set up, somewhere the humans won't find him. Even without August Leveraux, humans have three days to hunt us. I doubt by the end there will be anyone left who is strong enough to lead the Pack. I struggle against my Alpha's steely grip.

The Alphas who had gathered behind him—Esme of the 13th, Teresa of the 11th, Poul of the 10th, and Lorcan—stand away from him now. Lorcan looks shell-shocked, his mouth part open, his hair half in the little rubber band.

"How could you?" he whispers.

"I did," says Victor coldly, "what I have always done. What I *deemed* right for our Pack." He turns on his heel, his head high, waving dismissively at someone I can't see, but then jerks to a stop. He finally moves again, staggering back, his hand to his sternum, his mouth and eyes open wide.

A bright-red stain spreads over his bright-white shirt. Victor stares at Evie, shocked. His hand slides helplessly from the blunt, blood-soaked blade sticking out of his chest.

Then he lurches and falls to his knees, and Arthur, the least of all wolves, kneels in the mud beside him, waiting for him to collapse before pulling the butter knife from Victor's heart.

In the stunned silence that follows, the only sound is that of Victor's gurgling final breaths.

"I may be only a *nidling*," Arthur snarls at Victor's clouding eyes. "But I love my Pack as much as any wolf."

Evie's arms drop to her sides, and I run to Arthur, tripping over Victor's still-dying body to get to him. Arthur stares stunned at his hands, so when I lift his chin, I make sure that he focuses on me and understands that by marking him, I am not only giving him my reassurance, but also taking responsibility. Victor was dead one way or the other. I had already decided that. So if there is a price to be paid, I will pay it.

Evie looks around her Pack. All of them—the ones who followed her and the ones who didn't—are uncertain and worried, waiting for a decision. She pulls herself up, straight and strong, and calls to Silver, who has been watching from a distance, surrounded by huge, naked Pack anxious to mark her pups over and over, blotting out the lingering stench of steel and subjugation and replacing it with the smell of belonging.

"Quicksilver Nilsdottir," Evie says, her voice low and carrying and dominant, like the deep core of a Pack howl. "Your Alpha will have you as Deemer of the Great North."

Chapter 47

THERE IS A TENSE SILENCE. QUICKSILVER IS YOUNG. A runt. Mated to a Shifter. Hobbled when she is wild by a useless leg. But she is also strong of marrow, saturated in our stories, and wilder than any of us. She knows us. She knows that a moment like this requires decisiveness.

"Yes, Alpha," she says, jumping to her feet.

"As this"—Evie waves her hand toward Victor's body, Arthur, and me—"is a matter of law, I leave it to you, Deemer." And with that, she strides off, barking instructions to the Pack to prepare for the hunters that are coming.

Silver licks the tip of one of her sharp canines. "The murder of one Pack by another Pack is punished by death," she says.

"It was my decision, Deemer, and I am willing to take any punishment. I only ask that we wait until after the Iron Moon."

"I wasn't finished, Shielder," she says. "Victor was the one who determined that Arthur had no position in the hierarchy. 'A *nidling*,' I think he said, 'is not a place. It is the lack of a place.' Wolves cannot be denied the rights of the Pack and left only with the responsibilities. After the Iron Moon, Arthur Graysson will be clawed. That is my decision."

There is a deep intake of breath, both I think because he will not die and because the Great North hasn't had a clawing in two hundred years.

"When the time comes, I will carry it out. After, Arthur will not be comforted by any Pack, so he will know the pain and bear the marks. *But*"—Silver looks hard at Lorcan—"once he has healed, he returns to his echelon and his Pack as a full member. The Great North is done with *nidlings*."

Lorcan lowers his head to Silver, giving her the respect due his Deemer. As he turns away, he kicks dirt on Victor's body.

I feel for Arthur, holding his blood-soaked hand to his still smooth-skinned belly. I know the pain of being clawed, of needing comfort and finding none. But Arthur catches my eye and jerks upright, hands fisted to the side. "I will have the same marks you do, Shielder. And I will be proud to wear them."

He lowers his eyes to his Deemer, and with that, it is over. Everyone is thinking only of how to protect this sacred place now.

When two wolves pass by, dragging the blue tarp with the remains of the dogcatcher arranged down the center, Arthur takes hold of Victor's belt and wrist and unceremoniously dumps him on top. He takes a corner of the tarp and helps pull it toward the spruce flats and the coyotes, who have flourished because we are here, but who will also be collateral damage when the humans come hunting.

My hand drops from my hip where my fingers had been toying with the tail end of the scars that were supposed to mark me forever as an outcast but didn't because that is the strength of the Great North. The Beloved North who took me in and made me their own.

Elijah slides down the hill toward the access road,

followed closely by Thea. With bent heads, they listen carefully to Evie. As soon as she is finished, Elijah runs toward the Great Hall. Thea hitches her canvas gun case higher over her shoulder and talks to several wolves. Unlike Pack, she doesn't understand that you don't gather dominants and subordinates together and address them as though they are the same. But when she points to the Shifter car, the wolves unhitch the brake and roll it down the road.

At the curve below the Fire Tower, they rock it until it flips onto its side. Then slitting the tires, they buttress it with boulders.

Now the Goddess of the City of Wolves takes the rifle strapped to her back and fixes it to a tripod on the body of the car. The car moves slightly and Lorcan, my Alpha, runs off to the wood, returning with another smaller boulder that he crams into the gap under the car to keep it steady for her.

Tiberius, Tara says, is still too far away, so it is up to Thea to stop the hunters. This is not just a matter of delaying them until after our change but keeping them away for three whole days when we are wild, which is why when Elijah comes back, he brings an oilcloth bag filled with papers. Legal documents to refute any claim to access into our land. They are speaking softly, but softly for a human is loud enough for a wolf. Once they have moved beyond the law to other matters, I signal the wolves away to give them space.

She knows enough about wolves now to know that power is built on sacrifice, and if the humans get past her, Elijah will not be hiding. That her mate will be among the first to die. I watch her scratch the corner of her eye, then turn to him with a smile that has nothing to do with happiness. He leans forward and rubs her cheek and neck and hair. One side, then the other. He holds her hand as long as he can before heading to the trees and the mountains and the 9th. Thea rolls her shoulder, stretches out her neck, then settles in behind her improvised blind. She is still, quiet, fierce, and deadly as she readies herself to defend her Pack against her own kind.

Lorcan comes back to Evie, head bowed, waiting for instructions.

Pack have no time for regrets, so this is as close as a wolf is going to get to an apology. We also have no time for recriminations, so Evie simply nods and wishes her echelons *Eadig wap*.

Happy hunting and happy journeying and happy wandering.

"And be yourself not hunted," Lorcan replies, but instead of the quick and formulaic response, blurted out by Pack impatient for the change, Lorcan says it slowly and intentionally.

Then he repeats it to me. "And you, Varya. The 12th needs you." He puts his hand awkwardly on my shoulder. "I need you too."

He hesitates a minute and then tentatively leans in. When I don't move away, he marks me, the feel of his rough beard so different from that of my Arctic wolf. He doesn't mark my left cheek, just waits, the heat of his skin emanating to mine, until I lean closer and mark him.

"Good-bye, Alpha. Remember to take off your..." I point to the back of my head near where he has his little queue.

He doesn't have long if he is going to guide the 12th

on the long walk to the High Pines. Evie has decided to divide up her Pack again, sending the subordinate wolves up to the High Pines in the company of a handful of her Pack's Alphas, so that if the worst happens, there are still strong wolves who know how to lead.

The rest of the Alphas and Alpha Shielders will stay behind with Evie. If the hunters get through our lone human defender, we will disperse, killing them if we can, harrying them and keeping them away from the rest of the Pack if we can't.

At the very least, the hope is that our strong bodies will be trophy enough.

Chapter 48

NOBODY FEELS MUCH LIKE TALKING, SO WE SIT IN small groups, naked and in skin, waiting for the sun to set and the moon to rise. August Leveraux knew the patterns of our lives well enough. I doubt he had any interest in his wealthy, coddled, predator-hunters finding us writhing around in our grotesque between stage.

It just makes everything else sound so loud. The fly-over mallards, the warblers, the tree frogs rehearsing. The whipping of tree branches, less brittle now than in winter and frilled with young leaves.

Look at me.

Listen to me.

Love me.

Make life with me.

Then, in the distance, a wolf howls, broken and discordant, the sound of a wolf who has never sung before.

Evie cocks her head to the side, as do all the others here by the access road. None of them recognize the voice, because it doesn't belong to the Pack. It belongs to me.

Listening closely, I hear something else, something metallic and grinding. Loose stone. Another vast machine, only this one is ripping up rocks instead of trees. Eyulf howls again, warning me, warning us, in the only voice that will carry this far.

Alys us fram westendum and fram eallum hiera cræftum. Alys us fram westendum. Alys us.

We've gotten it all wrong. They're not coming by the access road. August Leveraux decided to circumvent our protections here and use the savaged land beyond the Gin.

I drop to the ground and lean into my hips.

"*Shielder!*" Evie kneels in the mud, her hand on my shoulder. "*You can't. You won't come back to us.*"

"They're already here. They're coming from the north."

"*Varya! Don't!*"

"I will try to slow them. I—"

It's too late. I wish I'd told her more. Told her that I loved the Great North, I loved Homelands, that I loved her. That however much I didn't say it or show it, in my own way, I loved this Pack as fiercely as any wolf could.

In the muffled isolation that follows, I wonder.

What do wolves who have made this final change miss?

Is it the damp breeze on your skin? Is it the delicate motion of fingers? Is it the sound of your name on a lover's lips? Is it the words to say the things I should have said and now never will?

Everything is gone, but I do feel Evie press my hand. My contorting phalanges cannot squeeze back. So that's gone too.

Will I remember anything? The Great North who accepted me more than I was ever willing to understand. My Alpha who I think understood me more than I was ever willing to accept. Will I remember Vrangelya? As the change takes over, removing one part of me at a time, I rehearse those segments of my life I would hope I can take with me. But not that. I think it is time to let Vrangelya go.

Then I pray to the moon, a different prayer than I've

ever made. I make this sacrifice gladly, but if we survive, please let me remember my wolf.

When I am done, I pull in a deep breath and sing to my wolf, my other self, the light to my shadow. My voice breaks like his did, though I'm not new to this.

The Alphas and Shielders stand aside to let me run. At the end, I pass Evie, who smiles sadly before lowering her head.

I try to absorb everything rushing past, the cabins for the mated wolves, the dormitories, the Bathhouse, the Meeting House. Past the little cabin far from everything else where they put the Shifter and the wolf who was always a little too wild. Not as wild as I will be.

Past the marshy shallows around Beaver Pond with its loosestrifes and cattails and bulrushes. Past the spreading tangles of blackberries near the Clearing where John died trying to save us.

Past the fragrant and fertile woods that have protected us and nurtured us for centuries. Up to the promontory with the best view north toward the machine with huge teeth and jaws tearing across the Gin. It's hard to see much through the pulverized stone, but clearly, if the machine is big enough, it doesn't take much to tear through our false sense of security.

Then just as suddenly as it started, the sound stops. The drifts of rock dust rise from between Westdæl and the High Pines. And just like that, the Gin, the wall that has built up little by little since long before the Great North first moved to this land, is breached.

A few loose rocks tumble down into the void.

Alys us fram westendum and fram eallum hiera cræftum. Alys us fram westendum. Alys us.

Now I don't dare call to him because in the silence,
the humans will hear.

*There is so much I will be happy to forget. But
please let me remember him. Yours. Mine. Please let me
remember just that much. Let me remember that much.
Yours. Mine.*

The slow truck moves backward, its job done, and
now I hear another equally foreign sound. The sound of
metal against porcelain, of glasses, of human laughter.
Keeping to the edges of Westdæl, I run along the tree
line until I can get a closer look.

A few hundred meters away, the humans are holding
a noisy party in long, open white tents on a low wooden
platform set over the muddy ground. One corner is
defined by eight ATVs parked in neat rows.

The netted tents are filled with tables and chairs and
laughing *westends* eating at once-white tablecloths now
stained with the wine and food of sloppy eaters. Of
course the hunters are eating first, because this hunt is
not about hunger.

Some have finished and are busy talking to less richly
dressed people. Their guides, I presume. I recognize
one of them. Anderson, I think. Owner of junkyards
and setter of traps. He is busy showing his client how to
use a high-powered light that even at this angle and this
distance sears my eyes. The idea, I suppose, is to blind
the Pack and then shoot us with the high-powered rifles
neatly stacked in racks on each ATV.

Once these men have geared up, the Great North has
no chance. We will be blinded and killed for no better
reason than dominion and brutality. There's a brightness
in my blood as I race toward the platform. The sun isn't

even fully set. Maybe being wild, I am more sensitive to the moon's pull on the currents of my body.

The other pull on the current of my blood appears beside me, running in perfect coordination. We turn together and leap together and run together. Together, we will bring chaos and confusion and the promise of pain to those who are here believing that the slaughter of the Great North is like a video game, a chance to kill something more powerful than yourself without actually risking anything.

I sail across the muddy trough to the platform that feels slick under my paws and with another leap land on the table. Without letting them think, I start on the hands. As many hands as I can. The bones are delicate and quickly damaged. Don't let them use their hands.

The screaming starts immediately. A gunshot and pain, but the shooter screams and I smell cold. I know the cold. YoursMine. Can't forget.

Never forget YoursMine.

The wild is growing in me, and I feel the strands that bind everything together running through me. I feel the fear of men as my jaws slash and break. Do not kill. No time to kill. Just hands.

Remember YoursMine.

New men and machines coming fast. More hands. Wrecked hands. The new men. New men arrive yelling. There are so many words said loudly. Words that I don't understand.

Snap.

Where is YoursMine?

There is confusion and screaming, and in the middle of it all, a new man sets himself before me, his bare hands out. He is not YoursMine. YoursMine is light and smells like cold. This man is dark and smells like evergreen and crushed bone.

He is talking more with words I don't understand.

I lunge at him, but no. I smell pups. I know that smell. I know those pups. They are my Pack. I don't understand. My pups and evergreen and crushed bone.

Where is YoursMine?

There is a light blinding YoursMine. He cannot see the man with the gun. But the man who smells like pups yells at him. Two shots. There are two shots. The human with the gun falls. There is a black hole in the middle of his forehead. Now red.

A man smelling of reeds at water's edge carries white fur and lays him in front of me.

YoursMine.

I snarl. The reeds man moves back, his hands held high. I nose YoursMine. *Bop.*

YoursMine, YoursMine.

I don't know your name anymore. But I know you. Look at me. Listen to me. Love me. Make life with me.

His eyes open, one green and one blue. Yes, that's right. Heaven and earth. He is bleeding. His leg. Only one leg. We have done this before, YoursMine. He struggles up and leans against me. Evergreen man says something. I show him teeth. He goes away, and I take YoursMine.

Home.

Epilogue

I ACKNOWLEDGE THAT BIG-GAME HUNTING IS A POTENTIALLY dangerous sport that could result in the loss of my life, the lives of others…

The law of humans is a beautiful thing sometimes.

I acknowledge and accept that my presence on the Property exposes me to many dangerous conditions.

And August Leveraux was very careful to protect himself.

In consideration of the privilege of trespass on the Property, I hereby release, protect, indemnify, and hold harmless the Property owners, their agents, employees, and assigns from any and all claims, demands, causes of action, and damages…

It goes on for several pages. Elijah says he couldn't have done better himself.

There is only one death, which I suppose is something. The others with their mangled hands are relearning how to eat. They will never, or so we've been told, shoot anything again.

I fold the document up again and, after a little throat clearing, take a deep breath.

"Nu is seo mæl for us leornian þine laga and sida."

My call to the law sounds through the hills louder than Victor's ever did or Gran Sigeburg's. It is picked up by those Pack who are wild. The howl starts high, goes higher, and then curls down with a little fillip at the end.

Being closest, the pups arrive first and tussle on the grass until the others arrive. A little group of Shifters, male and female; one Shifter mix, *min coren*; and one lone human, all of whom have other responsibilities, come running later.

Thea has an ear for the rough cadences of our language, but the Shifters are trying hard. Trying to understand our customs and our laws. And hopefully understanding that at the heart of everything we do, every law we've ever written, every story we've ever told is our sacred wild. I would say the Shifters have an edge there, what with being wild and all, but it turns out that Thea's understanding is better than the crappy Shifter wolves we have given refuge.

I'm not worried. I know from personal experience how glorious they can be. I can't help but smile when Tiberius sits beside me. When he grins back, he shows every one of those teeth that are too long, too sharp, too feral ever to be human.

I hadn't gotten far in the lesson when it starts, a rough howl rolling down from Westdæl. It isn't the gray wolf—we no longer call her Varya, because to name an *æcewulf* is to pretend to some claim on her—it is the white wolf calling from the Krummholz, the twisted forest at the top of Westdæl.

> *Winter-blasted, wind-twisted,*
> *The world's last sentinel.*
> *Forsworn, forsaken*
> *By all but the forever*
> *Wolf.*

The old song has come true, and Evie has done what she can. Westdæl belongs to the *æcewulfs* as does much of the land beyond that Tiberius inherited from his father. When we discovered that the gray wolf was pregnant, we cleaned out Ronan's cave, so there would be no human trace that would make them move on, looking for a better den.

There wasn't much: sleeping bag, some food containers. Clothes. But in a backpack was a worn pad with drawings. The last was of Varya. Of her sharpening a seax, looking as fierce as ever. Every mark on her hard body made beautiful. I would say even the claw marks across her torso, but maybe especially those.

I think Evie misses her friend, so though she put the notebook in the safe, she kept another page, one divided into panels each with a hardy Arctic flower.

She pinned it to her corkboard.

Varya had even less. Some wolf in the laundry found a matted ball of white fur in the jeans she had last worn. It must belong to the white wolf, but it didn't smell like anything anymore.

The Alpha has also commanded that when the *æcewulfs* call, any Pack who is wild must respond so that they know, whatever else they may have forgotten, that they belong. That we will fight as hard for them as we do for each other.

Clapping my hands once above the tussling pups, I point to the mountaintop to remind them.

They fumble to their feet and throw back their heads and howl their little *orrrooo*.

"*Nu.*" I begin classes like Gran Sigeburg always did. "*Sitt mid me.*"

Now, sit with me.

"And let me tell you the story of the Bone Wolf and the days that are coming. The days when men will be as wolves to men."

Here's a sneak peek at book one from
Maxym M. Martineau's Beast Charmers series

Chapter One

Leena

BY THE TIME EVENING FELL, THREE THINGS WERE CERTAIN: the gelatinous chunks of lamb were absolute shit, my beady-eyed client was hankering for more than the beasts in my possession, and someone was watching me.

Two out of the three were perfectly normal.

Sliding the meat to the side, I propped my elbows against the heavy plank table. My client lasted two seconds before his gaze roved to the book-shaped locket dangling in my cleavage. Wedging his thick fingers between the collar of his dress tunic and his neck, he tugged gently on the fabric.

"You have what I came for?" His heavy gold ring glinted in the candlelight. It bore the intricate etching of a scale: Wilheim's symbol for the capital bank. A businessman. A rare visitor in Midnight Jester, my preferred black-market tavern. My pocket hummed with the possibility of money, and I fingered the bronze key hidden there.

"Maybe." I nudged the metal dinner plate farther away. "How did you find me?" Dez, the bartender, sourced most of my clients, but brocade tunics and Midnight Jester didn't mingle.

I shifted in the booth, the unseen pair of eyes burrowing further into the back of my head. Faint

movement from the shadows flickered into my aware-
ness. Movement that should have gone unnoticed, but
I'd learned to be prepared for such things.

"Dez brought a liquor shipment to a bar I frequent
in Wilheim. He said you could acquire things." He
extracted his sausage fingers from the folds of his neck
and placed his hands flat on the table.

Believable. Dez made a mean spiced liquor that he
sold on the side—a cheap yet tasty alternative to the
overpriced alcohol brewed within the safe confines of
Wilheim. But that didn't explain the lurker.

Hidden eyes followed me as I scanned the tables.
Cobweb-laden rafters held wrought-iron, candlelit chan-
deliers. Every rickety chair was occupied with regulars
in grubby tunics, their shifty gazes accompanying hur-
ried whispers of outlawed bargains. Who here cared
about me? A Council member? A potential client?

My temple throbbed, and I forced myself to return
my client's gaze. "Like a Gyss."

The man sat upright. Yellow teeth peeked around
chapped lips in an eager smile. "Yes. I was told you
have one available."

"They don't come cheap."

He grimaced. "I know. Dez said it would cost me one
hundred bits."

One hundred? I tossed a sidelong glance to Dez.
Elbow-deep in conversation with a patron at the bar, he
didn't notice. One hundred was high for a Gyss. He'd
done me a solid. I could've handed over the key right
then and there, but I had a rare opportunity on my hands:
a senseless businessman in a dry spell looking for luck.
Why else would he want a Gyss?

"One-fifty."

He launched to his feet, nearly upending the table, and his outburst grabbed the attention of every delinquent in the place. Dez raised a careful eyebrow, flexing his hands for effect, and the businessman sheepishly returned to his seat. He cleared his throat, and his fingers returned to the thick folds of his neck. "One-fifty is high."

Crossing my arms behind my head in an indolent lean, I shrugged. "Take it or leave it."

"I'll find someone else. I don't need to be swindled."

"Be my guest." I nodded to the quiet tables around us. "Though none of them will have it for you now, if ever. They're not like me."

He hissed a breath. "Are all Charmers this conniving?"

I leaned forward, offering him my best grin and a slow wink. "The ones you'll deal with? Hell yes."

"Shit." He pinched his nose. "All right. One-fifty. But this Gyss better work. Otherwise, you'll have to find a way to make it up to me." With obvious slowness, he moved his fingers to his chin, tracing the length of his rounded jaw with his thumb. A faint gleam coursed through his gaze, and I crossed my ankles to keep myself from kicking him under the table. I needed the money, and I didn't want to dirty my new boots with his groin.

I barely kept the growl from my voice. "I can assure you the Gyss will grant your wish. One every six months."

"Excellent." He extended his hand, waiting for the shake to seal the deal.

"You know Gyss need payment for every wish, correct?"

His hand twitched. "Yeah, yeah. Fulfill a request, get a wish."

"And I'm not responsible for what the Gyss requests. That's on the beast, not on me."

"Fine. Get on with it already before Sentinels ransack this shithole."

Sentinels? He wished. The capital's muscle-bound soldiers wouldn't come near this scourge. The festering dark woods of the Kitska Forest were crammed flush against the west side of Midnight Jester. The errant, bone-shattering calls of monsters scraping through the air were enough to deter even the bravest of men.

No, Sentinels would never come here.

I clasped the businessman's outstretched hand. Clammy skin slicked along my palm, and a chill crawled up my arm. He moved away, reaching into his pocket for a velvet coin purse. As he pulled at the leather strings, a handful of silver chips and gold autrics clanked against the table.

One hundred and fifty bits. Funny how pebble-size pieces of flat metal carried such weight. Those of us living outside of Wilheim's protection had to fight for our coin. Ration our supplies. My last bits had gone to a much-needed new pair of leather boots. This man probably had fine silk slippers for every occasion.

With this kind of money, I'd have the chance to get something much more important than footwear. Sliding my hand into my pocket, I extracted a bronze key. Power vibrated from the metal into my palm, and I shot the businessman another glance. "Are you familiar with the Charmer's Law?"

His eyes skewered the key. "Buying and selling beasts is strictly forbidden—I know."

I rolled the key between my forefinger and thumb. "Not that. The Charmer's Law is meant to protect the beasts. If I find out you're mistreating this Gyss, I have the right to kill you. In any way I deem fit."

The man's face blanched, sweat dampening the collar of his tunic. "You're joking."

"I don't joke about beasts." I dropped the key on the table. Offering him a wolfish smile, I cocked my head to the side. "Still interested?"

He wavered for only a breath, then made a mad dash for the key. Thick hands pressed it flush to his breast pocket. "That won't be necessary. I'll treat the Gyss right."

As he pushed away from the table, he offered a parting nod. I jutted my chin out and kept my expression tight. "Think twice before wishing. The consequences can be extreme." A familiar sliver of unease threaded through me. I hated dealing in Gyss, but his needs seemed straightforward enough. Money. Power. He'd never be able to fulfill the boon the Gyss would require for more.

This Gyss wouldn't be used against me. Not like before. The breadth of their ability was dependent on their master, and this man didn't have the aptitude for true chaos. No, my exiled existence would be safe a couple hundred years yet. There were Charmers who lived well into their late two hundreds. At the ripe age of twenty-nine, I had plenty of time.

The invisible daggers, courtesy of my mystery lurker, dug deeper into my back. Maybe I was overestimating my life span.

Tracking the businessman's escape, I settled into the booth's cushions to count my coins. No need to rush with the stalker's eyes on me. A thief, maybe? Bits were hard to come by, and I had enough to get me to the south coast and back with room to spare. The Myad, and the opportunity to prove my worth to my people, was within my reach.

I just needed to acquire the blood of a murderer—given freely, with no strings attached. It was a necessary ingredient for the Myad's taming, and something that wouldn't happen in Midnight Jester where bartering patrons couldn't distinguish favor from paycheck. I'd deal with it in Ortega Key. For now, I needed to get there before the beast disappeared.

"You taking off?" Dez sidled into the opposite side of the booth, a toothy grin pulling the jagged scar running from his earlobe to his chin tight. With a square jaw and a nose broken one too many times, he had a rugged charm about him. "It's nice having you around."

I toyed with one of the silver chips. Living above the tavern had its perks. Giving Dez a quick appraisal, my mind flashed back to the night before when we'd been tangled in the sheets. A carnal release with none of the attachments, at least for me. We'd never broached that discussion, but I often caught his gaze lingering when it shouldn't have. I'd have to deal with that eventually. There was only so much of myself I was willing to give.

"I'll only be gone for a short while. There's been a rare beast sighting in the south, and if I hang around here, I'll miss it." Reaching for my coin purse, I slid my earnings off the table.

"You know you don't have to prove anything to anyone here." Voice low, he let his gaze wander from head to head. "Hell, you're easily the best person in this establishment."

"In your eyes." My people would rather welcome a flesh-eating Tormalac into their homes than allow me back into our sacred grounds. "Charmers are only as strong as the beasts they keep. I have to be prepared."

"Prepared for what?" Dez asked. I knew what he wanted. A little bit of honesty. An ounce of trust. I just couldn't cave. There was a reason I was the only Charmer for miles around, and telling him the truth meant he could be used to find me. The Charmers Council had worse rulings than exile.

"I'll come back. You know I love this place."

"You know you love me." Another glimmer of hope.

"And you know I don't do love." I leaned in, a slow smile claiming my face. "But that doesn't mean I don't enjoy your company."

His eyes shone. "I'll take that. For now."

Heat ignited in my stomach. Maybe a few more hours wouldn't hurt. "Can Belinda watch the bar?" All thumbs with her head in the clouds, the bar maiden skipped across the floor, sloshing frothy beers and ales as she went. She couldn't handle a serving tray to save her life, but her tits raked in money Dez couldn't ignore.

He didn't bother to look away and check. "She'll manage."

"Good." As I made a move to stand, a high-pitched whine sliced through my mind, and my feet cemented to the floor. Iky—my camouflaged beast I kept on hand during all black-market dealings. With senses sharper than a Sentinel's blade, he would've been able to discern any shift in the tavern's close quarters. We'd had a few brushes with two-bit murderers and thieves before. Nothing he couldn't handle. It looked like my unseen stalker was going to make his move after all. "Actually, we'll have to revisit that idea."

I scoured the tables. By all appearances, everything was fine. No one jumped. No one made a move to block the bar's only door. The regulars I'd grown to know over the years were neck-deep in their own worlds and not the least bit interested in my dealings. But with the weighted stare abruptly gone and the body count the same, something was definitely off.

"What? Why?" Dez shifted uncomfortably in the booth.

"Any shady characters in recently?"

He raised a brow. "Seriously?"

"Shadier than usual."

All humor wiped from his voice. "What's going on?"

"I'm being watched. Or I was. Iky noticed a shift."

Dez's hardened gaze spied the lopsided coatrack tucked against the wall. Forgotten threadbare coats clung to the hooks like leaves that wouldn't die. It was Iky's favorite place to lurk. Dez discovered Iky once when he most unceremoniously tossed another left-behind cloak and missed. A floating red garment gave even the regulars a scare.

"All right. Promise me you'll take care?"

"Of course." I rested my hand on his shoulder. "I'll be back before you know it."

"Sure." Dez stood, spreading his hands wide and gesturing to the crowd. "I just came up with a new special, folks! Cured pig with red flakes." A signal only local outlaws would truly understand: danger, potential spy.

For a moment, everyone stiffened. Eyes darted in

erratic patterns before the slow murmuring of mundane conversation—weather, the royal family's upcoming ball, anything other than what we were all here for—flitted through the air. With his coded warning in effect, Dez took up his place behind the counter, polishing glasses with one eye on the door and the other on his patrons.

Always assume they're snitches. Dez's previous warning rattled through my brain as I reached for the busted iron doorknob, a still-invisible Iky right on my heels. How long had my deal with the businessman taken? I'd stationed Iky behind me before that, which meant his hours in our plane were waning. I'd have to send him back to the beast sanctuary soon. With no time for delay, I pushed through the door and met the evening air with guarded eyes.

Staying in the tavern wasn't an option. What if the Charmers Council had finally caught on to my crimes? I couldn't jeopardize Dez or his establishment. This place was a haven for those who had nowhere else to go. Myself included.

I glanced east in the direction of Wilheim, our capital city. I'd never had the opportunity to pass through those gleaming white walls of marble and diamond. Stretching tall to kiss the underside of the clouds, the concentric, impenetrable towers guarded an impressive mountain where the royal family lived. Where the fortunate lived. Most of us scavenging on the outskirts were banned for one reason or another from passing through the magic-clad ivory gates.

Shaking my head, I quickened my pace. Though the royal family's jurisdiction technically covered the continent of Lendria, everyone knew that law didn't apply past those glistening stones. Out here, magic and darkness and questionable dealings reigned supreme. Iky let out another private whine, and my gaze jumped to the forest line. My stalker was back. Invisible to me, but not hidden from my beast's senses. My destination was the train station, but if this lurker was from the Council, I didn't want them getting a whiff of the Myad and stealing my beast. I needed to deal with the threat first.

I know you're there, creep.

Flipping the collar of my jacket up, I picked my way down the winding dirt path away from Wilheim and the train depot. Lure them out, trap them, free and clear. Easy enough. The descending sun crept toward the riotous treetops of the Kitska Forest. Steeped in shadows, the dark leaves shivered in the dusk air, and a small whistling meeting my ears. The sheer density of the woods invited a certain level of hysteria to the unfamiliar—out here, one couldn't tell the difference between a pair of eyes and oversize pinesco pods.

Needles and mulch crunched beneath my knee-high boots, and my feet screamed at the ache of unbroken leather pressing against my joints. Soon enough, I'd wear the boots in and be wishing for more bits to replace the holes.

A twig snapped in the distance, and I splayed out my right hand. One of the forest's many monsters, or my stalker?

The Charmer's symbol, a barren rosewood tree on the back of my right hand, exploded to life. A criss-cross network of roots inked down my knuckles and wrapped around my fingertips in gnarled directions. Iky responded to the flux of power and distanced himself from me. Searching. Pursuing. The lack of his watery scent left me unnerved, but I needed to give my lurker a chance to strike. Then Iky would snare him.

A frigid breath skated along the back of my neck.

I whirled, thrusting my hand forward and focusing on the well of power humming beneath the surface. But Iky had done his job without fault. Just beyond my reach stood a tall, slender man dressed entirely in black. With a voluminous pompadour, thin-rimmed silver specs and freshly polished dress shoes, he looked suited for a night in Wilheim—not a stroll in the Kitska Forest. With his arms pressed flush to his sides, an unused, glittering black knife limply dangled from his gloved fingertips.

I dropped my hand, and the ink work along my skin receded. "Iky, be a dear."

Iky materialized at last. Tall and amorphous with see-through skin, he adjusted his body constitution, color, and shape to suit my needs. With elongated arms, Iky had wrapped the man in a bundle, pressing him so tightly his chest struggled to inflate.

"Give him a bit more breathing room."

Iky loosened his arms, and the man let out a sharp gasp. The shadows clinging to the forest's limbs seemed to darken.

"Who are you?"

No response. Harsh ice-green eyes speared me. The high planes of his face sharpened, and a small vein throbbed along his temple.

"Why were you trying to kill me?" I glanced pointedly at the knife. He dropped it to ground, and Iky nudged it toward me with a newly formed extremity. It receded as quickly as it appeared, folding back into his body mass with a quiet splash.

The man pursed thin lips, and a rattling breeze ushered in more thin shadows. It was no secret that these woods were cursed, but this darkness was thicker. Unfamiliar. Something else was going on here.

Deal with the threat, and get the hell out.

"Iky?" I nodded toward my beast. Iky's arms tightened, and the man sputtered. "If you don't tell me something, this is only going to get worse."

The sharp snap of a splintering rib broke the silence. He wheezed, words I couldn't make out intermingling with pained gasps. I glanced at Iky, and he stopped.

Murder dripped from my would-be killer's glare. "I'd never dream of telling you a damn thing."

My brows furrowed. "That so? Iky, you know what to do." A new extremity formed, wrapping its way around the man's pinky finger. With a sharp and fluid motion, Iky snapped it.

The man swallowed a cry, face gone parchment-pale as I studied him. He wasn't a familiar presence in Midnight Jester. Most of the men and women who stumbled through the tavern were scarred, reeking of bad choices and worse fates, but this man? From his immaculately trimmed hair to the smooth glow of his clean skin, everything about him screamed privileged.

I resisted the urge to glance back toward Wilheim. "Who are you?" Taking a few steps forward, I studied his black garb. Long-sleeved, button-up tunic. Satin, no less. Slim-cut trousers hemmed just about his shoes. Not nearly ethereal enough to be a Charmer. Certainly not brilliant enough to be a Sentinel. Their armor threatened to outshine even the brightest diamond.

He glowered. "I don't see the need to repeat myself." In my peripheral vision, onyx tendrils slithered across the forest floor and edged toward me. A heartbeat pulsed from their swirling depths. Whatever monster watched us from the forest, we were clearly running out of time.

"You're too scrawny to be a Sentinel, though you certainly have the arrogance of one." I inched away from the cursed wood. "You don't have the emblem of a Charmer, so you're not one of my kind." Thank the gods for that.

"Are you done fishing?"

"No." I flicked my wrist, and Iky broke another finger. The man's scream rattled pinesco pods, sending misshapen dead leaves to the ground. Shadows devoured them whole. "You were trying to kill me, which means you're likely a murderer for hire."

A slow smile dared to grace his lips. "You won't make it out of this alive."

Oh, but I would. And a new idea was brewing in the back of my brain. One that had to do with favors and blood and the golden opportunity standing right in front of me.

I started to circle him, assessing his potential. The problem was, offering freedom in exchange for his blood didn't exactly mean the blood was "freely given." Semantics, but in the game of taming beasts, semantics were everything. "And why is that?"

"Because I'm a member of Cruor."

The world slipped out from beneath my feet. Heavy ringing filled my ears, and the treetops spun together.

I'd assumed assassin from the get-go, but *Cruor*? Who would go to such lengths as to hire the undead?

Realization struck hard and fast, and my gaze jerked to the pooling mass of darkness near his feet. He leached shadows from the corners and hidden crevices of the forest. Even the once-solid blade had dispersed, joining the curling tendrils around my captive. They licked his skin and gathered in his aura, waiting to do his bidding. That wasn't some Kitska monster gathering the darkness—it was *him*.

He'd been toying with me all this time, and I had seconds to react.

"Iky, serrated. *Now*." Iky shifted, coating his arms with thousands of miniscule barbs that punctured the man's clothing and skin, and locked him in place. Blood trickled from a multitude of pinprick holes. Gleaming red droplets that wormed their way out and oozed down his ink-black coat like veining through marble. Blood I couldn't use. The first wasted rivulets dripped from his fingers and splattered against the gravel path. He watched them with fierce eyes, and the dark wisps receded. Good. At least he had enough sense to realize when he was beaten. "If you try to dissipate on me, you'll end up as mincemeat. Why am I on Cruor's shit list?"

Irritation tightened his face as my beast and I so deftly turned the tables. "I'm not going to dignify that with a response. As if I'd tell a *job* the details of my work."

Egotism, even in the face of death. The Charmers Council had to be behind this. If they'd somehow caught on to my underhanded dealings, they'd sooner hire someone to kill me than leave the sanctity of Hireath. But

Cruor? I chewed on the inside of my cheek. Charmers valued all life. Execution was rare. Hiring someone who walked with the shadows all but guaranteed my death. With me already sentenced to a lifelong exile for a crime I most certainly did *not* commit, they must have felt a more extreme response was appropriate. No chance to plea my case. No chance to return to my people.

Gripping my hands into fists, I glared at the assassin. "Gods be damned. Killing was not on my agenda today."

A brittle laugh devoid of humor scraped through the air. "If you kill me, another will be sent."

He was right, of course, and I prayed my next words wouldn't be my death sentence. I needed this bounty gone. I had business in the south I couldn't postpone. The Myad was my only hope of ever going *home*. "Then take me to Cruor."

His green eyes widened a fraction. "Your logic escapes me."

"Good thing it's not your job to understand how I think. Take me to Cruor, or Iky will end you. Plain and simple."

"As if you could kill me."

Iky snapped another finger without my prompting, and the man hissed.

"What were you saying?" I asked.

"Fine." He rotated his head, peering around trees before jutting his chin to the left. "You won't like this."

Tendrils exploded in a swirling vortex that blanketed out the Kitska Forest. Rivers of black surged beneath our feet, and my stomach turned itself inside out. We were thrust forward, and yet we hadn't moved a muscle. Intertwining shadows sped through us, around us, careening us toward a destination I couldn't even begin to pinpoint. Tears pricked the corners of my eyes, and I sucked in a breath.

And then we came to a screeching halt, the outside world slamming back into us as the darkness abruptly receded. I white-knuckled a fist against my stomach and glared at the assassin in Iky's arms. His smirk was maddening.

The comfort of Midnight Jester was now what felt like a world away.

Slowly, I unfurled my hand and caught sight of my Charmer's symbol, weighing Iky's branch and my apparent insanity against his time. Every beast had a weakness, and his was a shelf life. Two hours of strength for every twenty-two hours of sleep. With every minute that passed, Iky's limb retreated to the base until it would fade from existence, forcibly returning him to the beast realm to regain his stamina.

I had fifteen minutes, give or take.

Stepping to the side, I gestured to the woods. "Let's get this over with. Iky, pick him up." His hooks retracted a fraction, and Iky cradled the man to his chest like an overgrown child.

The assassin scoffed, unintelligible curses dropping from his lips.

The void had transported us close, but I still couldn't see the hidden death grotto known as Cruor. Yet I could feel it. The weight of eyes and shadows. My hairs stood on end as we made our way through the suffocating foliage, darkness dripping from limbs like tacky sap. Above us, birds squawked and feathers scraped together as they took flight, swirling upward and chasing the setting sun into the horizon. A heavy branch creaked. A shadow more human than night rocketed from one tree to the next. The assassin stared after the figure without saying a word, but smugness laced his expression. One of his brethren, then, going to alert the others.

Icy hands wrenched my heart, and I gripped the book-shaped locket hanging about my neck—the miniature bestiary all Charmers carried—and begged the gods for favorable odds. I could have waited. Could have called forth another beast, but Iky's strength took a serious toll on my power, and my arsenal that could fight off the legendary might of Cruor was small. Besides, summoning another could be the difference between a peaceful negotiation and a declaration of war. The latter I would surely lose. I needed every chance to run I could get, in case negotiations went south.

Mangled iron fencing battled against the overgrowth of the cursed forest, marking the edge of Cruor's property, and I paused at the gates. In the distance, the evening sky birthed a manor shrouded in darkness. Alone on a hill and two stories tall, with more windows than my eyes could count, the guild was just shy of a castle.

Slate black and covered in vibrant red gems, a rycrim core glittered from between neatly trimmed hedges and the side of the house. Magic energy pulsed from it in an invisible dome over the mansion.

I'd begged Dez to invest in a rycrim core for months. Changing every candle by hand, warming the bathwater over a fire—I wanted the simplicity of self-lighting fixtures, a faucet that immediately poured scalding water. But convenience cost more bits than we could afford to spare. Murder apparently paid well.

Iky whined aloud, a low vibration thrumming through the air. Less than ten minutes left.

With a heavy breath, I pushed the gate open and tried to shake the eerie grating of hinges as I stared down the winding path leading me straight to death's door.

Terms used in
the Legend of All Wolves

Æcewulf: Forever wolf. Real wolf. The Iron Moon moves Pack along the spectrum of their wildness. Pack who are already wild at the beginning of the Iron Moon are pushed further along and become *æcewulfs*. There is no changing back.

Banwulf: Bone Wolf. This is what the packs call the wolf tasked with announcing the end of days. The wolf humans call Garm. "Now Garm howls loud before his cave; the fetters will burst, and the wolf run free." —Völuspá

bedfellow: A kind of mate-in-training. Since Pack couplings are based on strength, bedfellows must be prepared to fight challengers for rights to their bedfellow's body: *cunnan-riht*.

Bredung: The ceremony by which two Pack are mated. It comes from the Old Tongue word for *braiding* and symbolizes the commitment of an individual to mate and to land and to Pack. The commitment is iron-clad.

Clifrung: Clawing. The harshest punishment short of death by *Slitung* in Pack law. A wolf who is clawed becomes *wearg*, an outlaw.

cunnan-riht: Mounting rights.

Dæling: The ceremony that determines both the initial

hierarchy and pairings of an echelon. Since challenges are a fact of Pack life, this will change.

Eardwrecca: Banished. Packs are intensely social and exiles rarely survive.

echelon: An age group, typically of Pack born within five or six years of one another. Each echelon has its own hierarchy. Its Alpha is responsible to the Alpha of the whole pack.

Gemyndstow: The memory place. A circle of stones with the names of dead wolves and the dates of their last hunts.

Gran: An elder. The word does not imply blood relationship, as family ties are largely inconsequential in the face of the stronger ties of Pack.

Iron Moon: The day of the full moon and the two days surrounding it. During these three days, the Pack is wild and must be in wolf form.

lying-in: Pack's mutable chromosomes mean that pregnancy is rare. When it does happen, the last month is fraught as pups change into babies and back again. The mother must change with them before her body rejects them. It is exhausting.

nidling: A lone wolf at the bottom of an echelon's hierarchy. Because lone wolves are considered disruptive, the *nidling* is forced into a kind of indentured servitude to his or her Alpha pair. They rarely last long.

Offland: Anywhere that is not Homelands, the Great North's territory in the Adirondacks. Offlanders return to Homelands only for the Iron Moon and the occasional holiday.

Pack: What humans would call werewolves. Pack can

turn into wolves at any time and usually prefer to be in wolf form, but during the Iron Moon, they *must* be wild. These three days are both their greatest weakness and, because it binds them together, their greatest strength.

schildere: A shielder is a protector, the lowest degree of wolf pairing. From the Old Tongue. In the youngest Pack, shielders protect one another from being eaten by coyotes.

seax: The dagger worn by all full-fledged adult Pack when at Homelands.

Slitung: Flesh tearing. The ultimate punishment. Every wolf participates so that the whole Pack bears responsibility for the life they have failed.

Shifter: Shifters are not bound by the Iron Moon, and since humans are dominant, Shifters see no advantage in turning into something as vulnerable as a wolf. Unfortunately, they have adopted many of humans' less-desirable traits, while retaining the strength and stronger senses of a wolf-changer—the worst of both worlds for Pack. In the Old Tongue, they are called *Hwerflic*, meaning *changeable*, *shifty*.

Wearg: Among Pack, it means outlaw, bloodthirsty. Among humans, it means outlaw or monster and derives from the word for wolf.

westend: Waster, destroyer. Old Tongue for human.

Wulfbyrgenna: The wolf tombs. It is what the Pack calls the coyotes who eat their remains.

Year of First Shoes: This is the first year that pups start changing into skin and, as the name implies, the year they start wearing shoes and clothes. It marks their transition from pups to juveniles.

Acknowledgments

I would like to acknowledge salty licorice and Cheetos. Without them, this book never would have been finished, though maybe my spacebar wouldn't stick.

My one tiny piece of advice to anyone interested in writing is to make friends with fellow writers. Those I've met in person and virtually have been a constant comfort in a job that involves a disproportionate amount of time staring at a wall the color of dusky tobacco. I also continue to be in awe of the women of Sourcebooks—Susie Benton, Heather Hall, Laura Costello, Stefani Sloma, Kirsten Wenum, Ashlyn Keil, Beth Sochacki, Kaitlyn Kennedy, Cat Clyne, Mary Altman, and Dawn Adams—who have always been inexplicably kind and patient and supportive. Then there's my editor, Deb Werksman, who knew exactly how to talk me through when I was having trouble. To my astounding agent and advocate, Heather Jackson, what can I say? I am almost speechless with admiration. Almost.

Finally, the unimaginable has happened, and I am in a position to thank readers. During more than one Cheetos- and licorice-fueled wall-staring marathon, a reader said something kind and made me remember why.

About the Author

Maria Vale is a journalist who has worked for *Publishers Weekly*, *Glamour*, *Redbook*, and *the Philadelphia Inquirer*. She is a logophile and a bibliovore and a worrier about the world. Trained as a medievalist, she tries to shoehorn the language of Beowulf into things that don't really need it. She currently lives in New York with her husband, two sons, and a long line of dead plants. No one will let her have a pet.

Also by Maria Vale